I0716023

DARKNESS

AN ALEX WATTS THRILLER

WESLEY CROSS

JOIN THE STORY

To receive free books, get behind-the-scenes stories, and be the first to hear about new releases—sign up for the newsletter.
See the back of the book for details.

PUBLISHER INFORMATION

This is a work of fiction. Names, characters, businesses, places, events, and incidents are either the product of the author's imagination or used in a fictitious manner. Any resemblance to actual persons, living or dead, or actual events is purely coincidental.

Published by
Cerberus Prints
New York

ONE

New York City Mayor Victoria Sterling glanced at the gleaming hands of the Lady Datejust Rolex on her left wrist and stifled a sigh of frustration. It was eight twenty in the morning, and the golden hands of her elegant watch were spread out wide over a champagne-colored dial as if in a gesture of disapproval. The delegation was running late—an embarrassment she could already picture splashed across the tabloids, with some snarky headline questioning her administration's competence. Not exactly the image she wanted to project. She had fought too hard to let a simple delay mar what should have been a flawless victory lap.

Victoria allowed herself a moment to breathe, steeling her nerves. This wasn't just another ribbon-cutting. The building set to rise on Staten Island was more than a project; it was a symbol of her legacy, a testament to her vision for the city. Designed by Vanderbilt & Pembroke Architects—one of the most prestigious firms on the East Coast—it would be a bright jewel in the crown of New York's cultural scene. The final 3D renderings depicted a sprawling complex with a beautiful spire that seemed to defy the constraints of the urban landscape, a striking embodiment of timeless style and elegance. A seamless blend of modern design and classical grandeur. A building that would have critics raving and etch her name into the city's history.

Victoria had personally led the efforts to raise money for the project and lobbied the city administration while she was still a virtual nobody, long before she became the mayor. This was her project. Her baby. Her pride and joy. One of the core promises of her mayoral campaign—to breathe new life into the city. Being late for the ceremony would be in poor taste, and she was planning to leave the office early enough to make it to the construction site on time, but a last-minute phone call from one of her biggest donors delayed their departure.

She wanted to take a car, but Dean Graham, her first deputy and the bane of Victoria's existence, insisted taking the subway would be good for publicity.

"I'll call ahead," he said. "Ask them to make it look like they are not quite ready to start until you arrive. No one will be any wiser."

He wasn't wrong. It'd been a long time since Victoria mingled with the crowd, and while her approval ratings were decent enough, keeping up appearances seemed like the right thing to do. But of course, on the off chance a disgruntled constituent was going to confront her in front of the press or the ubiquitous cell phone cameras, it would create a great soundbite for Graham's campaign in the upcoming election season. A win-win for the deputy.

He didn't explicitly say one way or the other if he was going to run against her, but Victoria could feel it in her gut. The meetings he took, the lunches and galas he attended. People he rubbed elbows with. It wasn't obvious to most, but she could see exactly where the breadcrumbs were leading. He had been the right choice for a running mate at the time she announced her candidacy, locking down the conservative part of the electorate and the donors who came with it. Now, however, he was clearly itching to step out from under her shadow. It seeped through him even in their private conversations as he would grow impatient quicker than usual. He'd argue more stubbornly on policy and budget decisions, only to restrain himself before their conversation would turn hostile as if reminded by some inner monologue the time wasn't quite right for him to confront her.

Victoria had to be honest with herself. Graham had been a brilliant partner throughout her first term. Despite their differences, he had proved to be a dedicated and reliable second-in-command. Hardworking and loyal. At least when it mattered. But it was a political marriage of convenience, and she was using him just as much as he was using her. Graham had a certain charm about him. He knew what to say and how to say it, a natural politician. But behind that charm lay an ambitious man who would stop at nothing to achieve his goals. When the time came, the little weasel would take credit for every success she'd had and claim that every failure of her administration stemmed from her resistance to his brilliant ideas.

"Don't let them stifle innovation!" he said during one of the recent fundraisers. "When they try to bring you down, it's your time to shine ever brighter!"

The audience might not have been entirely clear about who was the "they" he was referring to, but Victoria knew.

As the train pulled into the station, Victoria immediately felt the intense heat and humidity rushing out of the tunnel despite the early hour. The heavy air seemed to cling to her skin as she made her way through the bustling crowd, her heels clicking loudly on the hard tile floor. She could see people starting to recognize her, their faces lighting up with excitement. An older woman broke away from the mob and walked toward her, followed by a man in his forties with his wife in tow. A young mother with a child strapped to her chest in a colorful baby sling also joined the group. Soon, Victoria was surrounded by eager faces, all wanting to greet and speak with her. Her well-rehearsed smile stretched across her face while she shook hands and engaged in polite small talk with each person. It was a familiar ritual, one she had perfected over her long career.

"Mayor Sterling." The woman with the baby sling offered her a hand. "Mia Zhang. I just wanted to say thank you for supporting teachers. It's nice to have a mayor who cares for a change. And it's good to see a woman in charge."

"Please, Mia. Call me Victoria." She took the woman's hand and gave it a firm squeeze. "If you asked me, teaching is one of the most important professions in the world. You're on the front lines of building our future. Helping you is the least we can do. What do you teach?"

"English. Middle school. PS 157."

"Wonderful." Victoria nodded toward the sling across the woman's chest. "And what's the name of this little pumpkin?"

"Tara." The woman beamed as she looked down at the child. "She's six months."

"She's beautiful. So calm. When my daughter was this age, it felt like she cried twenty-four-seven. My husband and I spent the first year of her life in zombie mode."

Victoria felt a pull on her sleeve and turned to see Graham gesturing at his watch. She dismissed him with a shrug. It was his idea to mingle, and now he was going to have to suffer through it. Talking to a crowd was an art form, and she was good at it. You had to control the flow, spending enough time with each person to make them feel you cared for what they said. Make them feel heard. But you couldn't do it for too long. That opened the door to awkward pauses and unwanted questions. Knowing how to leave the conversation on a high note, whether in person or in front of the cameras, could be the difference between a successful career and obscurity.

The train rumbled into the station, and the crowd flowed into the cars, but Victoria stayed behind like a rock on a beach during the low tide. She talked to more strangers and shook more hands, but soon, the station emptied out, leaving Victoria and her entourage alone.

"We'll take the next one," she said with the corner of her mouth when she saw Graham making a face again. "It's not like someone else is going to cut the ribbon before we get to the construction site."

"What was wrong with the train that just left?" He gestured toward the lights disappearing into the tunnel.

"Timing," she snapped. She opened her mouth to elaborate, but a sudden tickle erupted in her nose. Victoria's face contorted with discomfort as the sensation intensified, a searing pulse that spread down her throat like liquid fire. She desperately tried to suppress it, but it was no use—a violent sneeze escaped her, echoing off the walls in a harsh bark. The force of it sent jolts of pain through her body, making her shudder.

"Bless you," both of her guards said in unison while Graham made a face again, instinctively shrinking away from the mayor.

"Thanks." Her right eyelid twitched uncontrollably from a sharp, throbbing pain. Victoria reached for it to rub but missed, her finger stubbing painfully in the corner of her eye. As she glanced at her hand, her fingers visibly trembled.

"Mayor Sterling?" One bodyguard moved closer, a frown on his boyish face. "You look rather pale. Are you feeling all right?"

"I'm radioing for help," the second guard said, pulling out his walkie-talkie.

Victoria's throat burned with a scorching pain as if a hot iron had been pressed against her windpipe. She gasped for air, but each breath felt like razor blades slicing through her lungs. The agony spread like wildfire throughout her body, devouring every nerve and muscle in its path. She stumbled back, her legs giving out beneath her as she fell onto the unforgiving platform before anyone could catch her. It was a living nightmare, and she couldn't escape or call for help as darkness closed in around her.

The impact was distant. Her senses dulled as spasms racked her body from head to toe, leaving her in a disoriented haze.

"Victoria," Graham yelled, his face reduced to a pale fuzzy spot swimming somewhere above her like a deflated balloon. Featureless and out of focus. "Can you hear me?"

She could still hear him and the bodyguards. But as her muscles locked, freezing her in place, her world shrunk to a point and darkened. With strange detachment, she thought this was how animals swallowed by a large constrictor snake must have felt—as if passing through a series of ever smaller and more powerful vises. Getting crushed and suffocated at the same time. The time finally stopped, and the world outside completely disappeared. The last thing she heard after her heart gave out was the sickening crunch of snapping bones.

TWO

I watched the man from across my desk as he jotted his name on the check. The man was petite, his scrawny frame nearly devoured by the massive expanse of a black leather chair as he wielded the pen with odd intensity. It wasn't a particularly large amount of money, but it was much more than I would have dared to charge for a case like this just a few months ago. Rich Lizetti owned a small bagel shop in Queens and suspected his business partner, who also happened to be his brother-in-law, was stealing from him.

I wasn't sure why he came to me in the first place. Any decent accountant would have given him the same result in half the time, but I wasn't going to complain. If the man wanted to hand me his money, I was going to take it.

As Lizetti scrawled his signature, a row of zigs and zags with angles sharp enough to puncture a tire, he crushed the pen with a fervor that hinted at more than a mere financial transaction. The accompanying spectacle of his tongue sticking out, a gesture more reminiscent of a first-grader still grappling with the mysteries of penmanship, added an unexpected layer of absurdity to the scene. I briefly wondered if I should warn him one more time not to take the law into his own hands but bit my tongue. Lizetti wasn't a pleasant man, but a violent person he was not.

The weeks following the closure of the most significant case in my career had been a whirlwind. The Valentine Killer, the man with numerous aliases but whom I knew as Ezekiel Morton, had met his demise. The night at the mansion on Shore Road still haunted my dreams. The crumpled body on the floor. The dark stain on polished wood. The torture room at the end of the long hallway. Those images seemed to have claimed a permanent residency in some dark corners of my brain. As had the image of the strange book with a piece of a celestial rock embedded in its cover.

I hadn't seen or spoken to John Levy, the man who brought me Morton's case, since the end of the investigation. We'd exchanged a few pleasant texts and emails, but that was the extent of our relationship. I liked Levy, but I'd get evasive every time he broached the subject of meeting in person. Eventually, he stopped trying. I knew exactly why I'd been avoiding him.

Partially, it was because I feared seeing him would stir the memories I'd been desperately trying to suppress. And also, because I felt responsible for hiding what I knew about the rock and its connection to his family.

Of course, there was also the small matter of whether Lucifer was real or the storm, the killings, and the whole damn case were nothing more than a twisted line-up of bizarre coincidences. Perhaps letting my connection to John Levy and the mysteries of the Valentine Killer case fade away was the best decision I could make.

Over time, Ezekiel Morton's name slowly disappeared from the news. Whether he lacked kin or simply failed to attract anyone daring enough to claim his remains was unclear. But after the statutory waiting period was over, the city itself, in a twisted act of generosity, had offered an unmarked grave for his final resting place. And now, the psychopath who had once haunted its streets, leaving a trail of carnage in his wake in the span of several harrowing weeks, had become the city's forever resident. If it were up to me, I'd have

Morton cremated and dumped his ashes in the nearest landfill. Alas, I had to find solace in the fact he wouldn't have a tomb that aspiring serial killers could visit.

In the days that followed, despite my best efforts to stay under the radar, the press made me famous. I ignored the reporters camping outside my house for as long as I could. I turned off my phone and watched them from behind drawn curtains while sipping wine and munching on the canned food from my quickly depleting pantry. It was amusing for about five minutes, but after a few days, I grew restless while the gaggle on the street showed no signs of disappearing. Finally, my neighbor, Hanna Greene, marched over to my house, banged on my door, and, when I let her in, convinced me to give in to the frenzy and embrace my newly found notoriety. A couple of morning shows and one true-crime documentary deal later, as my caseload exploded, I retaliated by hiring her as my office assistant. The bagel shop owner slouched over the pen in front of me was just one of the many who felt my fame made me trustworthy.

"There you go," Lizetti said, offering me the signed check. "Thank you again for all your help."

"Ms. Greene will actually take it," I said, pointing at my assistant's desk by the wall. "It was my pleasure."

I tensed as he stood up, praying he didn't offer to shake hands, and averted my gaze, pretending to read something on my screen. Lizetti shuffled over to Hanna's table, and a few seconds later, the doorbell chimed, signaling his departure.

"Yikes," Hanna said. "What an unpleasant character."

"He's a charmer compared to some of my previous clients," I said, looking up from the screen. "Sorry. That was dark. What else have we got?"

"Simon Blackwood," she said, glancing at the clock on the opposite wall. "Should be here any minute. I've scheduled him for two o'clock."

"Oh yeah. Him." I chewed on my lip. I wasn't too thrilled about meeting the man. Perhaps because of the timing—I'd received the email with the not-so-descriptive subject line of HELP from Black-wood right after I got rid of the book that may or may not have been connected to Lucifer. Or perhaps because he alluded that the case was unusual.

After Morton, I'd avoided anything strange, only taking on cases that paid well and were as straightforward as humanly possible. Fraud, infidelity, surveillance—bring them on.

The fact that the Lucifer angle of the Valentine Killer's case wasn't known to the general public spared me from being flooded with cases from the crazies who surely would have come to my small office with all kinds of stories. I didn't know if Blackwood's case would entail anything paranormal. But his email called whatever he was looking for *peculiar*, which didn't sit well with me. Both because it was peculiar and because he used the word to describe it as such.

However, while I wasn't keen on peculiar cases in general and didn't take Blackwood's case immediately, his polite persistence eventually wore my defenses down, and I agreed to a meeting. I looked at Hanna, and she shrugged as if reading my mind. "Oh well. I guess it doesn't hurt to hear him out."

Simon Blackwood entered the office at exactly two o'clock. He was a tall, handsome man well into his sixties. His slim figure was clad in a crisply ironed white shirt and a bespoke coffee-and-cream three-piece. He wore the suit with undeniable panache, each element perfectly coordinated, from the brushed cotton jacket with a colorful pocket square to the sharp lines of his pressed pants to the meticu-lously knotted silk tie, showcasing the level of style and flair that surely turned heads.

Sharp, light-green eyes seemed to light up his tanned face from behind the thin frames of designer glasses. His salt-and-pepper hair was slicked back, and a sharp, mostly white goatee framed his thin-lipped smirk.

"Miss Watts, I presume?" he said, looking me straight in the eye as he stood in the middle of the room. He sounded like Morgan Freeman, if Mr. Freeman had spent a large chunk of his early years practicing Received Pronunciation in the posh southeastern parts of England. I nodded, and he briskly crossed the room, firmly shook my hand, and confidently took a seat in the leather monstrosity I called a client chair. He was the first person I'd seen who seemed genuinely at ease being inside the vast curves of the furniture monster. I threw a quick glance at Hanna, and she gave me a wild smile in return—I don't know if I liked Mr. Blackwood yet, but he sure seemed to have charmed my assistant.

"What can I do for you, Mr. Blackwood? Your emails were rather vague."

"It was by design, Miss Watts. I do not place my trust in electronic communications. One cannot entirely sidestep them in this contemporary age, but I make a concerted effort, nonetheless."

"Alex," I said. "You can call me Alex."

"Quite right, Alex." He elegantly crossed his legs, settling more comfortably into the chair. "You see, I consider myself a bit of a historian and a treasure seeker."

"You are a treasure hunter?"

"Yes," he flashed a quick smile, "I know there's a negative connotation attached to the profession, but I love what I do. I've traveled to the most exotic places on the planet and met some fascinating people. Obsessed historians, conniving thieves, con men, deadly mercenaries. It's exhilarating. But nothing comes close to the thrill of finding something of real value. Throughout the past few decades, I've amassed a rather modest collection of items that were, at one point, deemed irretrievably lost. There are some exquisite pieces of which I'm quite proud. However, recently, I've stumbled upon something I believe not only surpasses anything currently in my possession but could potentially be the most consequential historical discovery in modern times. Have you ever acquainted yourself with the tale of the *Flor de la Mar*?"

"*Flor de la Mar*?" The words rumbled through my mouth like hard marbles. I didn't know what it was, but it sounded exotic and made me think of spices and silk. "I don't believe so. What is it? Sounds like Spanish for *flower* of...something?"

"Flower of the sea," he said with an easy smile. "But it's Portuguese. Not Spanish."

"A ship?" I ventured a guess.

"Yes." His smile widened. "A carrack, to be precise. *Flor de la Mar* was built in Lisbon in 1502. During that era, she stood as one of the most splendid ships in the entire world. At four hundred tons, she also held the distinction of being the largest carrack ever to grace the high seas. Her maiden voyage from her home port of Lisbon to India was under the command of none other than Estevao da Gama, the cousin of the legendary Vasco da Gama himself. She proved to be somewhat difficult to maneuver when laden with cargo, but she led a busy life, participating in a few India runs and even saw some military action, which is not surprising as she wielded a frightening battery of fifty guns. But the most interesting part of her story came toward the end of her career during the conquest of Malacca.

"In 1511, while under the command of Afonso de Albuquerque, she was returning home, bringing the spoils looted from the Sultan of Malacca's palace to Lisbon, but was caught in a storm and sank off Timia Point in the Kingdom of Aru, Sumatra. The shipwreck has never been found."

"I'm assuming the treasure on board was valuable," I ventured.

"Yes." He gave me another sample of his thin-lipped smirks. "Some scholars believe the carrack to be the richest vessel ever lost at sea, valued somewhere in the two-to-five-billion-dollar range. You'll find others, of course, arguing the *San Jose* that sank in the Caribbean carried more valuable loot, but personally, I don't believe so. I think it was laden with just a fraction of what was thought to be on board when it sank. Hence, I am among those who consider *Flor de la Mar* to be the Holy Grail of lost treasure. But monetary value is not what makes it so valuable."

"Oh." I found myself leaning forward as he spun the story, clinging to every word. "Five billion dollars sounds pretty valuable to me. Though I fail to see how a private investigator from Brooklyn can be helpful in retrieving treasure lost somewhere in the Indian Ocean."

"I understand." He gave a subtle nod, his gaze turning inward as if recalling something important. "You see, before Malacca fell to the Portuguese, it experienced a golden age in the middle of the fifteenth century. Its own Renaissance. Under Sultan Mansur Shah, it expanded, absorbing massive amounts of land and collecting untold riches he stored in his palace. By all accounts, the sultan was a highly intelligent man. An avid historian and collector, he traded with many to acquire important artifacts from every corner of the world. You might have heard of the legend of Alexander the Great meeting a reclusive yogi while he was in India."

"I have."

"Good." He smiled in approval. "There's a lesser-known tale about the famous general meeting *someone* as his army camped at the Hyphasis River. Some say it was a local noble, or perhaps it was another yogi. Whoever they were, they presented Alexander with a fabulous helmet cast from solid gold and adorned with expensive jewels. The king loved the gift, but once he put the helmet on, he became disoriented at once. He quickly took it off, fearing he had been poisoned. The guards had the man who had presented the king with the helmet executed. But things got progressively worse. Within hours, Alexander stopped recognizing his own advisers and soldiers. Despite his confidants trying to keep a lid on what had transpired, the rumors spread through the camp like wildfire. Soon, the Hellenic army mutinied, putting an end to his eastward march. It's not a mainstream theory, but I believe the helmet somehow altered Alexander's brain and ultimately killed him."

"Fascinating. You think the magical helmet is on the ship?"

"I think it was. But not anymore." His voice became quieter, almost a whisper. "I think the carrack has been recently found, and most of the treasure salvaged. And I think at least two important pieces made their way to New York City. I believe one of them is the helmet that ended the reign of Alexander the Great."

"And the other?"

"I'm actually not quite sure." I saw Blackwood fidget in his chair, looking uncomfortable for the first time since he had waltzed through my door. "The descriptions I've seen are rather vague. But from what I understand, it was the sultan's most prized possession. He was a fairly progressive ruler at the time. A lot of the items in his collection were accessible to the public. He had a museum of sorts where artists and engineers could study some of the exhibits, and the general population could marvel at their beauty. But this particular *thing* was locked away in a special vault, guarded around the clock by his most trusted soldiers. He believed the item had immense magic powers."

"Do you believe in the supernatural, Mr. Blackwood?" The words escaped my mouth before I realized what I was actually saying. Perhaps it was mere curiosity. Or perhaps the shadow of the Valentine Killer case still looming over my head made me examine anything remotely unconventional with a magnifying glass. I needed to know what Blackwood's views on the subject matter were.

The man smiled, fished in his jacket pocket, and pulled out a deck of cards. "A long time ago, before you were even born, Arthur C. Clarke created the famous Three Laws. The third law, which I have no doubt you've heard, states that *any sufficiently advanced technology is indistinguishable from magic.*"

"A technology?"

He flicked his left wrist instead of answering, and the cards took flight, fluttering through the air like a swarm of startled birds. Each card moved with purpose, as if guided by an unseen hand, weaving through space and converging into his right palm with a loud clap. Blackwood plucked the card from the top of the deck and placed it facedown on the desk before me. "There's a very special card for you, Alex. Ace of spades."

I looked at the back of the card. It was inky black with intricate geometric designs painted in gold on its glossy surface, the pattern a hypnotic dance of lines and angles. I raised the edge of the card, stealing a quick glimpse. Then, with deliberate slowness, I pivoted it over, revealing the two of hearts. "Sorry."

"Oh my." Blackwood recoiled in his chair, a picture of shock on his face. "Perhaps I'm losing my touch."

I shrugged.

"But wait." He leaned forward again, a sly smile spreading on his thin lips. "I didn't say *this* was the card intended for you, did I, Alex? Why don't you check your jacket?"

I frowned, stuck my hand inside my pocket, my fingers brushing against the hard edge of a card, and pulled it out. I'd be damned—an ace of spades. I heard Hanna gasp at the other end of the room. "Clever. How'd you do it?"

"Magic, love." He gave me a thin smile. "My point is, Alex, things can *appear* as magic when we don't understand them."

"Okay. What do you think was the magic item? You surely have at least some ideas?"

"Not a clue." He shrugged. "All I know is it was of the greatest importance to the sultan. And that the sultan considered it dangerous enough to hide it from the public eye. That's good enough for me. Personally, the only description of the item I've ever seen had one word: *Darkness*."

THREE

"I don't understand," Hanna said as she flipped the card back and forth as if checking for some hidden mechanism. "He didn't even come close to you."

"He shook my hand," I said.

I found myself more irritated than amazed by the parlor trick. The way Blackwood effortlessly ensnared me into thinking the card laid out on the table in front of me was the one I ought to be paying attention to. Misdirection was a principle known to any practitioner well-versed in the art of sleight of hand. Make your audience focus on what you want them to witness while you clandestinely engage in a wholly different endeavor. It was a tactic that should have worked on a crowd of impressionable adolescents. Not someone like me.

"He did," she agreed. "But I don't understand how he could reach your jacket, let alone put something in your pocket. You stayed behind the table the entire time."

"I don't know." I shook my head. "Perhaps it was a sign for us to install a couple of hidden video cameras in this office. It doesn't matter. There will be no more tricks performed by Mr. Blackwood here as I won't be taking the case."

"You won't be?" There was genuine surprise in Hanna's voice. "You negotiated pretty hard for someone who wasn't going to be working for the man."

"I know." I chuckled, reflecting on the back-and-forth. While Simon Blackwood was eager to hire me for the case, he drove a hard bargain. There was no sign my newly found notoriety had affected his judgment. I told him I'd consider his offer. But my gut was telling me to stay away from Mr. Blackwood, and I was determined to listen. Judging by the disappointment I saw in his eyes as he took leave, it seemed he understood my intentions.

"I just wanted to see if he was real," I said. "But there's something I don't like about this treasure hunt. I don't know exactly what it is, but my Spidey senses are tingling. Call it a hunch. The last time I had a similar feeling, I didn't pay attention. And we both know how it turned out. Perhaps this time, I should."

Hanna opened her mouth to say something but then pursed her lips and went back to her desk.

Besides John Levy, she was the only person who knew the part of the Valentine Killer case that wasn't included in the true-crime documentary. I hadn't planned on telling her. It just happened. We had been friends for a while, but after she guided me through the notoriety crisis when reporters camped on my front porch, we became closer than ever. One late Saturday night, after I had one too many tequilas at her place and her husband and their kids were already asleep, she asked me how I was coping. And instead of the usual noncommittal *fine*, I told her about the manuscript, the stone, and the crazy reason Morton had been killing his victims.

Perhaps there was something about talking to therapists after all. I've always scoffed at the idea that talking to other people about your problems did anything other than burden other people. But who knows, maybe that was precisely the point? As she quietly listened, sitting still at the other end of the table, watching me with those dark, almost black eyes, an empty glass in her hand, I felt how the terrible weight I'd been carrying lifted off my shoulders and dissipated in the air. Not all of it was gone, of course. I'm fairly certain some parts of the horror story I had to live through will stick with me forever. But it became easier to breathe, for which I was grateful.

To this day, I don't know what conclusions Hanna drew from the story. Perhaps she believed it all, or perhaps she thought rationality wasn't something you applied when you dealt with true madness. Whatever she thought about my tale, she kept it to herself. I could hardly blame her—I still don't know what to think of it myself.

"There's a case, however, I'm contemplating taking," I finally said as I watched her type away. She paused and glanced up at me from the computer. "Victoria Sterling. I'm not convinced she died from natural causes. There's something fishy about the reports, the cookie-cutter press release, and the general lack of media coverage of what should have been the main story of the month. Maybe it's nothing but my imagination running wild, but I want to take a closer look."

"You've read the article too, haven't you?"

"What article?"

"On *Gotham Tales*," she said, referring to the popular true-crime blog run by a mysterious figure only known by his pseudonym, the Merovingian, in the nod to the character from *The Matrix* trilogy. Every now and then, the blog coughed up some juicy bits you couldn't unearth anywhere else in cyberspace. They beat legacy media to the punch when reporting that Morton's first victim met her unfortunate end right around Valentine's Day, sparking the birth of the infamous Valentine Killer nickname. But it was a fringe outlet, the majority of its content dedicated to conspiracies, UFOs, poltergeists, and other equally trustworthy topics. You needed to pinch your nose and wear rubber gloves to sort through its sordid content if you were hoping to find any real pearls. And there was no guarantee your search would end up being fruitful, anyway.

"I haven't seen it. What are they saying?"

"They mentioned a few interesting things." Her fingers danced on the keyboard, and a moment later, she turned the monitor so I could see a stock, black-and-white picture of the entrance to the subway station cordoned off by yellow police tape. "For starters, the area around the train station was closed for too long, considering the official cause of Sterling's death was a massive heart attack. Almost twenty-four hours."

"That's hardly unusual," I said. "She was the mayor. Can't blame the NYPD for going above and beyond. The pressure on the guys must've been enormous."

"Well, but this is where it gets weird," she said. "The Merovingian claims, and I'm quoting here, *'In the dead of night, the area was visited by a specialized NYPD van, and after closing off the entire block to divert any late passersby, it was inspected by two workers wearing biohazard suits. The reasons or the findings of the search are still unknown. We've reached out to the NYPD but haven't heard back.'"*

"Biohazard suits? That...changes things. Are there pictures?"

"No." She scrolled the page up and down. "Some unverified witness reports, that's all. And the NYPD refuted the story when someone reached out to them from cable news."

I took out a phone and pulled up my former partner's contact. "I'm going to regret this, aren't I?"

Detective Dominic Deluca and I might have patched things up over my last famous case, but I needed to tread with caution. The last thing I wanted to do was to abuse the fragile friendship we'd reestablished. I stared at the screen for a few seconds, uncertain, and then hit the Dial button. The call connected on the first ring.

"Alex?" the gruff voice barked at the end of the line, followed by some noisy breathing. "Tired of running down cheating husbands yet? Is it the call where you tell me you're ready to come back to the precinct where you belong?"

"Sometimes. And no. But at least I don't have to sing and dance every time Cap looks at me funny," I punted back.

"Fair. What can I do for the famous private investigator?"

"Victoria Sterling."

"The mayor?"

"Yes." I chewed on my lip, contemplating how to play it. Just because we were friends again didn't mean DD was going to roll over and tell me what I wanted to know. "I'm hearing rumors. Did you hear anything strange?"

"We don't run on rumors. I'd have to direct you to the official statement," he said without missing a beat. "Every news outlet in the country has reported she died from a heart attack. Not much to tell you besides that."

One of the first things you learn as a cop was how people deny being involved in anything because they are afraid of getting in trouble. It's not something set in stone, of course. I've met some very talented liars in my career who could convince you they were Jesus reborn if you weren't careful enough. But most of the time, when the answer to whatever question you're asking is a simple "no," that word is usually the first thing that parts their lips before they say anything else. They might qualify their answer, but the natural instinct is to say "no" first and qualify it later. Deflection and speaking in the third person are immediate red flags, and DD was pulling them out like a magician unveiling an endless string of handkerchiefs from a seemingly empty hat. I wasn't pleased. My magical tricks cup was already full after Blackwood's performance.

"I guess things really have changed since I left," I said, contemplating how far to push it.

"How do you mean?"

"When I still wore the badge, we never sent teams with hazmat threads to review the scene of a cardiac arrest. But I guess you can't be too careful these days. Perhaps it was a contagious heart attack."

DD said nothing for a few seconds, but the silence told me enough. "Alex—"

"Come on, man. Give me something."

"You're such a pain in the ass sometimes." He sighed. "The official theory is still a heart attack."

"But?"

"But there are some," he paused, as if looking for the right word, "potentially troubling findings. Before I tell you anything, you have to promise me to keep it under wraps."

"Pinky swear," I said. "You don't have to ask."

"I'm serious."

"I swear, I promise."

"All right." There was more thunderous breathing on the other end of the line as DD gathered his thoughts. "First of all, the witness testimony was alarming. The mayor appeared to be choking before she collapsed. Both of her guards and her deputy said she behaved strangely. She turned extremely pale quickly, stiffened, and appeared to have had a seizure. The seizure was strong enough to snap some of her bones. All of it could still be attributed to the heart attack, which was confirmed by the autopsy, but it was weird enough to request a deeper dive. There was nothing on her skin, but the lab found extremely faint traces of synthetic organophosphorus compounds on the sleeve of her jacket. Thiophosphonate."

"She was poisoned?" I ventured, ignoring the unpronounceable words DD was throwing at me.

"We don't know for sure," he said. "It's too inconclusive. They could have been false positives. When I say faint, I mean it's a small miracle we found them at all."

"Anything on CCTV cameras from the station?"

"Nothing useful. The side of the platform where the accident took place has only one barely functioning camera covering it, and the mayor happened to stand where the view was blocked by a column. You can only see a part of her face. Perhaps this was by design, but it doesn't appear so. She strolled onto the platform pretty fast with her entourage in tow and almost immediately went to greet people. If someone did try to alter her path, it's too subtle to see."

"And those she talked to?" If traces of poison had been found on her sleeve, it probably meant it was delivered by a handshake or direct touch. I recalled a case where a mob hitman sprayed his victim's hand with poison as he walked past him on a crowded street in Times Square. A stunt like that would have been impossible to pull off on a tight subway platform with lots of eyeballs.

"We counted twelve people who interacted closely enough with her to have the opportunity to do something, but we've only identified seven by cross-referencing video feeds from the train, other stations, and aboveground surveillance," he said. "I don't think we will find the other five. At least not all of them. We are still working different angles, so it's possible we'll ID one or two. All five? I doubt it."

"The bodyguards?"

"Sterling hates them," he coughed, "*hated* them. They were trained to hang back and not interfere in meetings like these."

I thought about it for a moment, trying to recall my brief chemical agent training. "What exactly is a thiophosphonate?"

"VX." He cleared his throat. "Or most likely a derivative. I'm no chemist, so I can't tell you for sure."

"The nerve agent? Holy shit." What DD was referring to was one of the ugliest relics from the Cold War era—an extremely toxic nerve agent, "Venomous Agent X," or VX for short. A single drop of this tasteless and odorless, amber-colored liquid was enough to kill an adult human through direct exposure. A light touch was all you needed to send someone to the grave. "How is it not all over the news?"

"It's under the tightest of tight lids," DD said. "Nobody wants sensational headlines in every newspaper in the country, only to find out in a couple of days the traces were false positives. All the whackos will never stop running conspiracy theories and claiming we buried the information. You know how this works. We need to be sure. A specialist is coming in from Virginia tomorrow morning to look at the results. If they also rule it a homicide, it'll be hard to keep it secret for much longer. The genie will be out of the bottle. But if not, we skip a whole lot of unnecessary headaches."

"I see." I glanced at Hanna's face as I chewed on my lip again. She didn't seem to be thrilled by the prospect of me taking a case involving nerve agents. But I couldn't help it. There was an itch inside my brain that couldn't be relieved by anything else but digging just a little deeper. "I'd need to talk to Sterling's deputy. Can you set up a meeting?"

"With Graham? Are you nuts? Absolutely not."

"DD—"s

"Don't you DD me," he snapped. "I've already given you more than I should have. You just don't know when to stop."

"Fine." I paused, carefully weighing my next words. "How about a compromise? Can you tell me where I can meet him without too many in his entourage so I don't endanger your position?"

There was a long silence on the other side of the line, followed by a heavy sigh. "Fine. I'll let you know."

"I'd like to ask you two questions before you do anything," Hanna said after I hung up. "It's the mayor. Aren't we going to step on other people's toes if it's a murder? And, more importantly, who's going to pay us?"

"We always step on somebody's toes," I said. "It's part of the job. As for the payment? I'm not sure yet. We'll work it out when the time comes."

"Great," she said, raising her hands in mock surrender. "Another pro bono case. You better start dating the landlord then, so by the time we run out of money, he can stop charging us rent."

"Would there be anything else, sir?"

"Pardon me?" Simon Blackwood stared at the waitress for a moment, startled. He sat in a Midtown cafe, so lost in his thoughts he didn't see the woman until she seemingly materialized out of thin air beside his table.

"Will you be ordering anything else?" she repeated with a polite smile and gestured at the plate in front of him.

"No, thank you. It was lovely. You can ring me up." He pushed the remnants of his lunch aside and cradled a cup of coffee in his hands as the waitress nodded. He paused, then gave her a wry smile, reaching into his jacket pocket and then taking his hand out. "Oh, here's my card."

Her brow furrowed as she realized he wasn't holding anything, just empty air. She glanced at his hand, then back at his face, puzzled. "Uh...?"

"Oh," he murmured, as if remembering. "Sorry, love. It's already in your check holder."

She blinked, flipping open the check holder, and a tiny puff of smoke curled out, disappearing as fast as it came. She jolted back slightly, her eyes widening as she stared down at his credit card resting neatly inside.

"Magic, love," he said with a casual smile, lifting his coffee cup to his lips.

The waitress nodded, still half-staring, before retreating into the back to ring him up, her bewildered expression never leaving her face.

He took a slow sip, the warmth spreading through him, but it did little to dispel the uncertainty gnawing at his thoughts. Alex Watts was not going to take the case. She didn't quite say it, but he could feel it in his bones. He was certain there were dozens, perhaps even hundreds of others who would no doubt be happy to take it on and even happier to pocket his money. But Blackwood didn't want anybody else. He wanted Alex Watts.

He couldn't quite articulate at first why he had been so fixated on this particular private investigator. Blackwood had been following the former detective's career since she briefly became a person of interest in the Valentine Killer case. He wasn't alone, of course. Her name was everywhere in the days following the death of the serial killer, but as Blackwood dived deeper into what was known about the events leading up to the dramatic standoff in the Bay Ridge mansion, he became convinced the official story was lacking some important details. There was something otherworldly about the case. He was sure about it.

Intrigued, Blackwood set out to find out what wasn't written on the front pages of the New York papers. After all, despite their vast differences, Simon Blackwood and Alex Watts were, in many ways, kindred spirits. She was a private investigator and a former detective, a master of unraveling mysteries and uncovering hidden truths. While Blackwood was anything but a detective, he had spent most of his adult life hunting for lost treasure, a pursuit that demanded a similar set of skills. Both were driven by an insatiable curiosity and a tenacity that refused to let them quit. Their paths might have been different, but the essence of their work—following leads, piecing together clues, and navigating the shadows of uncertainty—was strikingly similar.

But there was something else. While Blackwood grew up in a Catholic household, he wasn't much of a believer himself. Part of it was the circumstance—both of his parents died in a car crash when he was only twelve, and while he loved his grandmother, who took on the duties of raising him and his two younger brothers, he didn't see her as much of an authority on the subject of spirituality.

As he grew older, as it often happens, Blackwood wondered if there was something beyond the realm of the physical world.

Perhaps it was the slow realization of his own mortality, or perhaps it was his professional experiences that made him question if there was something more behind the curtain.

Despite his extensive search, he wasn't able to find definitive answers about the Valentine Killer's case apart from some vague references to occult items allegedly found on the scene. It was only reported by a fringe online source that didn't inspire confidence, but his intuition suggested there might be a grain of truth to it. Thoughts swirled in Blackwood's mind as he watched the busy New York streets through the café window, the city's never-ending hustle a stark contrast to the stillness within him.

A few times during his career, he came across phenomena he couldn't explain with science alone—the most significant experience happened a mere two years ago when he was traveling through South America with a group of adventurers on the hot tip of a lost city in the Amazonian jungle. Deep in Yanomami territory, they crossed paths with a group of indigenous people, and their shaman wasn't too happy to see them. Blackwood's guides tried to reason with the short, stout man, but it only seemed to anger the shaman more. The man cursed them as he danced in front of them, screaming and shouting, his colorful headdress shaking as if alive. The guttural ramblings of an ancient tongue that seemed to vibrate through his bones were unsettling, but Blackwood and his companions only scoffed, dismissing it as the ravings of a primitive man.

Science had been their compass, logic their map. There were eight hard, experienced men. Blackwood traveled with two other treasure hunters, Milo Diaz and Drew LeClerc. There was also a doctor and four local helpers—two hired to carry their tools and luggage and two guides. If the locals had any concerns, they showed no signs of them.

At first, nothing happened, and by the end of the week, as their group marched on, Blackwood almost forgot about the encounter with the tribe and the angry shaman.

But then came the deaths. One by one, his companions fell victim to a relentless string of misfortunes. First, at night, a large jaguar dragged the group's doctor into the jungle. They awakened to his screams and scrambled after the poor man, shouting and firing their rifles into the air, hoping to scare the animal. It didn't help, and soon, the wailing stopped, swallowed by the dark jungle. As they followed the bloody trail at the first light of the dawn, they found nothing except the good doctor's left shoe and a sleeve of his shirt. The blood had soaked into the fabric, turning it a rusty, brownish-red. The sleeve was shredded, with tattered threads hanging off its edges like frayed ropes.

They buried the doctor's scant possessions in a shallow grave under a simple cross and moved on. But as they trudged forward, the mood turned dark, a shadow of doubt creeping over the group like a malignant fog. The once-boisterous camaraderie was replaced by a heavy silence, broken only by the rustling of leaves and the distant calls of unseen creatures. Whenever they stopped to rest, Blackwood saw glints of paranoia in the eyes of his compatriots, fingers twitching near triggers, ready to defend against an invisible threat.

A few days later, in the morning, both men who had carried their things woke up with a fever. They shrugged it off at first, insisting on continuing the journey, but before noon, neither could move, their faces pale, their breathing laborious and shallow, forcing their group to stop. By the time the sun went down, the two men were delirious, suffering from severe bouts of diarrhea, and despite Blackwood and his comrades taking turns watching them overnight, both were dead before sunrise.

Blackwood wanted to continue, but the guides wouldn't have it. Gripped by fear, they refused to proceed deeper into the jungle and insisted the group turn around. No amount of begging, cajoling, and outright threats seemed to help. A week later, Simon Blackwood was staring out the window of the rickety plane, the vast green expanse of the Amazon shrinking into a mosaic of emerald and ochre as he headed back to civilization. As he watched the jungle below him be replaced by the structures made by men, he found himself wondering, not for the first time, if the supernatural wasn't just silly superstitions of uneducated men. Those deaths left a mark on Blackwood's soul that couldn't be erased by mere logic or science.

The waitress returned with his card, and Blackwood signed the bill and went outside. He paused on the sidewalk for a few moments, feeling the warmth of the afternoon sun on his face. The bustling sounds of the city surrounded him—honking cars, chattering pedestrians, distant sirens. It was a familiar noise, and he took comfort in it, but he couldn't shake off the haunting images of his ill-fated expedition.

Perhaps this was why he had been drawn to the PI, he thought with a sudden realization. He needed to work with someone who had been through a similar experience. In a sense, working with someone else who had never encountered the paranormal would be like if an alcoholic tried to work through his issues with a group of people who had always been sober. They could sympathize, of course, but they could never fully understand. If Alex Watts had encountered the unexplainable before, she would be uniquely suited for the task.

The taxi pulled up to the curb, and Blackwood got in, giving the driver an address in Brooklyn Heights. The streets passed by in a blur, but his thoughts remained firmly anchored in the past. If Alex Watts wasn't going to take his case, there were only two men he could think of capable of understanding the stakes, but only one was a friend—Milo "Magellan" Diaz. He worked with the industrious

Mexican twice—the first time successfully pursuing a collection of Renaissance paintings stolen during World War II and the second time during the doomed expedition to the Amazon. The news of the treasure from the famed *Flor de la Mar* would surely excite the old man.

Diaz occupied a quaint brownstone with white-trimmed windows and a modest garden out front. The wrought-iron gate creaked open as Blackwood made his way up the stone pathway lined with overgrown shrubs and colorful flowers. Reaching the front steps, he raised his hand to ring the bell but stopped halfway—the door was slightly ajar.

Blackwood nervously looked around, his heart pounding in his chest as he pushed the door open. The hinges creaked in protest, and he stepped into the house, immediately assaulted by the overwhelming smell of decay that hung heavy in the air. Against his better judgment, he crept through the dimly lit hallway, each step echoing ominously in the silence.

As he approached the doorway leading into the dining room, a sense of dread washed over him. His eyes widened in horror as he saw a pale foot sticking out from behind the doorframe, unnaturally still. Blackwood's breath caught in his throat as he crept closer, fear gripping him with icy talons.

He stuffed his nose into the crook of his elbow and inched closer until he saw it. Milo Diaz lay sprawled on the floor, eyes wide open in a frozen expression of terror. Flies buzzed around the corpse, drawn to the stench. Diaz wore only pajama pants, his arms and legs splayed out at odd angles. His skin was pale and gaunt, with visible rib bones protruding under thin flesh. The man's mouth was hanging ajar as if in a frozen scream.

"Bloody hell," Blackwood murmured as he tried not to gag. He retraced his steps, almost running, until he was outside again, gratefully gulping handfuls of fresh air. He stood there for a moment, trying to comprehend what he had just witnessed. He knew he couldn't leave without reporting this, and his heart raced with uncertainty. The body. The flies. The images of the Amazonian forest and two listless bodies slumped on the ground flashed before his eyes as he struggled to regain his composure.

Blackwood loosened his tie, feeling a bead of sweat trickle down the back of his neck despite the cool breeze that now brushed against his skin. His hands trembled as he pulled out his phone, fingers fumbling for the emergency dial button. With a shaky breath, he pressed the numbers and brought the phone to his ear.

"911, what's your emergency?" a calm voice answered on the other end.

Blackwood cleared his throat, trying to steady his voice as he spoke. "I... I need to report a death. You need to send someone immediately. It's...it's Milo Diaz. He's dead. It seems like he's been dead for some time."

The dispatcher took down the information while Blackwood recounted the grim scene he had just stumbled upon in Milo's home. The dispatcher assured Blackwood help was coming and advised him to stay put until the authorities arrived. Hanging up the phone, he paced back and forth in front of the brownstone, his mind racing with questions. How long had Milo been dead? What had happened to him? And why did he feel a lingering sense of unease, like a shadow creeping over his shoulder?

Minutes stretched like hours until the police car's flashing lights cut through the dusk. Two officers came out of the vehicle, and Blackwood stepped forward, raising his hand to catch the attention of a middle-aged detective.

"I'm the one who called it in," he said, his words coming out in a rush. "I came to visit him and found the door ajar. I probably shouldn't have gone in, but I was worried."

"That's okay." The tone was soothing, but the detective's eyes didn't match his words as he scanned Blackwood up and down suspiciously. He waved toward the second policeman. "Hang here with Officer Miller for a minute, will you? I'll go take a peek inside."

The detective disappeared inside the brownstone, leaving Blackwood alone with a young, fresh-faced cop who looked like he had just graduated from the academy. Miller avoided eye contact, fidgeting with his belt as if unsure what to do.

Blackwood turned away from the young officer and fished out his cell phone. There was someone else who needed to know about Milo's death—Drew LeClerc. He wasn't a fan of the big Frenchman, but Milo and Drew went back a long way, and the man deserved to learn the bad news from someone he knew.

He dialed the number from memory and held his breath as the phone rang, wincing in anticipation. After a few rings, a soft female voice answered. "Hello?"

"Hello," Blackwood said, clearing his throat. "May I speak to Drew LeClerc, please?"

"Who is this?"

"This is Simon Blackwood." He hesitated for a second. "A friend."

There was a strange sound on the other line, like a long sniffle. "I'm sorry. This is Sarah, Drew's wife. I'm afraid he can't come to the phone."

"That's quite all right." He tried not to sound relieved. "Could you leave him a message?"

"I'm afraid not," she said, and this time he recognized the sound. The woman was crying. "Drew passed away last night. Completely unexpectedly."

"Oh."

"They said it was a heart attack," she said between sobs, "but I don't know if it was. He collapsed when I was in the kitchen. I heard him fall and ran back to him, but he was already not breathing. And he was so stiff. I've never seen anything like this before."

The streetlights flickered and came on, casting long, eerie shadows that danced along the pavement. As Blackwood stood there, helplessly thinking of anything to say to console the widow of a man he never liked, he got the strange feeling his troubles were only starting.

FIVE

I watched the entrance to the fundraiser from across the street. For the past fifteen minutes, I'd seen one German or Italian car after another glide up to the red-carpeted sidewalk, pause long enough to spit out men in tuxedos and women draped in designer gowns, and then disappear into the night. But now, the stream of luxury vehicles had finally started to slow. The event, an annual gathering of the city's most influential, was held at a fancy restaurant tucked under the arches of the Queensboro Bridge. A place sparkled in the gritty darkness of the city around it. And I needed to be inside.

The fundraiser was supposed to be for a good cause—at least on paper. But everyone knew the truth. It was just a convenient excuse for the city's elite to rub shoulders, sip vintage wine from crystal glasses, and sample caviar from silver trays carried by waiters who looked like they stepped off magazine covers. There'd be auctions of overpriced luxury items, but the real action would be in the side conversations. And Dean Graham, the acting mayor, would be right in the middle of it all. He was somewhere inside, no doubt, working the room, making deals that would turn his temporary title into a permanent one. People like him didn't just want power. They craved it.

I had to find the way in if I wanted to meet him, but while DD told me Graham was going to be at the fundraiser, despite his name being absent from the list of attendees, my former partner's help didn't extend as far as getting me a ticket. That part I was going to have to figure out myself.

I changed for the occasion, swapping my usual jeans and leather jacket for an evening gown and Valentino shoes I borrowed from my sister Tina. The simple necklace that flickered in the light of the street-lamps was hers, too, and I made a mental note to resist the urge of trying to figure out its value. I'd sleep better. The only two items that belonged to me were the Kelly bag I got to keep after the last case and a scratchy thong that drove me crazy. It surely was an invention of a man, as no sane woman could come up with something so uncomfortable to wear.

As I watched the entrance, I saw a silver-haired gentleman step outside, the glow of a cigarette illuminating his face in the dim light. He was alone, his expression one of casual boredom, a man who had seen it all and found it lacking. Perfect.

I checked my reflection in a darkened store window, adjusting the necklace, took a deep breath, and crossed the street.

"Excuse me," I said as I reached the man, a touch of urgency in my voice. "I'm sorry to bother you, but I'm in a bit of a predicament."

He looked at me, his eyes momentarily narrowing as he took in my attire. But the suspicion didn't last long, the apparent value of my ensemble putting him at ease. "How can I help you, miss?"

I gave him an apologetic smile, glancing back at the grand entrance to the restaurant as if expecting to see someone emerge at any moment. "My name's Alex Smith. I was supposed to meet my fiancé here, but I can't seem to reach him, and he has the tickets."

"Did you try to call him?"

"Of course. But it goes straight to voicemail, and now that I let the driver go..." I trailed off, waving my hand toward the street as yet another German car spat out a glamorous couple from its belly onto the sidewalk.

The man took a long drag on his cigarette, his eyes never leaving my face. "And your fiancé's name?"

"David. David West," I replied smoothly, leaning into the lie with practiced ease. "He's in finance. Tall, dark, curly hair, wearing a black tux. You might have seen him. He really should be here by now."

He nodded slowly, his gaze softening even more, and flicked the cigarette into the bushes. It flew, sparkling like a meteor, and disappeared into the night. "Perhaps, Miss Smith. There are almost a thousand people in there. Come on, then. Can't have a lady in distress, can we? I'll get you inside."

He stuck his elbow out, and I took it as he led me up the steps and past the doorman and two security guards who barely glanced at me.

"You say Mr. West is in finance?" the man said as he walked through the airy foyer and into a large, open space. The domed ceiling of the restaurant made for some interesting acoustics, intensifying music and conversations into jet-engine-level volumes. "What does he do, exactly?"

"Investment banking," I said, almost yelling against the background noise.

"Ah." His smile remained on his lips, but I could see a heavy dose of boredom creeping into his dark-gray eyes. "I hope you find him, Miss Smith."

I nodded, letting go of his elbow, and turned around to scan the room. The regular dining tables had been removed and replaced with tall standing ones for the occasion. Their round, white, cloth-covered disks loomed in the restaurant's dim light like small islands temporarily sheltering different groups of people as they migrated from one tasting station to another.

A large podium stood in the middle of the room, with a giant TV suspended above it from the ceiling. Its bright screen displayed an impressive running tally of the funds raised. Beneath the setup, a small band played a lively, jazzy tune, filling the air with infectious energy. I snagged a flute of champagne from a passing waiter, the cold glass sweating in my hand, and, ignoring the raised brows from the musicians, climbed onto the stage behind the band.

From my elevated vantage point, I scanned the sea of affluent faces until I spotted Graham. He was at the far end of the restaurant, surrounded by an attentive crowd. They hung on every word, their laughter punctuating his story. I frowned at the naked display of whoring for power and status and climbed down the podium, my heels clicking against the thin wood. As I moved through the crowd, I pulled out a phone and typed, "We need to talk about the murder of Victoria Sterling." It might have been my imagination, but the usually friendly glow of the phone's screen seemed to have taken an ominous hue in the dim light of the restaurant.

I approached Graham's group from behind and slipped through the throng of admirers with confidence I didn't feel. Some faces turned, a few murmurs of annoyance flaring behind me as I made my way closer, but I kept my eyes on Graham.

Reaching him, I stood by his side, my shoulder touching his, my posture casual. He stopped mid-sentence, his eyes narrowing in surprise and annoyance. But before he could say anything, I subtly held up my phone, making sure he was the only person able to read the message.

His frown deepened, his gaze flickering to the text and back to me, and I tipped my head toward the other side of the restaurant. Graham glanced around, his politician's instincts kicking in, masking his concern with a practiced smile. "Excuse me, everyone," he said. "Duty calls."

He extricated himself from the crowd and followed me without a word. I led him through the bustling room until we reached a door marked Staff Only and went into what looked to be a maintenance closet, the chatter and music of the party all but disappearing as Graham shut the door behind him.

"Who the hell are you, and what do you want?" he demanded as soon as we were alone. He was short and heavyset, with a prominent belly that gave him the distinctive shape of a question mark. But his diminutive stature didn't take away from his aura. The man radiated raw power with such intensity I was sure it could be seen from space.

"My name is Alex Watts," I said. "I'm a private investigator, and I just want to help."

His dark-brown eyes narrowed as he scanned me up and down, but then I saw a flicker of recognition, and his face softened. "Wait. *The* Alex Watts? You caught the Valentine Killer, didn't you?"

"The one and only." I gave a mocking curtsey.

"I don't understand." His lips formed a frown again. The change was so quick, for a moment, I wondered how much Botox was required to keep those cheeks from creasing. "I thought you were some yellow press, and the last thing we need right now is a conspiracy theory running amok, upsetting the fragile status quo after such a horrible tragedy."

"You mean upsetting your chances of staying as the mayor? I'm sure that'd be terrible," I blurted before I could stop myself.

"Continuity is important, Miss Watts," he said, ignoring the barb. "You can mock my ambition all you want, but the public needs to know the city remains in steady hands. But I thought you said you were here to help. All I've heard so far is insults."

I had to give it to the man. He was unfazed. I made a mental note to do a deep dive on Dean Graham at the first opportunity I got. But for now, I was on a different mission.

"Perhaps we've started on the wrong foot." I gave him one of my most charming smiles. "I might not care for your agenda or opportunism, but I am here to help. I don't believe Victoria Sterling died from natural causes. And if she didn't, you might be in danger as well."

"Says who? I've personally read the report from the NYPD that said it was a heart attack. I was there too, remember? She just collapsed and went into shock."

"Had you noticed anything suspicious before she did? Anyone acting weird or saying something that didn't sound right?"

"No." He shook his head. "Which you would know if you had read the police report. They interviewed me, along with Victoria's bodyguards and a few people who talked to her at the station. Where are you going with this?"

"I can't tell you where this is coming from," I said, "and will deny I told you anything at all if you ever put me on the spot, but I think she was poisoned."

"Poisoned? How?"

"I don't know yet." It was my turn to shake my head. "But I would like to look into it."

"I don't like this." Graham crossed his arms and started pacing back and forth, his face contorted into a deep frown. "If you have something, why don't you go to the cops? You're famous now. I'm sure they would listen to you."

"I don't have enough, and frankly, I'd like to keep it on the down-low for the time being."

"Oh, I see. You're trying to make some dough." He stopped abruptly in his tracks, turning to stare at me, his dark eyes boring into mine with a mixture of suspicion and anger. "And here you were accusing me of opportunism while trying to milk the city for a wild-goose chase. I think we're done here."

"I don't care about the money," I blurted.

"Good, because the city won't pay you a dime."

"That's fine. All I need is a mandate. I want to question people. To gain access where normally I wouldn't be allowed."

He nodded as if considering. "I can't just not pay you. You can't waste the city resources either, is that clear?"

"Crystal."

"What do you want from me exactly?"

I reached into the depths of my Kelly bag, pulled out a piece of paper, and handed it to Graham.

"What's this?"

"A description of powers you will be temporarily granting me in order to investigate the mayor's death."

Graham took the page and quickly scanned it. "You want access to the NYPD database? That's all you need? You better not be wasting my time."

"I won't. Do we have a deal?" I offered him my hand.

He looked at it for a few long moments and then finally took it and gave it a firm squeeze. His fingers were cold as a lizard's skin. "Fine. I'll open some doors for you."

"Open doors are all I need."

SIX

"I didn't like him," I said as I scrolled down Dean Graham's Wikipedia page. I had to admit he had an impressive resume. An Ivy League school grad. Went on to become a senior partner in a major VC firm prior to entering politics. He'd been married for the past fourteen years, with two beautiful daughters. Not even a hint of a scandal. Until now, that was, when he became NYC's acting mayor when his fairly young boss conveniently cleared the path for him after a devastating heart attack.

"You think he has something to do with it?" Hanna asked me as she continued typing.

I looked over the screen at my assistant and frowned. "I don't know yet. Just a gut feeling. He's clearly very ambitious. And his hands were cold."

"That's, um," she chuckled as she threw me a sideway glance, "a very scientific reason to suspect someone. 'Your Honor, it doesn't matter if he has an alibi. His hands felt like icicles.'"

"Laugh all you want," I said, returning my gaze to the screen. "There's something about him that just doesn't sit right."

Of course, Wikipedia wasn't going to be my principal source of information, but you've got to start somewhere. Most people, especially those in power, live double lives. There's the version of themselves they show to the public—carefully crafted, every detail scrubbed clean. It's the shiny, polished version, like a well-lit portrait. Even the flaws they present are controlled, designed to make them seem relatable, more human. Nothing too damaging. Just enough to make you think, *Hey, they're just like us.* It's an illusion, though. Their real self? That's hidden in the shadows, behind the smiles and speeches. That's the version I needed to find. The cracks, the secrets. The stuff they never put on the record.

Everybody does it, at least to some extent. Think about job interviews. When the interviewer asks you to share a weakness, no one says anything juicy. Nobody's going to admit, *Oh, I'm a raging alcoholic,* or *I've got a serious gambling problem.* No, it's always some harmless fluff like, *I'm too detail-oriented* or *I'm such a perfectionist, it slows me down.* It's a clever way to sneak in another strength wrapped up as a flaw.

Politicians? They're pros at this game. But they do it with more finesse. They toss out a flaw, something for the media or their opponents to latch onto, hoping it keeps everyone too busy to dig into the real dirt. It's all misdirection, like a magician pulling your focus to one hand while the other hides the trick. Meanwhile, the things that could actually sink their careers stay buried, away from the prying eyes.

I like starting with official profiles because they tend to drop a few clues, whether they mean to or not. Sometimes, it's what gets hammered home a little *too* hard. Like, if the guy's constantly talking about his family, always showing up in public with his wife clinging to his arm, you've got to ask: Is he truly the devoted husband, or is there more to the story? Maybe there was an affair, and now she's not letting him out of her sight.

Or take the ones who make a big show of being frugal, turning down fancy dinners, and bragging about their old cars. Sure, it could be discipline. Or, it could be just as easily a cover-up for something else, like debts piling up behind the scenes that would be seen as compromising their integrity. Career-ending stuff. Either way, these profiles give you a starting point, a thread to pull on until the real picture starts to unravel.

Starting with a public profile is like washing away the makeup from someone's face. Sometimes, the person underneath is not that different. There might be a few wrinkles here and there and perhaps a pimple or two, but overall, they are almost the same. And sometimes, you start with a princess and end up with a cackling witch with a giant wart on the tip of their nose.

"Did you get an email from DD?" I asked, referring to the CCTV files from the subway station where the mayor had died.

"Not yet," Hanna said. "But he promised to get them before two o'clock. You really think there's something there?"

"Nothing obvious," I said, glancing at the clock on the wall. To be honest, I wasn't quite sure what I was expecting to find in those videos. Quite a few people from the NYPD must have gone over those files multiple times. The chances of them missing a clear clue were slim to none. But as any seasoned investigator would tell you, detective work sometimes comes down to a hunch. If there weren't any obvious clues in those videos, I was hoping there was *something* that would send me in the direction where I could find some answers.

My phone rang just as I started researching Dean Graham's financial disclosures. I reached out to pick it up but stopped when I recognized the number.

"Who is it?" Hanna asked, watching my reaction.

"Blackwood."

"He's very persistent."

"Sure. Persistence is one way to describe this." I looked at the phone again as it stopped ringing, making the decision for me. Then it started ringing again. I sighed and answered the call, putting him on speaker.

"Ms. Watts." His charming British accent boomed from the

phone. "I apologize for disturbing you, but I think you'll find this information valuable."

"All right."

"You see," he cleared his throat, "after our conversation, I had a feeling you were hesitant to take my case. I don't really know the reasons why you're reluctant to help me, although I have a theory. However, I'm hoping you would reconsider after you learn some of the new developments."

"Don't keep us in suspense then, Mr. Blackwood."

"Fair enough. There are two important pieces to this. First is the artifact itself. It's true there's not much known about it other than a description I've come across in some historical texts. *Darkness*. Not a whole lot to draw from it, but there's something evil about this arti-fact, Ms. Watts. I can feel it."

"I'm sorry," I said, ignoring Hanna's stare. "I don't believe in voodoo, astrology, or any other mumbo jumbo."

"I'm not entirely sure I believe this item possesses any supernat-ural abilities, either," he said. His voice took on a tone I couldn't quite understand. "But it doesn't matter what you and I believe, does it? It only matters if *someone* believes in it. I think, of all people, you should know that."

"What's that supposed to mean?" I felt blood rushing to my cheeks.

"Don't be upset with me, Miss Watts," he said, seemingly unper-turbed. "I'm not a detective, but in many ways, we do similar work. We look for clues. We draw conclusions wherever they might lead us. Your last case wasn't as straightforward as some others, no matter what newspapers said. I've looked into it. The Valentine Killer might have been a madman, but he *believed* he was onto something. I'm sure, to a degree, you'd wondered if he was onto something as well."

I looked at Hanna, and she gave me a *don't-look-at-me* shrug. I turned back to the phone again. "And you think there's someone who believes the artifact has some kind of magical powers?"

"Yes, and here's where the second part of the story comes in. A couple of years ago, I went on an expedition to South America with two more explorers and a supporting crew. Something happened during that trip. Something I can't quite explain. I don't know if it was just a string of unfortunate events. Or, perhaps, it was something more. What I do know is a few people from our crew died. When it became clear to me you were not interested in taking up my case, I reached out to two people who had been with me on the trip. I figured if anyone would understand what I was dealing with, it would be them."

I tensed, somehow sensing where it was going. It was unsettling enough that Blackwood learned something about the Valentine Killer that seemed to have eluded newspaper reporters and even the police. To most but a select few, he was just a crazed killer who got off on ritualistically murdering his victims. But it wasn't so simple. A series of images flashed in my mind—each one more disturbing than the other. The freakish storm that wreaked havoc in the city. The gleaming of the pallasite stone from an ancient meteorite. The leather-covered tome with grooves for sacrificial blood. And the most disturbing memory of them all—the calm eyes of a psychopath watching me as I dangled helplessly suspended in the air. I've had a few brushes with the Grim Reaper. Both as a detective for the greatest city in the world and as a private investigator. None were as close as when I tracked down the weirdest case of my career.

"I take it something happened to them?" I finally said, doing my best to push the images out of my head.

"They are both dead. Seemingly within days of one another."

"How?"

"Natural causes, if you believe the police reports."

"You don't believe them?"

"I am not a doctor," Blackwood said, a hint of annoyance in his voice. "Although there were two people with me during that expedition to the Amazon, I was only friends with one of them—Milo. We'd been on a few trips together. A wonderful man. He was dead when I arrived at the house. Probably had been for a few days, judging by the smell. I wasn't sure if it was a good idea, but I called 911 and waited for help. When the police showed up and had a chance to take a look at him, one of the cops said it was most likely a heart attack.

"But I'm not entirely convinced. There were some...irregularities that made me wonder if it was foul play. I found Milo on the floor in his dining room, but the front door was unlocked and slightly ajar. Surely, there could be an explanation for that but he was only wearing his pajama pants. I find it strange he'd be walking around the house half-naked while his front door was opened."

I chewed on my lip. It was weird, but there could be, indeed, a million reasons why the door was opened. Maybe he heard something and peeked outside, and that's when he felt ill. Tried to go back and find a phone and then collapsed before he could call for help. "And your other friend?"

"LeClerc. We weren't really friends," Blackwood said. "But he and Milo went a ways back. I thought it would be proper if he heard about Milo's passing from me. But when I called, his wife told me he was dead, too. Also a heart attack. And then she said the most peculiar thing. She said he was unusually stiff right after he collapsed. As if rigor mortis set in immediately."

I sat up straight, a rush of nervous excitement going through my veins. Victoria Sterling died from an alleged heart attack and also appeared unusually stiff. Now, Blackwood was telling me two of his friends met the same fate. I had no idea what connection the late mayor could possibly share with my would-be client, but my Spidey senses were tingling again. I could potentially solve two cases in one go. Getting paid in the process wouldn't hurt, either.

"Good timing," Hanna said as soon as I hung up the phone after setting up another meeting with Blackwood. "Just got the email. You want to see it now?"

"Sure."

My computer pinged, and a small window for a shared playback popped up on my screen. I clicked on it, and it expanded into a grainy, black-and-white video.

"It's less than eight minutes long," Hanna said. "Not a lot to work with."

I dragged the slider from left to right, trying to capture the bigger picture first. The platform was crowded from the start, but the poor quality of the image made it difficult to distinguish people's features. Most faces except those closer to the surveillance camera were mere blurs and smudges, barely discernible in the dim light.

With a click, I returned the slider to its original position and pressed Play. The screen flickered to life, showing a bustling platform filled with people hurrying about their day. At the one-minute mark, there was a commotion at the end of the platform, drawing my attention to where Sterling was approaching the camera. She was flanked by two imposing bodyguards, and just behind her, an unhappy-looking Dean Graham could be seen striding forward with purpose. The mayor stopped abruptly, only a step away from being fully visible on camera, her face partially obscured by a nearby column. A semicircle of individuals quickly formed around her, each eagerly vying for her attention with smiles and handshakes.

This went on for a few minutes until a train arrived, and the crowd around the mayor dissipated as people climbed into the car. Then, a few seconds later, Sterling took a couple of unsteady steps and collapsed away from the camera, her legs visibly convulsing. It was hard to watch, but we went through the tape two times, hoping to see something the NYPD had missed.

"It might be nothing," Hanna said as we were watching the tape for the third time, "but can you go back to 2:48?"

I did, watching Sterling greeting people and shaking more hands. "I don't see anyone doing anything suspicious."

"Not other people," Hanna said. "Watch the mayor."

I restarted from the same spot and watched it again. Nothing. "I don't get it. What do you see?"

"Watch her face."

I started the playback one more time, concentrating on the half of Victoria's face that was visible on the camera. I almost missed it this time, too, because of how fleeting it was. We couldn't see who she was talking to. The column was still in the way, but for a split second, there was something in the late mayor's face. A flicker of recognition that was immediately dismissed and washed away. Just like when we see someone in a crowd and wonder for a moment if we know them, only to forget it the next moment after seeing the stranger's face. Sterling might not have been even aware of it herself.

"I'll be damned," I said, looking up and meeting my assistant's eyes.

"Yes." Hanna flashed a big smile across the room. "She thought she saw someone she knew."

SEVEN

To an outsider, the brick fortress in Williamsburg's Northside was just another old structure in a city full of them. But anyone who knew anything about Brooklyn real estate understood the truth: this place was a hidden gem worth much more than a casual glance could ever suggest. The squat, red brick building didn't scream luxury. It barely whispered. With its broad, almost defiant stance, the building could have been mistaken for a warehouse or some forgotten commercial space. The heavy front door, fitted with one-way glass, perched above a lone granite step—unwelcoming, almost daring someone to try their luck. The sidewalk outside was bare, save for a couple of spindly, half-dead maples that seemed to cling to life out of sheer stubbornness. Black panel windows, all fitted with custom shades, kept the secrets of the house locked away from curious eyes. Nothing about it invited you in, and that was precisely the point.

I might not have my sister's eye for luxury real estate, but being a Brooklyn native, I knew enough to realize this place wasn't just expensive—it was worth a fortune. We're talking high seven figures, easy. Drew LeClerc either struck it rich in some treasure hunt straight out of a fairy tale or—and this was far more likely—he married into some serious cash. I'm a cynic—sue me.

Blackwood's tale about his traveling companion's death had all the right notes—it was compelling, tragic, even believable. But I wasn't in the business of taking stories at face value. Not anymore. If I was going to touch this case, I needed more than words; I needed proof, and I needed it without him knowing I was digging. In my line of work, trusting the wrong person could get you killed. Homework wasn't just a formality; it was often the difference between life and death. So yeah, I was going to check things out for myself. Quietly. Thoroughly. And if Blackwood had something to hide, I'd be the one to find it.

Finding Drew LeClerc wasn't exactly a challenge. A quick search through public records, and there he was—only one LeClerc in the entire borough. Easy. Almost too easy. But locating his residence was the simple part. As I stood outside the red brick building, watching its dark windows, I wondered if I made a mistake.

Normally, I'd try to learn what I could before showing up at the doorstep like this. But something held me back from diving in, from prying into his family life, his past, his connections. Call it instinct, call it caution. I wanted my first impressions unspoiled.

"How may I help you?" The voice crackled through the raspy intercom, and maybe it was just my imagination, but there was something in her tone—an undercurrent of sadness that cut through the static.

"My name is Alex Watts. I'm sorry to bother you during this difficult time, Mrs. LeClerc," I said, keeping my voice steady. "But I'd like to ask you a few questions about your late husband."

There was a brief pause, just long enough for me to wonder if she'd already hung up. "Did you know Drew? And...what kind of questions?"

I hesitated, weighing my options. I could spin a story and tell her what she wanted to hear, but I decided to play it straight. "No. Not personally. He was a friend of my client. Or rather, someone I am considering taking up as a client."

"I'm not sure it's a good idea," the woman said, her voice tightening. "Have a good day."

Before she could hang up, I blurted, "He might have been murdered." The words spilled out faster than I intended. "I don't know this for sure—"

The door buzzed, followed by the sharp metallic clang of a lock disengaging. I wrapped my fingers around the heavy handle and pulled, the massive door yawning open. Stepping inside, I found myself in a vast, open space that oozed industrial chic. The foyer stretched out into what looked like a converted garage, the concrete floors polished to a blinding shine. In one corner, a vintage Land Rover Defender sat like a relic from another era, its rugged lines a stark contrast to the sleek surroundings.

I took it all in, my eyes drifting across the room and landing on a high-quality reproduction of a Marc Chagall painting, bold and colorful against the exposed brick wall. It seemed out of place, yet somehow fitting.

"You are a fan of Chagall?"

I turned to the sound of the voice just in time to see an elegant middle-aged woman coming down the stairs. She wore a simple silk pantsuit. Her silver hair was twisted neatly into a perfect, classic bun, not a strand out of place. Her thin, aristocratic face must have turned heads when she was younger. Perhaps it still turned them even now.

Whether Drew LeClerc had been a successful treasure hunter was still up for debate, but I didn't need any more clues to figure out where the money had come from. This woman, standing before me like she'd just stepped out of a boardroom or an art gallery, was the source. The purse behind the man.

She reached the bottom of the stairs and paused, her cool green eyes giving me a once-over that felt like a cold breeze cutting through a warm room. It took everything I had not to fidget under her gaze.

"My mom was," I said, stealing another glance at the painting. "Nice copy."

"Thanks." The woman's smile was polite, but it didn't reach her eyes.

She didn't bother correcting me, but the way her gaze lingered told me all I needed to know. I felt a flush creep up my neck as I realized my mistake. Of course, it wasn't a copy. It had to be the real thing.

Her smile faded, replaced by a cool, appraising look. "Now, who are you exactly, and what's this about murder?"

"I am a private investigator," I said, trying to regain my footing. "A man approached me to take up a case. At first, I wasn't interested —just another wild-goose chase, I figured. But as I started digging, things got...complicated. A few people connected to his search turned up dead—all within a week. All seemingly from natural causes, but there were clues. Not enough to be conclusive. But enough to make me want to start asking more questions."

Her eyes narrowed, but her expression remained calm. "Were they all"—she waved a hand, almost dismissively—"adventurers, like my late husband?"

I leaned in, lowering my voice. "Can you keep a secret?"

She cocked her head, studying me for a moment as if weighing whether I was worth her time. Then, with a slow, deliberate nod, she answered, "Sure."

I hesitated, the name heavy on my tongue. This wasn't just another name to drop; it was a bomb waiting to go off. "The third was Victoria Sterling."

I thought she was going to pepper me with more questions, but she remained still, her green eyes studying me intently.

"There's something you should know," she said, her voice tinged with hesitation, as if weighing a decision. Finally, she seemed to make up her mind. "Come with me."

I followed the woman up the staircase, my hand brushing against the polished oak banister, smooth as glass. At the top, she led me down a quiet hallway until we stopped at a small door. She opened it without a word, revealing a large, rectangular balcony overlooking a walled-off backyard below. The garden was perfectly manicured, with tall hedges and flower beds that looked like they were straight out of a magazine. The red brick walls surrounding the yard were covered in ivy, giving the space an old-world charm, like something you'd find in a European estate.

"Take a seat," she said, gesturing to a pair of wrought-iron chairs with beige cushions and a small round table between them. "I'll be right back."

When she returned, she was holding an old, faded manila envelope. There was something handwritten on one side, but before I could make it out, she set the envelope facedown on the table between us and rested her left hand on top of it.

"You know," she said, her eyes narrowing as if piecing something together, "I've seen you on TV. You caught the serial killer. I guess the city owes you some gratitude."

I slowly nodded, trying not to flinch at the word "caught." At least she didn't say "killed," which was what I usually heard. People meant well, and I got that. Logically, I knew Morton being dead was a good thing, and the world was safer now. But logic didn't stop the nightmares. In those dreams, I was always back at the mansion by the shore, facing Morton again—the man who truly believed he was about to become Lucifer himself. Those nights had nothing to do with logic. They were about fear, raw and unfiltered.

"Drew was acting strange right before he died," she said, a sad smile tugging at her thin lips. "But then again, he's been acting strange most of his life. That's part of why I married him. He was always searching for something beyond the horizon, always chasing after the next adventure. The eternal romantic. My family didn't approve of him. Thought he was too unpredictable, too wild. But I didn't care. I wanted to follow him wherever he went and see the world through his eyes. Feel what he felt."

She paused, her gaze drifting as if she was remembering those times. "I couldn't always go with him, though. Running a large estate spanning two continents is harder work than most people realize. But it was always the same pattern. After an expedition, he'd come back satisfied for a while. But then, sooner or later, he'd get restless again. He'd start talking to his old friends, digging through dusty books, studying ancient maps."

She sighed, her fingers tracing the edge of the envelope. "It'd been a couple of years since he last went anywhere, and I thought maybe it was just that time again. Time for him to hit the road, find whatever it was he was looking for. But it was different. There was something else driving him, something darker."

"What do you mean?"

"He got..." She hesitated, searching for the right word. "Paranoid? Maybe that's too strong of a word. More like worried? He just wasn't himself for the past few weeks. One day, I saw him deleting cookies from every computer in the house. I didn't think much of it at first, but then I caught him doing it again the next day. When I asked him about it, he got all strange, muttering something about glitches."

I didn't want to ask the obvious question, but sometimes, the simplest explanation was the right one. "Was he a faithful husband?"

She smiled softly. "Yes, I believe he was. Not just because he loved me, though he did. Despite my father's doubts, our marriage was strong. But Drew was also practical. He knew without my family's money, he couldn't keep chasing after his dreams, doing what he loved most."

She looked away, her eyes distant. "That's why his behavior worried me. He wasn't one to hide things. Not from me. And then, two days before his death, he gave me this envelope."

I glanced at the faded yellow envelope, but her hand stayed firmly on top of it, pressing it against the table. "Did you open it?"

She shook her head. "No. He told me to give it to one of his travel companions if anything ever happened to him. Said it wasn't worth anything, but it might help them if they were in trouble. The whole thing was cryptic, to be honest. At the time, I didn't think much of it."

I stayed quiet. She wanted me to take the envelope—it was obvious. But if I pushed too hard, she might back out. Sometimes, to get what you want, you have to act like you don't want it at all. "Anything else suspicious happen in the past few weeks?" I asked, steering the conversation back.

She didn't answer my question. Instead, her eyes narrowed, studying me. "You said you were thinking about taking a case but hadn't decided yet."

"That's right."

"Can you tell me the name of your potential client?"

I didn't respond, keeping my gaze steady on her face. Technically, Blackwood wasn't my client yet, so I wasn't bound by confidentiality. But something about giving up his name didn't sit right. Not until I understood the motive behind her question. "Why?"

It was her turn to fall silent. When she spoke, her voice was low and deliberate. "Because Drew told me there were two people who would benefit from what's inside this envelope. One of them, he said, was someone he couldn't stand, but he'd trust with his life in a heartbeat. The other man he called a close friend for years, only to discover he was the type who'd stab you in the back if he had to."

She paused, letting the weight of her words settle. "Here's the deal—give me the name of your client, and I'll hand over the envelope. Or...I won't. Your call."

She knew she had the upper hand and wasn't shy about playing it. I hate being trapped, but sometimes, there's no way out.

"Your move," she said, her fingers tapping rhythmically on the faded yellow paper.

"Simon Blackwood," I said. "I didn't want to take his case. Wanted to look into the mayor's death instead. But it turns out there might be a connection."

She didn't respond. Instead, her slender fingers plucked at the edge of the envelope and flipped it over. She slid it across the table, stopping it just inches from me.

My eyes locked onto the scrawled handwriting: "For S. Black-wood," written in a quick, decisive cursive.

I picked it up and nodded. "May I ask you one more question?"

"Of course."

"What was the other name your husband mentioned? The one he said couldn't be trusted."

Her expression shifted, something flickering across her face I couldn't quite read. If I didn't know any better, I'd say she looked concerned—for me. Which was odd, considering we'd only just met.

"Be careful should you decide to take up this case," she finally said, her voice tinged with something that sounded like regret. "You don't know what these people are capable of. His name was Graham. Dean Graham."

EIGHT

The facility was just off the highway. It was weirdly small for a storage place: a gray concrete slab tucked between a strip mall and a lumber yard. I parked between a beat-up van and a dusty pickup truck and got out of the car, Drew's widow's envelope crumpled in the back pocket of my jeans. It was one of those automated self-storage locations—windowless, isolated, anonymous, the sort of place where things go to be forgotten. Or hidden.

My heart was doing this weird skip thing in my chest, and as I looked around, I couldn't quite understand why. Save for a few cars, the entire plaza looked deserted, but it was just past noon, and the midday sun left nothing to the imagination—no shadows to conceal movement, no bushes to hide behind, just vast, empty, concrete flatlands littered with sunbaked, dusty cars, their bodies shimmering in overheated air. Perhaps the emptiness itself was putting me on edge; if someone were to attack me here, there would be no one around to help. Or perhaps the cryptic message of Drew's widow was what unnerved me. Before I could stop myself, my hand grazed the back of my jeans, feeling the bump of the pistol in its hidden holster.

I strode across the empty lot, the crunch of gravel underfoot the only sound cutting through the stillness. Despite the afternoon heat, my fingers were cold. Reaching the gate, I punched in the code. It squeaked open—just like every other storage facility I've ever seen, right? Wrong.

I stepped into a long, narrow corridor, expecting the usual—a row of dented roll-up doors with oversized, faded numbers spray-painted on them. Maybe a rusted padlock or two. But this? This felt like I walked into a sci-fi movie. Everything—and I mean *everything*—was pristine, brilliant white. The floors were polished like marble, the walls impossibly smooth, reflecting the glow of spotlights overhead, each one glaring down like a miniature sun.

I blinked, trying to adjust to the brightness. The row of doors was there, but they were nothing like I'd imagined. No rough, dented roll-ups; no gritty texture. These were sleek, white panel doors. Perfect. Seamless. Something you'd expect to find in some top-tier law firm, not a storage unit. No doorknobs either. Just digital pads, each one as blindingly white as everything else. Sterile. Clinical.

"What the hell is this place?" I muttered under my breath, my voice bouncing off the unnervingly clean walls as I walked past the rows of identical white doors. Each door's digital display flashed a number. I scanned them as I walked, my eyes darting from one to the next until I stopped in front of unit number 7. I pulled out Drew's paper and double-checked the code. 493432401.

I punched it in. There was a soft click. That's it—just a tiny sound, barely audible in the silence, and the door glided open. I braced myself, instinctively expecting...I don't know what. Something. Anything. But when the door swung wide and the lights came on, I found myself staring into a small, ordinary room.

I let out a breath I didn't realize I'd been holding. The tension seeped out of me, replaced by a flicker of disappointment. I mean, all the build-up, and this was what I get? The inside of the unit looked like a sad little corner of someone's attic: Dusty shelves leaning slightly to the left. A few cardboard boxes stacked haphazardly, their edges soft from age. A pile of old books slouched in the corner. Just a mundane room full of old junk.

I spotted a small leather pouch tucked behind one of the boxes and picked it up. It was light and the soft, worn leather gave under my grip. I opened it carefully, my fingers brushing against something inside—an old manila envelope, a carbon copy of the one Drew's widow had given me. Next to it, a small leather-bound journal. My pulse quickened. The room might be underwhelming, but this seemed to be the reason why I was here.

I tore along the edge of the envelope and pulled out an old black-and-white photograph. It's a group photo. Seven young people in hiking gear, tall backpacks looming over their shoulders, were grinning toward the camera. The landscape behind them was pretty—a mountainous zigzag of a horizon, small puffy clouds. I'm no botanist, but the lush greenery framing the group on both sides seemed tropical. Exotic. I flipped the picture over, half-expecting some kind of note scribbled on the back, but it's empty. Just blank paper, spotted and yellowed from time.

I flipped the card back and study their faces. Six men and one woman, their faces slick with sweat, stare right back.

"Wait, holy shit." My fingers tightened as a jolt of recognition ran through me. The woman. She was much younger here, her hair shorter, wild from the wind, but her face—those sharp features and the intense look in her eyes were unmistakable. Victoria Sterling. Blackwood was right. Somehow, the late mayor was part of whatever this was. A chill ran down my back—this meant, without a doubt, her death wasn't a heart attack. I didn't have any evidence yet, but I was now convinced it was a murder. I took out my phone, snapped a picture of the old photo, and texted it to Blackwood.

He called me back just a few moments later, the excitement in his voice almost palpable. "Alex? Where did you find this picture?"

"It doesn't matter." Blackwood might have gained a few trust points, but I wasn't sure I wanted to share everything with him just yet. It seemed prudent to keep a thing or two to myself for now. "It looks like you were right. Victoria Sterling was mixed up in something."

"Not just Sterling." Blackwood's voice dropped a notch, like he was about to tell me something important. "The other two are in this photograph as well."

"Who?" I asked before I could stop myself. "Your travel buddies?"

"The man on the very left with the most ridiculous mustache is Drew LeClerc. We never quite got along. He was brilliant but, like most Frenchmen, a bit of a pompous twat. And the one to the right of Victoria, the chap in the white hat, that's Milo. Milo Diaz."

I glanced down at the photo, studying the two men. LeClerc's mustache was something straight out of a bad '70s detective flick, and Diaz looked like a guy who could talk his way into—or out of—just about anything. But my eyes kept drifting back to Victoria.

"She's way too young," I murmured, more to myself than to Blackwood.

"Sorry?"

I tapped the photo, my finger hovering over Sterling's face like I was pointing out the obvious, even though he couldn't see me. "Look at her. She's in her late twenties or early thirties. This must've been taken at least twenty years ago, maybe even more. If this was the expedition that found whatever you think was on the *Flor de la Mar*, and it was very valuable, why the hell did it take so long for the items to surface? Why now?"

There was a pause that stretched just a little too long, and I knew Blackwood was chewing on the same question. "I don't know," he said finally. "But there must be a reason. I thought the find was recent, but you might be right. Perhaps it had been found a long time ago."

I stared at the photograph, trying to piece together the puzzle. "Do you know where this was taken?"

"I don't know exactly, but I'm certain it's Sumatra. Look closely at the plant behind LeClerc."

I squinted at the picture. At first, I didn't see it, but then it jumped at me—a massive flower next to the Frenchman, nearly as tall as he was. "Wait. Is that...a flower?"

Blackwood let out a dry laugh. "Yes. The titan arum—or as it's more commonly known, the corpse flower. Magnificent in person, but it smells like a decomposing body. It's native to Sumatra. You won't find them anywhere else in the wild."

I chewed on my lip, studying the monstrous bloom. "The timing really bothers me, though. Did you know anything about this expedition?"

"Not a thing. Neither Milo nor Drew mentioned it to me, either. But then again, you have to understand. Treasure hunters are secretive people. Sometimes, they partner up when they need each other's expertise and skills. But unless it's a necessity, no one will tell you what they are looking for or why."

"Do you recognize anyone else in the photo? Anyone who might give us a lead?"

"Sorry, no. I've never seen any of these people."

"Okay." I tucked the photo back into the pouch, my mind racing. If Victoria Sterling, Drew LeClerc, and Milo Diaz were part of whatever started this, and all three of them were already dead, that left a hell of a lot of questions unanswered. In fact, all I had for now were questions. "Thanks, Simon. I'll keep you posted."

"Wait," he said before I got a chance to hang up. "Does it mean you're taking the case?"

"Yes, um, no." I paused, trying to collect my thoughts. "Maybe. I'll let you know as soon as I can."

I hung up before I opened the journal. I was sure Blackwood could shed some light on whatever was inside of those pages but I wanted to have a chance to process it first. To understand what should be revealed and what cards I needed to keep close to my chest.

The journal felt heavier than it looked as I flipped it open. There's no title or a name. Just notes written in a neat, precise handwriting of a man who takes himself too seriously.

The artifact we found—"Darkness," as it is called—holds a power none of us fully understand. And it should remain that way. Without the key, Darkness is nothing more than an object, ancient and dangerous but inert. To keep it this way...to keep it safe...the key must never become whole. Not in anyone's hands.

I see it as fate the key was made of seven pieces. Seven people with seven pieces scattered across the globe. We all agreed. No one could be trusted with the power alone. We are now bound to each other by this secret, by this burden.

Seven parts for seven of us. One for each, to guard, to hide, to protect. If even one piece is lost, the key cannot be reassembled. Darkness stays sealed.

No one must try to reassemble. Not without all of us in agreement. Not without understanding the consequences.

The Mind's Eye—held by the Scholar
The Ace—held by the Joker
The Blade—held by the Soldier
The Helm—held by the Captain
The Elixir—held by the Alchemist
The Feather—held by the Hawk
The Shade—held by the Phantom

I stopped reading and leaned back. My head was spinning. The Scholar. The Shade. The Joker. What the hell are those names? Clearly, he's referring to the people in the photo, but what's up with all this cloak-and-dagger? Darkness... That was what Blackwood called it, too. I rubbed my temples, trying to make sense of it, but my mind kept drifting back to the place I really didn't want to go to. The Valentine Killer. The storm. The fight at the mansion.

Now, as I stared down at these ludicrous nicknames plucked from a third-rate graphic novel—I could feel that same cold prickle at the base of my neck. The sense you got when you're about to step into something much bigger than yourself. Something dark and dangerous. I tried to shake it off, but it wasn't working.

"Damn it," I whispered to myself, running my finger over the words again. It felt like a riddle I didn't want to solve. But then again, I've never been good at walking away.

I wanted to keep on reading, but this wasn't the time or the place, so I closed the journal and slid it back into the leather pouch, my pulse quickening. Whatever this was, whatever *Darkness* was—it just got a whole lot messier.

I stepped out of the storage room and back into the stark-white corridor, the words I'd just read still turning over in my mind. The place felt tighter, the fluorescent lights harsh and unrelenting, the air so sterile it's suffocating. I needed to get outside, feel something real.

I pushed open the door and stepped into the parking lot, but whatever sunny day I'd left behind was gone. The sky was a thick, sullen gray, clouds hanging low and heavy, ready to split open any second. The temperature had dropped...not enough to make you shiver, but enough to feel it in your bones.

"Great," I mumbled as I hurried across the plaza, the images of the storm from my last case flashing in the back of my mind. "We are only missing the baseball-sized hail now."

Movement. Just a flicker in my peripheral vision, but enough to snap me back. My instincts kicked in, the sort you don't question. They'd pulled me out of the fire more than once. I ducked low, not thinking, just reacting. Then, *crack*—the sharp sound of a gunshot ripped through the air. A car window exploded just inches from where I'd been standing, glass spraying the concrete like confetti.

"Shit!"

I rolled to the side as I ripped the HK from my back holster. I crouched behind the nearest car, my heart pounding in my chest. I risked a glance at the shattered window—a clean hit just where my head was a mere second ago. This was no stray—it was meant for me.

I crouched lower, my back pressed against the hot metal of the car, eyes scanning the lot, trying to spot the shooter. But there's nothing—just silence, heavy and thick. My pulse hammered in my throat. Whoever they were, they were not messing around. And they got me pinned.

Two more shots. The first one slammed into the engine block of the car I was using for cover. The second bullet hit a tire—there's a loud, angry hiss as it deflates, sinking the car lower to the ground. I cursed under my breath. I'm a sitting duck here. I need to move. Fast.

I glanced over at my car, parked just a few spots west, but it might be as well ten light-years away. But I couldn't stay here, either. That's a death sentence. I lifted the HK, its comforting weight in my hand, and steadied myself. There was no time for marksmanship—I just needed to give them something to chew on. I twisted around the car and fired off two quick shots toward the attacker, not waiting to see if they hit anything.

Then I bolted.

My feet pounded against the asphalt as I made a mad dash toward my car, keeping my head low. My breath was ragged, heart thudding in my ears, and I swear I could feel another bullet coming for me any second. But before I reached my car, I heard something else—the sound of a car door slamming shut.

I froze for a split second, listening. The rev of an engine followed, then tires screeched against the pavement as a car I still couldn't see tore out of the lot. I whipped around, gun still raised, scanning the plaza. But it was too late. Whoever it was, they were gone. The stakes just got a hell of a lot higher.

And now, I've got a target on my back.

NINE

"I'm glad you've decided to take on my case," Blackwood said, his eyes flicking down to the printed copies of two pages from LeClerc's journal. The man was composed, his three-piece as elegant as ever. In fact, he was too composed for my liking. As if we were discussing something entirely routine and not something tied to mysterious deaths, including the mayor's, an ancient artifact that allegedly had some supernatural powers, and God knows what else.

"Against my best advice," I heard Hanna Greene mutter from behind her desk. She didn't bother lowering her voice, but Blackwood either didn't hear or pretended not to.

After the would-be assassin had fled, I returned to the office in one piece. Still, my nerves were like high-tension wires. To distract myself, I buried myself in the journal, hoping it would offer more than just cryptic warnings and a group photo.

To my disappointment, the rest of the journal was...well, mostly fluff. Off-the-cuff notes about LeClerc's exploits, anecdotes, enough ego-stroking to make anyone cringe, and some cryptic drawings. But the second page—that was *something*. A riddle. Something tied directly to Darkness. Whatever the hell that was.

"I'm actually still on the fence," I said, leaning back in my chair. "What's in it for you? You said yourself it was buried in the ocean. Someone found it. From where I'm sitting, it seems it belongs to whoever figured out the location of the wreck."

He smiled that annoyingly British, thin-lipped smile of his—the one that said he had a thousand secrets, and he'd only ever let you in on the ones that suited him. "Ms. Watts—"

"Alex."

"Alex." His smile deepened. "I've been doing this for a very long time. With practice, you start to recognize when you're after something rather extraordinary. You learn to trust your hunches. I don't know what the artifact is, but I am convinced whoever is holding it right now might not be aware of its full potential. If we find it, I intend to acquire it."

"And if you fail?"

He shrugged. "What can I possibly do? Sometimes you win, and sometimes you lose. But I think you might be beginning to realize I'm right."

"Beginning to realize?" Hanna snorted, shaking her head. "She just got shot at because of your stupid artifact. This isn't a game."

"She's right." I nodded toward my assistant. "I think whoever has the artifact already knows exactly how valuable it is. And they aren't shy about using force to keep us from getting close. Fortunately for you, bullets don't scare me off. If anything, they make me even more stubborn."

"It's settled then," Blackwood said, his eyes back on the journal pages spread across the table without missing a beat.

Hanna shot me a look that said everything her mouth didn't. She wasn't happy about this, not even close. And when Blackwood left, I knew I'd be in for an earful. But for now, I turned to my copy of the riddle as well.

"To find my piece, seek joy and glory,
    Where stone and sea tell the same story.
    A watchful man stands tall and proud,
    Above the city's endless crowd.
    His feet on land, his gaze to the West,
    In angel's shadow, the secret rests."

"Joy and glory," I said, tapping the page. "This almost sounds biblical."

Blackwood stroked his goatee, his eyes narrowing like he was sifting through old memories. "I doubt it. Drew wasn't a religious man. Far from it. He spent his early years in the Bérets Verts of the French Navy, running covert ops and getting his hands dirty in places most people can't find on a map. Then, after he left the service, he played mercenary for hire. For a good few years, too. Eventually, he married into a wealthy family, got his payday, and settled down. The man was an adventurer, an opportunist. But religious? Not a chance."

I nodded. "The Soldier, then," I said, almost to myself.

"Beg your pardon?"

"The nicknames." I pointed at the journal's copy. "The Soldier. That's him. He must have the Blade piece, then. Whatever that is."

He nodded in agreement. "It fits."

"Joy and glory," I repeated, tasting the words. "It's got to be more than a phrase. Something tied to him. His life."

"Which reminds me," Blackwood said. "Where did you say you found the journal and the photo?"

"I didn't," I snapped. "And I'm not going to."

He raised his hands in a half-surrendering, half-I-don't-want-to-fight gesture.

"It sounds like a large statue to me," Hanna said from her

computer. "A watchful man, standing tall and proud above the city's endless crowd."

Blackwood raised an eyebrow. "An excellent guess, Miss Greene. Perhaps you're onto something."

I nodded and typed "biggest statues in NYC" into a search bar.

"Anything?"

I scrolled through the list, weeding out the usual suspects. "Statue of Liberty, no. John Lennon memorial, no. Atlas in front of the Rockefeller Center? Doesn't feel right. Wait—Columbus! It's gotta be Columbus. LeClerc clearly saw himself as an explorer. No wonder he would feel connected to Christopher Columbus."

"His gaze to the west," Hanna said. "It makes sense. If the statue faces the west, this could be another clue."

I pulled up an online map of Columbus Circle and switched to street mode, zooming in on the statue. There, carved into the side of the monument, was the inscription in Italian.

LA GIOIA E LA GLORIA

I didn't need a dictionary to translate the sentence. "Joy and glory. And he's facing the west. I guess we are taking a trip to Columbus Circle. Hanna, are you coming?"

She pushed her chair back and stood up. "I found your statue... you bet your ass I'm coming."

As the cab slowed to a stop at Columbus Circle, I felt a knot tighten in my gut. Just a few hours ago, someone had tried to put a bullet in me, and here I was, stubbornly chasing down clues to uncover the artifact those killers were so desperate to protect.

I stepped out onto the sidewalk, taking a quick look around. The crowd was thick but looked harmless—tourists, commuters, the usual hustle of the city. Nothing seemed out of the ordinary, but I was still on edge.

"Have to give it to Drew," Blackwood said, craning his head as he looked at the towering monument. "It's a bold move to hide it here."

"Let's just hope no one's paying too much attention to us," I said.

Hanna was already walking around the fence surrounding the

monument, her eyes scanning the memorial with a mix of curiosity and impatience. "Where do we even start?" she asked, shading her eyes with one hand as she squinted up at the towering figure. "That thing's huge."

I followed her gaze, my eyes landing on the angel perched beneath Columbus, holding the globe. The riddle replayed in my mind: *In angel's shadow, the secret rests.*

"It's gotta be somewhere near the angel," I said, stepping closer. "But where? Is there a hidden compartment somewhere? I don't see any place where you could hide something."

"Could it be behind those metal thingies?" Hanna said, pointing above the angel.

"What *thingies?*" Blackwood asked.

"The pigeon spikes?" I offered, though it didn't feel right.

"No, right below them," Hanna said, pointing again. "The thing that looks like a miniature fence. Right above the angel."

Blackwood's face lit up with sudden realization. "Ah, the cresting! Of course."

I surveyed the area. People milled about, taking pictures, chatting, and generally minding their business. If anyone was paying us extra attention, I didn't see them. I saw no cops around, either. Timing would be everything. I waited for a moment when the crowd thinned, then nodded to my companions.

"Cover me," I said, hopping over the fence.

Without waiting for a response, I climbed the three stone steps in front of the statue, grabbed the ledge beneath the angel's feet, and pulled myself up until I was face-to-face with her.

"Sorry about this," I muttered, stepping onto the globe she held and then onto her head. From there, I could just reach behind the iron cresting. My fingers rummaged through dirt and stuck leaves until they bumped against something—small, solid, taped to the inside of the cresting. A square box.

I yanked it free and tucked it into my jacket. As quickly as I could, I climbed down, doing my best to ignore the small crowd that had gathered behind the fence. As they watched me, their faces lit up with a mix of curiosity and mild alarm.

I hopped over the fence, held the box up like a trophy, and shouted, "He finally proposed! And I said YES!" Without hesitating, I grabbed Blackwood and planted a firm kiss on his lips. He caught on fast, playing along as the crowd erupted into cheers and applause. I tugged on Blackwood's sleeve, pulling him and Hanna away from the monument as the onlookers continued to clap behind us.

"Well, I guess making Page Six is better than ending up in a holding cell," Hanna muttered as we power-walked up West Fifty-Ninth Street, heading toward Seventh Avenue.

"My deepest apologies, Miss Watts," Blackwood said. "I assume this wasn't your idea of a good time."

"For the last time, it's Alex," I snapped. "And trust me, I've done worse. Call it...going undercover."

Hanna shot me a look. "You're not going to look at what's inside?"

"Not yet," I said, my fingers tightly wrapped around the box. "We'll wait until we get back to the office. And until I can make sure it doesn't come with any extras."

Blackwood raised an eyebrow, already flagging a cab. "Extras?"

"Yeah," I said, sliding into the back seat. "Like something that goes boom. I don't think opening boxes planted by former mercenaries without some precautions is a good practice."

"You think—"

"Don't worry," I said. "It's unlikely. I'm just being thorough."

As the cab weaved through traffic, I let my gaze drift to the sky, the dull gray shifting into something deeper, heavier, as if the clouds themselves were plotting. The sun had long since thrown in the towel, leaving the city under a thick shroud of gloom. It felt like an all-too-fitting reflection of where my life was heading. Fate had a funny way of playing its hand. Taking John Levy's case—the one that spiraled into the showdown with the Valentine Killer—felt like the key that had unlocked a door to all things otherworldly. It reminded me of a book I read as a kid—the one where if you gave someone your real name, they could always find you. Well, someone out there had my real name now. And the hunt was on.

The cab pulled to a stop outside the office, and the three of us climbed out in silence. Once inside, I wasted no time getting to work. I laid the box on my desk, Blackwood and Hanna hovering just behind my shoulders, and started my examination.

First things first—booby traps. I grabbed a pair of gloves, carefully examining every inch of the box. There was no obvious wiring, no hidden compartments. Nothing that seemed out of place. I tapped it and then gently shook it, listening for any suspicious clicks or hisses. Nothing.

"Okay," I said, pulling a letter opener from the drawer and slipping it under the seam of the box. "You might want to step back—just in case."

I waited until Blackwood and Hanna retreated a few steps and pressed on the letter opener. There was a soft click, and the box popped open. Inside was a small object nestled in a piece of folded velvet cloth.

I pulled it out, my breath catching for a second. It was no bigger than the nail on my thumb—an intricate, steampunk-looking contraption that looked like a telescoping knife. The craftsmanship was astonishing—gears and levers interlocked in a way that seemed both old-world and futuristic. I pressed a small round button on its side, and a symmetrical double-edged blade shot out with a slick click, retracting just as quickly when I released it.

"I guess this is the Blade," Blackwood said.

"Looks like it." I pressed the button again, studying the blade. It had seven round holes right in the middle. A grouping of four smaller holes and three larger ones. "What are these for?"

"They aren't just round," Blackwood said, pointing at the holes.

I grabbed a magnifying glass from my desk, leaning in closer as I slowly pressed the side button that extended the blade. Holding it under the light, I examined the intricate design. The treasure hunter was right—the inner edge of each hole had tiny, segmented rings, almost like the aperture of an old-fashioned camera lens, opening and clicking into place as the blade slid out of its pocket.

Each piece seemed to move independently, designed with a precision that bordered on impossible. As I moved the blade out, they slowly opened fully and retracted as the blade went back when I released the button. This wasn't just a key. It was part of something far more complex. A puzzle within a puzzle.

"Incredible," Hanna said as she leaned in to get a better look. "But what do we do now?"

"I actually have an answer to this," Blackwood said. He strolled over to the oversized leather monstrosity we called the client chair and sat down.

"Please enlighten us."

"We need to find the other pieces of the key."

"Thanks, Captain Obvious," Hanna scoffed, not even bothering to do an eye-roll. "And how exactly do you propose we do that?"

"I don't know where all the pieces are, Miss Greene," Blackwood said with the patience you'd expect from a kindergarten teacher dealing with a not-so-bright child. "But we know the guardians of at least two."

"We do?"

"Yes," I said, pushing the blade aside and sitting down as well. "Milo Diaz and Victoria Sterling."

"Milo was a funny guy," Blackwood said, his eyes meeting mine. "I'm not a betting man, but if I had to make a wager, I'd say Milo Diaz was the Joker. I can go back to his house and see if I can find anything. I also need to introduce you to a good friend of mine. She's a librarian and has a vast knowledge of lore that surrounds many forgotten relics. Perhaps she could fill in some of the gaps. Frankly, I should have thought of this sooner."

"Fantastic," I said, my voice dripping with sarcasm. "I guess it means I'm going to visit the late mayor's place. I'm sure the cops are going to love this."

Blackwood ignored the comment, his eyes focused on the blade as if in a trance. "You do realize," he said softly, "the closer we get to these pieces, the more dangerous this becomes?"

"Yeah," I said, tucking the blade back into the box and putting it into the drawer. "I noticed when I got shot at this morning."

Blackwood smiled faintly, a hollow grin that didn't quite reach his eyes. "All the more reason to stay a step ahead of them."

TEN

Blackwood held the car door open for me as I slid into the back seat. I was going to argue I could open my own doors, thank you very much, but I just looked at him, standing there in his three-piece, and gave up. He followed, giving the driver an address, and the engine hummed as we pulled into the steady flow of morning traffic.

"You'll like Parker," he said. "I think she could help us."

I raised an eyebrow. "She any good?"

"Charlotte is one wonderful, deadly package," he replied with a chuckle. "Sharp as they come. We met at one of Milo's infamous poker parties. She cleaned us all out that night. Played us like amateurs. Still doesn't let me live it down."

"You said she's a librarian?"

"Well, sort of," he said. "The woman's got an eye for rare things. She mostly deals in rare books. Hard-to-find first editions, signed copies, rare variants. Things that make collectors drool. But she does other things, and she has an absolutely first-class network of dealers. If you have something of real value—she will find you a match. For a fee, of course."

"Of course," I echoed, my voice hollow as I stared out the

window, watching the bay as we eased onto the Shore Parkway. From this angle, the Verrazano Bridge seemed to stretch on forever, its pale-blue arch looming over the dark water like some giant, indifferent sentinel. Puffy clouds drifted lazily through the clear sky as if the universe had conspired to create the perfect day. A day where you're supposed to feel at ease.

I didn't feel any of that.

There was a knot in my chest, a tightening sensation no amount of sunshine could smooth out. It was easy to write it off to the events of the last twenty-four hours, but it wasn't quite that. Something was off, and my body knew it before my brain could catch up.

Blackwood, ever perceptive, cut through the silence. "Are you all right?"

His voice snapped me out of the spiraling thoughts. I sat up straighter, the tension thickening. The address he gave the driver—it had been gnawing at me, poking at a memory I didn't want to revisit. I turned to him. "Wait. What's the name of her shop?"

Blackwood glanced at me, confused. "Secret Scrolls. Why?"

And just like that, it all came flooding back.

I leaned back against the soft leather of the seat. Secret Scrolls wasn't just another bookshop. John Levy had been there, chasing leads on that cursed manuscript of his. The Valentine Killer had been relentless, believing that each victim brought him one step closer to some kind of twisted ascension. And right behind that very bookstore, in the dumpster, they found three bodies. A coincidence? I had an issue with coincidences. I thought they were as real as Santa.

"The Valentine Killer case," I said, the words coming out like they left a foul taste in my mouth.

Blackwood winced. "Bloody hell. I should have made the connection sooner. I didn't even think..." His voice trailed off, and for a second, he just looked at me with genuine remorse. "Apologies. I know it must be hard being around places tied to that awful case."

"It's not just that," I said, shaking my head. And it wasn't. This was more than just revisiting a crime scene in my head. There was something else simmering beneath the surface, something darker. The last thing I wanted to do was to connect the craziest thing that ever happened to me to this. Because if I did, it meant I was tangled up in the same kind of mess. Again. It wasn't a rabbit hole I wanted to dive into.

Charlotte Parker was nothing like I imagined. I had pictured someone more, well, bookish. An older, frail woman with oversized glasses perched on the edge of her nose, maybe a bit of a stoop from poring over musty tomes all day. Instead, I found a tall, flat-chested, sturdy woman in her late forties or early fifties with a robust build that suggested she could wrestle a bookshelf into place all by herself if she had to. Her jet-black hair was pulled back into a sleek ponytail, and she moved around the shop with an energy that would put most men to shame. There was nothing fragile about her.

"Alex Watts," she said, her voice crisp as she sized me up, eyes gleaming with sharp intelligence. "Blackwood tells me you're quite the investigator, and he's not the generous kind when it comes to compliments."

"Depends who you ask."

She shot me a grin, but I didn't smile back. There was a lot going on behind those dark eyes, and I hadn't decided if I could trust the woman yet.

"Would you like some linden tea?" she asked. "A friend of mine brought me some exquisite tea from Austria last week."

I opened my mouth to politely decline. Tea wasn't really my thing, and I was more interested in getting straight to business. But before I could get a word out, Blackwood beat me to the punch.

"Thank you, Charlotte. Tea would be lovely," he said, his accent making it sound like we were about to negotiate world peace.

"Come," she said, already moving toward the back of the shop with a speed that suggested she didn't like wasting time. "We have some time to chat before I have to open the shop. Can you tell me what brings you here? Simon's been extraordinarily cagey."

I glanced at Blackwood, and he gave me a subtle nod. "We think someone found a shipwreck and brought a rare artifact to the city," I said. "We were hoping you could help us figure out what it might be."

"Only if you tell me which shipwreck you're referring to," she said coyly.

"It must be difficult to keep such a big store organized," I said, changing the tune, just trying to be polite.

"It's more than a full-time job," she said. "It helps that I live upstairs. My commute is just under sixty seconds."

We stepped into a small office tucked behind a maze of shelves. If the store felt like a library, the office was a different beast entirely.

The space was cluttered but not in a messy way—more like controlled chaos. Piles of books stacked on every available surface. The air had the familiar scent of leather-bound books and something else—old wood, maybe—mixed with the faintest whiff of dust.

A heavy wooden desk with a double monitor dominated the center of the room, paired with a tall leather chair behind it. Parker gestured to the two smaller chairs against the wall.

"*Flor de la Mar*," I said as I watched her fuss over a small table in the corner, pouring the steaming golden tea into delicate white china cups—old-school, elegant. They were so thin I was afraid they'd shatter if you sneezed wrong. Blackwood, of course, sat down with perfect posture, looking like he'd just stepped out of a BBC drama. I wasn't nearly as graceful, but I followed suit.

"You're not playing around, Alex. Straight to the major leagues. You think some of it has been found and brought here?" She handed us the cups, took one for herself, and settled behind the desk.

"I think all of it was found—"

Her laughter cut me off, a deep, resonant sound that echoed through the room, bouncing off the shelves packed with old tomes. "You really believe that? That someone could pull off something that monumental? Three countries—Portugal, Indonesia, and Malaysia— are claiming rights to the wreck. Not to mention if anyone had found it, the treasure-hunting community would be in an absolute frenzy. Do you know how massive that haul would be?"

"Yes." I fought to keep my voice even as a flush crept up my neck. "Somewhere in the neighborhood of two billion dollars."

She leaned back, smirking. "Try closer to ten. But that's not what's important. You understand it wasn't stacked in the form of bearer bonds, right?" Parker's eyes gleamed with excitement as she leaned forward, tapping her fingers on the desk. "We're talking sixty tons of gold, two hundred gem chests filled with diamonds, rubies, emeralds... God knows what else. You can't just stash away an operation like that."

"What do you think happened, then?" Blackwood interjected, trying to save the conversation.

Parker leaned back in her chair, tapping a finger thoughtfully on the armrest. "The most likely scenario? Some complete amateur stumbled on the wreck by accident. Maybe someone local. Then, realizing they were in way over their head, they brought in someone more experienced. They probably scouted it, picked out what they thought was the most valuable, and then bailed, hoping to return later."

"Why would they leave the rest?" Blackwood asked, skepticism creeping into his voice.

"Most likely because they couldn't. Either they didn't have the resources to pull off something this big—or someone else found out. And if they did, I guarantee they shut those amateurs up for good."

I pondered what she said. "You're saying the actual haul hasn't been touched yet?"

"Exactly," Parker said. "The real run on the wreck hasn't even started. Which means there's still time for the vultures to circle. And whoever made the first move might not be around to tell the tale." She glanced between me and Blackwood, her expression growing darker. "If you're not careful, you might end up joining them."

"I see."

"You remind me of someone," Parker said, her eyes locking onto mine with that amused glint, like she knew something I didn't.

"Oh, yeah?"

"Many years ago, I had this business acquaintance..." She smiled. "Well, more than an acquaintance. He was a client at first, bought a few interesting pieces through me and then we just hit it off. The man just *loved* secrecy and lost treasure stories. He had a place upstate. A proper castle, if you can believe it. Threw some of the most extravagant parties I've ever been to."

I glanced at Blackwood again, and he gave me another subtle nod. "As exciting as it sounds, we're not after the whole treasure. We're looking for one particular piece."

"Let me guess." Parker flashed a toothy smile. "Alexander the Great's helmet?"

"No." It was a simple word, but somehow, I found it difficult to say it out loud. The whole "if they know your real name, they'll find you" feeling overcame me again. As if just by voicing the word, I'd break some protective spell and expose myself to some evil entity hiding in the shadows. "We're looking for *Darkness*."

She didn't respond for a few seconds, looking at me. There was only a brief moment, but I saw it—an almost imperceptible shadow of disappointment on Parker's face. I had no idea how she took Blackwood's money at that poker game. I could read her like an open book. That woman couldn't bluff me to save her life.

"Darkness?" she finally echoed, her voice light, amused even.

"Yes," Blackwood cut in. "What do you know about it?"

"Really, Simon?" She turned to face him. "Darkness? That's what you've reduced yourself to—chasing fairy tales?"

"A fairy tale?"

"Oh, please." Her voice took a mocking tone. "The legendary artifact that can only be opened with a key assembled from seven sacred pieces? And each piece is hidden by seven mystical protectors sworn to protect them with their lives? Come on, Simon."

I leaned forward. "You know about it?"

"Of course I know about it," she scoffed. "Everyone and their mother knows about it. You might as well be looking for Thor's hammer. Or Zeus's lightning bolt. Excalibur, King Arthur's crown jewels. Take your pick! The results are going to be exactly the same—nothing. Because none of those items are real. At least Alexander's helmet, as unlikely as that story is to be true, had some merit to it. There could have been an actual helmet that, over time, collected all kinds of stories. This? This is pure fantasy."

I looked at Blackwood. "Can we trust her?"

He gave me a solemn nod. "Yes."

"Okay," I said, settling back into my seat. I reached into my jacket pocket, pulling out a small box. "What if I told you we've already found one of the keys?"

Parker's eyes flicked to the box. "I'd say you're full of shit."

"Open it," I said, sliding the box across her desk.

She stared at it like she wasn't sure if she wanted to touch it. Then, with a flick of her wrist, she opened the box.

Her smile vanished.

The room fell into silence, her dark eyes, usually sharp and playful, turning cold and focused.

She reached into the box and plucked the key out, the polished metal gleaming like something alive, catching every bit of light in the room. Parker turned it over in her hand, eyes narrowing as the weight of the thing registered. She wasn't just looking at it, I could tell—she was *feeling* it, sizing up something she wasn't sure she wanted to understand.

"Well, fuck me," she muttered, her thumb finding the small button on the side of the piece. With a faint click, the tiny triangular blade shot out, glinting dangerously in the light. She released it, watching the blade retract. "The Blade. Right here, in my hands."

"You think it's real?" I asked, my voice low. I already knew the answer, but I needed to hear her say it. I needed her to confirm it wasn't some elaborate toy. A counterfeit.

Parker stayed quiet. She just stared at the key, her expression shifting from disbelief to something harder. "I thought I'd seen it all," she murmured, almost to herself, like the world around her had shrunk down to just her and that cursed piece of metal. "Looks like I spoke too soon. This is as real as it gets. Too bad."

"Too bad?" I echoed, leaning in. "I don't understand. You said it was real. Why is it too bad?"

Her gaze flicked up to mine, the intensity in her dark eyes hitting me like a physical force. She let out a slow, almost reluctant breath like she was about to admit something she'd been running from for a long time. "Because it means Darkness is real, too."

The words hung in the air, cold and final. Perhaps it was my imagination or the lingering PTSD from my last case. But I could have sworn the room seemed to shift. The air thickened, heavy with something I couldn't name. Fear? Dread? No—something older. Something primal.

I swallowed hard, fighting the urge to look over my shoulder, as if expecting something to crawl out of the walls. It was ridiculous. But in that moment, it didn't feel like paranoia. It felt like instinct.

Parker gently laid the key back into the box, snapping the lid shut with a finality that echoed through the room. She leaned back in her chair, folding her arms across her chest like she was trying to put some distance between herself and what she just touched. But I could see it in her eyes—whatever sense of control she had, whatever smug superiority she'd walked in with, was gone.

"Before I tell you anything else, I suggest you keep this," she nodded at the box, "and whatever other pieces you find here. No one will connect either of you to me, and if one of you is compromised, you can ensure the pieces are safe."

I thought about it for a moment. "I'm good with it. Simon?"

"Sure." He nodded in approval. "It's probably a wise thing to do."

"Tell us what you know," I said. "I want to understand what we are getting ourselves into."

"You sure you're ready for this?" she asked, her voice low, almost daring me to say no.

I wasn't sure. Not really. But that didn't matter. "Yes."

"You know how this story goes. There was an ancient order.

Powerful. Untouchable. Until they weren't. Then the rebels showed up, guns blazing, so to speak. The war dragged on for ten long years. Blood, betrayal, all the good stuff. They wiped out most of the old guard. Threw some in chains. But a few—well, a few managed to play the game right. They switched sides, threw their lot in with the upstarts, and somehow came out the other side looking like heroes. But not all of them were as loyal as they seemed."

"You've got to be kidding," Blackwood said, his voice thick with something I couldn't quite place—incredulity, fear, maybe both.

Parker didn't even glance at him. "But the one who sided with the rebels? Yeah, he'd ended up betraying them, too."

"Hold on—what? A war that lasted ten years? An ancient order? Rebels?" I shot a look between Blackwood and Parker, completely lost. "What the hell are you two talking about?"

"She's talking about Titanomachy," Blackwood said. "The ten-year war between Titans and the new gods, led by Zeus."

"The Titan who joined the new gods was named Prometheus. And, well...you know the story. When Zeus learned Prometheus turned traitor," Parker said, her voice low, "he wanted revenge. So he went to Hephaestus, the master craftsman, and ordered something special. Not a weapon. A woman. Beautiful. Flawless. Built for one purpose. The gods all gave her gifts, but Zeus's gift was different. When she was ready, he gave her a box and told her—*This is my own special gift to you. Don't ever open it.*"

"Are you kidding me? Pandora?" I said, my voice thick with disbelief. "This is what it's all about?"

Parker's eyes locked onto mine. "Yes. The key, made of seven pieces, is the one that opens it." She leaned forward, her voice almost a whisper. "Pandora's box."

ELEVEN

I kept coming back to LeClerc's journal, flipping through the pages for what felt like the hundredth time. My fingers itched to find something—anything—I might have missed. That persistent whisper at the back of my mind, gnawing at me like a toothache. Telling me there was more to this. Something I hadn't caught. Something crucial.

Maybe I was just looking for a distraction to take my mind off the insanity of the conversation Blackwood and I had with Charlotte Parker back at the rare books shop. Zeus? Prometheus? Pandora's box? It sounded absurd. Mythological nonsense. How could any of it possibly be real? It didn't make any sense.

But then again, it didn't have to.

I thought back to my last case. That nightmare had shaken the foundations of what I thought was real and what wasn't. It didn't completely destroy them, but the cracks were still there, and I didn't want them to widen. None of this mattered, though. Whether or not I believed in the ancient gods, one thing hadn't changed. My job was still the same. I wasn't a cop anymore, but even when you strip away the badge and the rules, the mission stays pretty damn similar.

Morton thought he was on his way to becoming Lucifer himself.

But honestly, he could've believed he was about to be the Dalai Lama for all I cared. He was leaving a trail of bodies to get what he wanted. That's all that mattered. Somebody had to put an end to it.

And now, if someone was killing because they thought they were after Zeus's gift? They needed to be stopped, too.

And so, I kept on reading the journal. About halfway through, my thumb snagged on a page, and I stopped. It wasn't the usual scrawl or another snarky anecdote but a drawing—rough, hasty, but precise in its way. It was a door, plain and unmarked, except for a sign overhead. *The Pulse*, it read, but the "S" was styled like a dollar sign, making it jump off the page.

Below the sketch, a note: *Unlocks third Friday at* 10. 777

I blinked, staring at the words, the gears in my brain turning. My gaze darted to the corner of my computer screen. Today was, in fact, the third Friday of the month. And the number "7" again.

I opened the internet browser and ran a quick search. "The Pulse, New York."

Boom. There it was. A nightclub. Large, loud, trendy. A place where music never seemed to stop, and neither did the bodies. Curious, I pulled up a street view of the building, and my own pulse quickened. The sign above the entrance was an exact match to the sketch—the "S" in *Pulse* was the same dollar sign.

The whisper in the back of my skull turned into a full-on shout. This was a neon-lit, bass-thumping, pulsing clue.

"Hey, Hanna," I called out, not taking my eyes off the screen. "You ever been to a club, the Pulse?"

She glanced up, holding a stack of papers. "No, but it does sound familiar. Is it in the Village? Why?"

"The Village, yes," I said, my fingers drumming on the desk. "A drawing from LeClerc's journal. The design of the sign matches. And get this—underneath, it says it unlocks on the third Friday at 10."

Hanna raised an eyebrow. "Third Friday? As in the third Friday of the month?"

"I think so."

"That's today."

I swiveled my chair to face her. "Exactly. I'm going to check it out. Worth a shot. You wanna tag along?"

She chuckled, shaking her head. "You're aware I have kids and a husband, right?"

"Yeah, yeah." I waved a hand, though part of me wished she could come. She had a keen eye for details and, sometimes, a fresh pair of eyes could be really beneficial.

It was 9:30 when I stepped out of the cab, and the bass from the Pulse hit me before I even reached the entrance. The place was alive. Neon lights flickered along the exterior like a cheap Vegas knockoff, but it had the unmistakable vibe clubs in the Village always did—wild, untamed, and loud as hell.

A line snaked down the block, a mishmash of twenty-somethings, hipsters, students, and tourists all dressed to the nines, eager for their night of debauchery. I made my way toward the entrance, slipping through the crowd. At the door, a bouncer built like a brick wall barely looked at me as I handed him a twenty. He took it, the note disappearing in his huge, meaty hand, nodded and gestured toward the door.

Inside, the place was a sensory overload. Strobe lights flickered in time with the pounding bass that seemed to vibrate through the floor and walls and straight into my bones. The air was thick with sweat, perfume, and pheromones. It was still too early for things to get weird, but the night was young.

I pushed through the crowd, my eyes scanning every corner of the club. To my left, a bar stretched along the back wall, bartenders moving with practiced speed, sliding drinks across the counter like it was an Olympic sport. One tried to flag me down when his eyes met mine, but I moved on. That wasn't what I was here for.

I wove my way through the dance floor, pulsing under the flashing, colored lights. The crowd was a mass of limbs, bodies grinding together, lost in the music. Above them, two cages hung from the ceiling, each one swaying slightly. Inside, two barely clothed dancers—

one male, one female—gyrated suggestively, their movements hypnotic under the strobe.

The noise was deafening. A DJ stood on a raised platform, twisting knobs and hyping the crowd, his voice distorted through the speakers as the bass dropped again, sending a ripple of excitement through the room. I pushed farther in, trying to get a better sense of the layout. There had to be something else here—something more than sweaty bodies and overpriced drinks.

I glanced toward the bar again, and something caught my eye—a waiter slipping into a service corridor. Normally, I wouldn't think much of it. Staff coming and going. It was a club, after all. But then, as the door swung shut, I saw it. Barely visible in the dim lighting, scrawled on the wall next to the corridor entrance—777.

The number from LeClerc's drawing. "Unlocks third Friday at 10. 777." My pulse kicked up a notch.

I made my way toward the bar, trying to blend with the crowd, moving in time to the music. A young man grabbed my waist, his fingers firmly planted on my ass, and swung me toward him, a huge drunken grin plastered across his face. He shouted something to me, unintelligible in all the noise, but I frowned and pushed him back. He shrugged, unperturbed, and turned away. No one else seemed to be watching me—perfect. I slid past the bar, checking to make sure the bartenders were too busy to notice as I slipped into the service corridor.

It was long and narrow and dimly lit, the music fading into the background. It smelled faintly of stale beer and kitchen grease. I passed a bustling kitchen, the clang of pots and pans muted behind closed doors, and then a few managerial rooms—nothing out of the ordinary. But then, near the end of the hallway, there it was—an unremarkable door with a keypad. Above it, painted faintly in the same dull color, was the number 777.

I stopped, listening for any sounds behind me, but apart from the subdued thumping of the bass coming from the dance floor, there was nothing. No one's coming.

I tried the handle—it's locked, of course. My fingers hovered over the keypad, hesitating for just a second before I punched in 777. For a split second, nothing happened, and I wondered if maybe this was a dead end. Then, with a soft click, the lock disengaged.

I pulled the door open, and it resisted—much heavier than I expected. As it swung open, the air beyond felt cooler. I stared into a long tunnel. It was damp and dark—there was an underpowered light every twenty feet or so, but they were so dim that, if anything, they made the tunnel feel even darker.

I stepped through, the faint smell of earth and concrete hitting me as the door swung shut behind me with a solid thud, sealing me in. I could no longer hear the music, not even the bone-vibrating bass. I guessed I had no other choice but to go on.

The tunnel stretched out before me, narrow and cold, its walls rough with concrete. The air here grew heavier and cooler, as if the weight of the earth was pressing down from above. And the farther I went, the harder it was to shake the feeling I was trapped in a different world. Alice, tumbling down the rabbit hole.

A few rooms branched off from the main tunnel, their doors unlocked, but when I peeked inside, there was nothing—just empty, unused spaces with old chairs or dusty shelves. They hadn't been used in years. Nothing worth my time. Until I found one door, slightly ajar, and it felt different even before I opened it.

It looked like an office. Nothing fancy—a wooden desk, a wrinkled leather chair, a few file cabinets lining the walls. It all looked old, but it was frequently used. There were papers scattered across the desk, and the faint smell of cologne or perfume lingered in the air.

I stepped in, drawn to the desk, and started searching. Papers, notes, nothing of interest—mostly ledgers and receipts—but then, I opened the top drawer and bingo. It was small—a carbon copy of the one that held the Blade. My heart skipped.

I carefully pulled it out, feeling its weight in my hands. When I opened the lid, nestled inside was another steampunk-looking device, as small as the last—no more than the size of my nail. It was shaped like the letter *A*, with intricate designs on the sides. As I tilted it under the dim light, marveling at the tiny gears built into the device, the patterns looked familiar, almost like the spades symbol on a deck of cards.

The Ace.

I turned it this way and that, but before I could ponder it further, a sound pierced the stillness of the tunnel—soft at first but growing louder.

Chanting.

I froze, every muscle tensing. The rhythmic, low hum of voices was coming from deeper within the tunnel. An icy chill snaked up my spine as I slipped the Ace into my pocket, closed the drawer, and moved toward the door, listening. The chanting grew stronger, and with it, the unmistakable pull of something dark. Whatever was happening down here, it was no good. And it was calling.

The chanting drew me in, tugging me deeper down the tunnel like a thread winding tighter around my chest. As I got closer, the sound filled my ears—a low, hypnotic murmur. The walls almost seemed to vibrate with its resonance, like the tunnel itself was alive, thrumming with the strange energy of their voices.

I rounded the corner and saw it—a large open area, some kind of underground chamber. The ceiling stretched much higher than I expected. Multiple tunnels branched out in every direction, like veins feeding into this dark heart.

There, hooded figures stood in a loose circle, all of them focused on the person in the center, the one leading the chant. Their voices rose and fell, the strange language twisting in ways that made my skin crawl.

I leaned into the shadows, watching. I didn't recognize the words, or even the language—Greek? But there was something deeply unsettling about the ritual. Like they were calling out to something. Or someone.

While I stood there, trying to decide on my next move, another figure emerged, moving quickly and purposefully. I almost didn't register it at first—the way this person walked with intent made me think it was part of the ritual. And then a gunshot cracked through the air, shattering the eerie calm.

The lead figure in the middle stumbled, their chant choking off as the bullet hit. Chaos erupted in an instant—screams echoed off the walls and the hooded crowd scattered in every direction, fleeing back into the tunnels. But the assassin didn't retreat. He rushed forward, straight for the fallen leader.

Instinct kicked in before I could think.

I leapt from my hiding place, rushing toward the assassin. He was already bending over the body, his fingers searching for something. I crashed into him, driving my shoulder into his side. He stumbled back, startled, and for a second, I thought I had him.

But he recovered fast, jumped to his feet, and bolted back into the tunnel.

I wanted to chase him, but I forced myself to stop. The figure on the floor was still, too still. I knelt beside him, pulling back the hood just enough to see his face. He was older—in his late fifties. And, oh yes, he's famous and very, very dead.

"Shit."

My eyes drifted to his chest, where his robe had fallen open, revealing his bare chest. There's a strange tattoo. It was small, sitting right on top of his sternum. A heart-shaped symbol, dark ink stark against his pale skin. It was a strange design. I didn't have time to study it, but it felt...wrong.

I stole a wild glance around—I was still alone—and took a picture of the tattoo. I was about to get up when I noticed something clutched in the man's hand.

I couldn't believe my luck, but it was another key. And not just any key—it was a small, intricate piece with that same steampunk design. My heart beat so hard, I was afraid it was going to break my ribs.

I pried the key from his fingers, still warm, and slipped it into my pocket just as the sounds of more footsteps echoed down the tunnels.

It was time to go.

Without thinking, I took off into one of the dark tunnels. I didn't know where it led, but I didn't have any other options. The air was thick and stale as I sprinted down the passageway, hoping—praying—it took me somewhere safe. If history was any indication, my chances were slim.

TWELVE

After the initial chaos—when the shot rang out and the man leading the chant hit the ground—there was a strange, brief moment of quiet. A heartbeat of stillness before the world tipped back into its usual madness. By now, the place could be crawling with cops, or maybe no one dared to call them. Maybe they were all too scared, too deep in whatever secret world they were part of. The man's body was cooling on the floor in silence, and I had no way of knowing what was happening behind me. But I wasn't sticking around to find out.

The tunnel stretched ahead, a yawning darkness that swallowed everything. As the dim light from the cavern disappeared behind me, I had to slow down and turn on the flashlight on my phone just to see more than a few feet ahead of me. The ground beneath me changed. The solid concrete floor gave way to gravel first, crunching beneath my feet, then to dirt. It was getting colder, damper, and soon, the soles of my shoes were soaked through, wading through shallow, foul-smelling water that reeked of things I didn't want to think about.

I checked the phone's battery—already halfway drained. Great. No telling how much longer the light would last. I had no idea where this tunnel was leading, and I prayed it'd connect with the subway network, not the city's sewage.

I kept moving, the beam of my phone light bouncing off the damp walls. Soon, I reached a fork in the tunnel. Of course, there was a fork. It couldn't just be a straight shot, could it? I slowed to a stop, scanning both paths, but all I saw was more darkness. No clues, no signs pointing me in the right direction—just two ways to get even more lost.

I knew Parker and her ludicrous story of Zeus and Pandora's box was to blame, but standing there in the dark, I couldn't shake the creeping sense I wasn't just running blindly through the tunnels with a murderer on the loose but was sinking deeper into something ancient. Dangerous.

I glanced at the walls again. They seemed to close in, the narrow passage narrowing even more, the air turning thick and cold. The irrational thought clawed at my brain: *This isn't just a tunnel. This is the Labyrinth.* But I wasn't Theseus, and I sure as hell didn't have a magic thread to guide me out. I stood there, paralyzed for a second. Left, or right? One way might lead me back to the city, to freedom. The other? God only knew.

"Great," I said out loud, more to break the suffocating silence. It failed, the sound of my voice defeated by the dampness of the foul-smelling air.

I glanced back at the tunnel that I came from, tempted for a moment to risk it and return to the land of the living through the nightclub. But it was a dumb idea, and I knew it. Even if nobody called the cops yet, eventually, this was going to be discovered. And when that happened, everyone and their mother would remember a filthy woman stinking to high heavens, making her way through the dancing crowd and out of the club. The only way to get out of this place was to go forward.

I went right.

A lifetime ago, back when DD and I were scouting a giant aban-doned warehouse—a tip from his shady informant came in about a smuggling ring—the place had been pitch-black. Shelves were every-where, as if someone had tried to create a maze out of cheap plywood and rusting metal. It was supposed to be simple: run in, grab some evidence, and get the hell out of Dodge. Instead, we ended up crawling our way through what felt like a place that had been designed to trap rats. I remember only half-jokingly telling my partner we were going to get lost, wandering around until we ran into the smugglers. He snorted like a water buffalo and told me about the *hand on wall* rule.

"It's simple," he'd said, his whisper loud enough to rattle shelves nearby. "If you ever find yourself lost in a maze, keep your hand on the wall. Figuratively speaking. You don't have to actually touch it. Just follow it, no matter how many twists and turns. Eventually, you'll find a way out."

That night, we'd wound our way through the death trap and emerged on the other side without having to test the rule. The smug-glers never knew we were there.

Now, here in this damp, suffocating tunnel that seemed like it was pulling me deeper into something I didn't want to find, I could almost hear DD's voice in my head, calm as ever: *Hand on the wall, Alex. Just follow it.*

I powered down the phone and stood there for a few long moments, fighting the primal fear as the darkness enveloped me. It was absolute, the kind of darkness most people never experience in their entire life. Every fiber of my being wanted to turn the light back on. To see *something*. But I knew it would be counterproductive. The floor was level, and if I moved slowly, I didn't run the risk of stum-bling over anything or falling into a well. I needed to preserve the light for later if I could.

I reached out, placed my palm against the cold, clammy stone, and started moving again. I might have decided to go right, but it didn't matter. As long as I kept my hand on the wall, I'd find my way out—or at least, I hoped to God I would. If I was going to die in this tunnel, I swore I'd turn into a ghost and haunt DD forever.

I started to move forward, making long, deliberate shuffles, testing the floor in front of me with each step, cautious as if the ground might drop out from under me at any second. One foot first, the other dragging to follow. The tunnel seemed to stretch on endlessly, a black hole swallowing time itself. Soon, I slipped into a kind of trance—my brain on autopilot, my body stumbling forward like I was one of the undead: one hand scraping the wall, the other cutting through the thick darkness like a blind person trying to find their way.

I lost track of how far I'd gone. My legs moved because I told them to, but everything else—the sense of direction, the purpose— had dulled. Then, somewhere between one shuffle and the next, something changed. It was subtle at first—almost imperceptible—but after God knows how long of walking in absolute blackness, I felt it. The darkness around me wasn't quite as thick anymore. There was something ahead, something faint—just enough light for me to notice the shift. My brain, groggy from the constant press of the dark, slowly clicked back into gear.

For the first time in what felt like forever, my spirits lifted. There was light ahead—finally, an end to this cursed tunnel. I wasn't imagining it. My legs picked up speed on their own, the exhaustion that had dragged me down replaced by a flicker of hope.

I wanted to break into a run, get to the light faster, to see the exit. But then, just as I was about to quicken my pace, I froze. The sharp, unmistakable sound of metal sliding into place echoed through the tunnel, cutting through the twilight like a knife.

Someone was racking a pistol.

I stopped breathing, every nerve on high alert. The sound was faint, but it was enough. It wasn't coming from behind me either, which would've been bad enough, but worse—it was ahead of me, somewhere between me and the light. The way out was blocked.

I swallowed hard, instinctively flattening myself against the wall, trying to control the rush of panic clawing at me. The assassin seemed to have played his cards right. Instead of trying to engage me at the cavern, he came here first and waited for me to stumble straight into his trap. And I almost walked right into it.

Options ran through my head. Turn around? Head back into the tunnel and pray I found another way out? Or take my chances and confront whoever was ahead? Neither choice was good.

He must've heard me, too. Had to. That's why he racked his firearm, getting ready to pounce. But he didn't know where I was yet. Not definitely, at least. Otherwise, I'd already be facedown in the muck, a bullet in my chest, bleeding out into the grime and God knows what else down here.

I stayed still, pressed against the wall, ears straining for any other sound—a footstep, a breath, anything that would tell me where he was. My pulse thundered in my ears, loud enough to drown out everything else, but I knew if I moved too fast, too carelessly, I'd give myself away. And if that happened, well, the next sound I'd hear would be the crack of gunfire, then would come pain, and the light up ahead would be the last thing I'd ever see.

Nope. I wasn't about to go down like that.

I moved as slowly as I could, keeping my breathing shallow and controlled. My hand reached under my jacket, fingers brushing the cool grip of the HK. The weight felt right and familiar, and I pulled it out of the holster with ease. Time stretched out. Every tiny sound seemed amplified in the silence.

With the gun in my hand, I knew what came next, and it wasn't going to be pretty.

With a deep breath, I crouched and lowered myself into the shallow, grimy water. The stench hit me immediately, sewage and rot clinging to the air like a wet blanket. It took everything I had not to gag right there. I swallowed hard, forcing the bile back down, and pressed forward.

The water soaked through my clothes instantly, cold and filthy. I could feel it seeping into my underwear, and the slimy texture made my stomach churn. I wanted to jump up and shudder in disgust, but I couldn't. Not now. The exit was just ahead. I could see the faint light from here. But somewhere between me and freedom, there was a bastard with the gun.

I steadied myself, gripping my HK tighter, and began to crawl. Slowly. Inch by inch. The sludge pulled on me, making every movement harder, more revolting. My elbows and knees sunk into the grime, but I kept on moving, closer and closer toward the light—and the assassin waiting for me at the end of the tunnel.

The light grew brighter as I inched forward. My heart hammered in my chest as I realized what I was seeing: a turn in the tunnel and light streaming from somewhere behind it. The way out. But there was a catch—a silhouette.

I could see him now—right there. Waiting for me. Tall, armed, half-hidden behind the bend. The light was behind him, casting his form in shadow and masking his face, but the glinting outline of the pistol was unmistakable. And I was close. Too close. If he spotted me, I'd be a sitting duck.

No cover. No options. Just me and the muck.

I couldn't stay here forever, though. If he got impatient and came my way, I was done. Time for a gamble.

With my left hand, I searched the ground around me, fingers sweeping through the wet, slimy dirt. There. A pebble. Small but solid. It would have to do. I picked it up and threw it hard against the opposite wall, the clatter echoing in the tunnel.

The assassin reacted instantly. His head snapped toward the sound. He stepped out from behind the bend, gun raised, and fired toward the noise—two shots. Fast and precise.

My turn.

I squeezed the trigger. One shot, center mass.

His yelp of pain and anger echoed down the tunnel, but the bullet only seemed to have grazed his arm. I saw him stagger, gripping his wound. For a second, I thought he'd come at me, but he stumbled back, retreating toward the light.

I heard the stomping of his boots on metal, the sound of a gate slammed shut, and then silence.

Slowly, cautiously, I crawled toward the turn, keeping my HK ready, just in case his flight was nothing but a ruse. When I reached the bend, I peeked around and finally saw it—a shaft with a steel ladder leading up to a grate. My way out.

I didn't waste any time. I climbed the ladder, leading with my pistol, in case more surprises waited for me on the other side. My every muscle ached, every part of me filthy and exhausted. When I pushed the grate open and climbed out, I found myself in a storm drain behind a warehouse.

I took a deep breath, the fresh, cool night air hitting my face. Freedom. But I was a mess. Covered in grime, drenched in sweat, and dead on my feet. And the smell. Oh man, the smell alone could kill. It was weapons-grade stuff. But it didn't matter. I was alive, and I'd retrieved two more pieces of the key.

I just needed to go home.

THIRTEEN

I pulled out the phone as I stood there, still dripping with grime, and long-pressed the power button. It took a few seconds—long enough for me to start wondering if the thing was dead, but then the screen flickered to life. 3:14 a.m. Great. Not exactly prime time for getting a ride. But then again, no cabbie in their right mind would let me in looking like this. I tried smoothing out my blouse but got another whiff of myself and stopped. Yeah, that wasn't happening. Somehow, I smelled worse than the sewer.

I thought about calling John Levy. He'd probably come in a heart-beat, but I couldn't do that to him. It wouldn't be fair. DD would come right away, too, but that would probably mean a long lecture, and I was fresh out of patience for those. But more importantly, I'd have to explain what exactly I was doing in Manhattan looking like this without somehow telling him about the past few hours. Scratch that.

That didn't leave a lot of other options. I scrolled through my contacts, found Hanna Greene's name, and pressed Dial. My stomach knotted. Hanna was a lot of things, but she wasn't exactly the "let me get up at 3 a.m. and drive all the way to Manhattan to pick up your sewer-smelling ass" type. The phone rang once, twice, three times. I sighed, already prepping myself for the tongue-lashing I'd get when she finally picked up.

Then I heard her voice. "Alex?" She sounded...relieved. And there was noise in the background. People talking in loud voices. Something banging. "Thank God you're okay. I've called you like a thousand times!"

"Wait, what?" I blinked, thrown off. "What the hell are you talking about?"

Right on cue, my phone buzzed in my hand—one notification after another. Texts, missed calls, voicemails—the screen was lighting up like I'd hit the jackpot on a slot machine. While I was playing cat and mouse in the tunnels, something happened. Something big.

"Where were you all this time?" she asked, completely ignoring my question.

"I'm in the city. There's a tunnel network under the Pulse, apparently. It's a long story, but suffice it to say there was a murder, and someone tried to kill me, too. I escaped through the tunnels. Now I'm..." I paused, stepping onto the street and squinting at the sign at the corner. "In the East Village, not far from FDR. You need to pick me up, and...well, I smell. Bad. But what the hell happened on your end?"

Hanna let out a sigh. "A call from your alarm company woke me up—they said your office had been broken into. While on the phone with them, I went downstairs to look at your house. Just in case. That's when I saw some movement outside."

"Movement?"

"Yeah. I looked out the window and saw your lights were on, and somebody was going through your house."

"What the hell—"

"Yeah. Since I was still on the line with the alarm company, I told them to call the cops, but I also turned on the lights in my front yard, which spooked them. I saw at least two men, but maybe they had someone waiting for them, too. As they ran off, one of them tried to set your house on fire—he threw a Molotov cocktail at your door."

"Holy shit." My stomach dropped.

"Don't worry. I grabbed the fire extinguisher and put it out before it could spread. It didn't take, luckily. But there's some damage to your front door, and your foyer is covered in residue from the fire extinguisher."

I couldn't speak for a second, trying to process the image of my place trashed and nearly torched.

"Spots?" I asked, referring to my cat, a stray I found a few months ago while trying to solve the Valentine Killer's case.

"He's fine. I set him up in the kids' room for now. You can pick him up later when you're ready."

"Thanks. I'll get him when I come home."

A pause hung on the other end. It was brief. Just a fraction of a second too long to feel natural. Something else was wrong. Something big. "What else is going on?"

Hanna's voice, usually cheerful and steady, faltered. "I don't know how to tell you this. Did you get any calls from DD?"

"No. Wait, I guess I don't know. Hang on." I pulled the phone away and scrolled through the sea of missed calls and texts that had flooded in once I got service back. Sure enough, there it was—a missed call from DD and, worse, a voicemail. My stomach churned. Nothing good ever came from voicemails in the middle of the night. "I've got one. I'm guessing it's not a check-in, is it?"

"No," she said. "The shooting in the club is all over the news."

I felt a wave of confusion crash over me. "Already? How—" I stopped mid-sentence, my mind snapping back to the cavern. To the lifeless body sprawled out on the stone floor—his face all too familiar. Richard Van der Meer. The powerful man with enough clout to make the news cycle spin faster than your washing machine. I grimaced. "The senator?"

"Yes."

"Shit." My throat tightened. "This is bad."

"It's worse than bad," Hanna said. "You're the prime suspect. You should lay low for a few days... You can stay with us."

"No." I furiously shook my head, even though she couldn't see it. My chest tightened, eyes burning, and not just from the sewer fumes. "I can't put you or the kids at risk."

"I could at least drive you somewhere."

I hesitated, weighing my options—which, right now, were nonexistent. "No, it's fine. If I'm not heading back to Brooklyn, there's no point dragging you out here. I'll figure it out. I know a place not far from here. Wish me luck."

"Wait—"

"I gotta go." I cut her off before she could say anything else. "Take care of Spots for me until I'm back."

I needed to get off the street, find a place to curl up, change clothes, and take a shower. But there was something I needed to do first.

I took a deep breath and pressed Play on the voicemail, holding the phone to my ear. Immediately, DD's noisy breathing filled the silence—his signature sound. There was a moment of hesitation that made me picture him rubbing his face, pacing back and forth like he always did when weighing his words.

"Alex," he finally said, his voice a gruff growl. "What kind of trouble did you get into this time? I swear, one day, I'll stop waking up wondering if this is the day someone's going to call me with another crazy story about my old partner. But clearly, this day is not today."

He let out a sigh. "Van der Meer is dead. But you already know that. Of course you do."

I tensed. Yeah. I knew.

"What's worse," he went on, "is you're on tape entering the Pulse. Somebody called it in. And there are witnesses."

He paused, letting that sink in. "Witnesses, Alex, who say they saw you go to the room with him, and then they heard a shot."

My jaw clenched so tight I thought my teeth would crack.

Witnesses? Who the hell were they? Liars, every last one of them. I didn't shoot Van der Meer. But someone had, and they were working hard to pin it on me.

"I'm not gonna lie." DD's voice dropped lower. "It doesn't look good for you. You need to turn yourself in."

A sharp laugh escaped me—bitter, without humor. Yeah, right. I'd turn myself in, and then what? Go to prison for the murder I hadn't committed?

DD kept going. "But there's more, Alex. Somebody put a bounty on your head. An anonymous donation. We are talking big money. That means every whack job in the city is going to be gunning for you. Not just cops. Bounty hunters. Criminals."

A chill ran down my spine as if the temperature suddenly dropped. My brain struggled to process the fact I wasn't just a fugitive anymore—I was prey. There would be no safe places, no shadows dark enough to hide in.

DD's tone softened, almost pleading now. "I can't protect you if you're out there, Alex. Please. Turn yourself in. We'll figure it out together."

The voicemail ended with a click, leaving me standing there in the middle of an empty street, the weight of DD's words pressing me down. My mind raced. Witnesses? I didn't even pull my gun out until after the assassin was gone. But people under stress aren't reliable storytellers. You learn that quickly as a cop. There are exceptions, of course—I still remember a case when a bodega owner got robbed in front of his store. Despite late hours and poor lighting, the description he gave to the sketch artist was so precise it could've been a photograph. The perp was caught before the day was over.

But most people weren't like that. Something traumatic happened in the cavern. They heard a loud noise, and somebody fell down. Their startled brains drew conclusions that someone must have murdered the victim. And then they saw me over the body, doing something. Their frightened imagination filled in the blanks. Maybe even convinced them that they saw me shoot the senator. Or holding a gun. Somebody said it out loud when questioned. Another agreed. Confirmation bias. Herd mentality. I shuddered—it was going to be hard to disentangle myself from this.

I opened the contact list and stared at my phone for a good minute, thumb hovering over John Levy's name. I wasn't sure I wanted to open that door again. But here I was, covered in grime, no other options, and of all the people I knew, John would get it. He'd understand what it felt like to have the world chasing you for something you didn't do. He'd been in my shoes once before—on the run, dodging cops, framed for murders he hadn't committed. If anyone could handle this situation, it was him.

I hit the Dial button. He picked up on the first ring, his voice rough with sleep. "Alex?"

"Yeah. I need a favor."

He didn't hesitate. "Where are you?"

I could hear the worry in his voice, but there was something else —excitement. Like he was glad I called, even at this hour. "East Village. I'll send you the exact location. Can you pick me up?"

"You're in luck," he said, already rustling in the background. "I'm staying in the city. Be there soon."

True to his word, he showed up quickly, a gray Toyota Corolla pulling up to the intersection in less than fifteen minutes. He stepped out, his face lighting up when he spotted me—until the smell hit him.

"Whoa," he said, taking a step back, trying not to laugh. "You smell like you haven't showered since I last saw you."

"It's been a rough night," I muttered.

He didn't push, just opened the car door. "Let's get you out of here. We can talk at my place."

His place was a tiny two-bedroom in Battery Park City.

"It's nice," I said, stepping into the small living room. The decor was sparse—just a gray couch, a coffee table with a decorative vase, and a TV—but the view stole the show. Manhattan's skyline was spread out beneath us, twinkling like it always did. The constellation of eight million stars, each shining in its own way. "Yours?"

"No." He shrugged. "Rental. I'm still keeping my place in Brooklyn for now. Just trying to see how it feels to be back in the city."

I said nothing.

Levy disappeared for a moment and came back with a towel and a fluffy bathrobe. "Shower first," he said, holding them out like an offering. Or perhaps just keeping his distance because of the stink. "Before this smell gets embedded in my walls."

I didn't argue. I needed the shower more than I cared to admit. As the hot water hit me, I scrubbed until my skin was raw, but the grime of the tunnels washed away. I started to feel human again. The heat soothed the aching muscles, and for a moment, I was at peace. No bounty. No dead senators. Just the water stripping it all away.

When I returned, clean and wrapped in the bathrobe, there was a cup of tea and a croissant waiting for me on the table. Levy was on the couch, too, pouring himself a cup. I glanced around. "Where'd you put my clothes?"

He gave a brief nod, like it was nothing. "It's in the washer. Your gun and all your stuff is on the table over there."

"You didn't have to—" I started, but he cut me off with a laugh.

"Oh, trust me, I had to."

I couldn't help it—I laughed, too. It was strange, considering everything that'd happened. I sat down, took a sip of chamomile tea, and felt the warmth spread through me. It was almost normal.

I glanced out the window, the blinking lights staring back at me, took a breath, and laid it all out—Blackwood's case, the murders, the tunnels. I watched his face as I talked, saw his worry deepen with each word, his green eyes darken. But he didn't interrupt. He just let me get it all out.

And when I was done, I finally felt like I've gotten my feet back under me, even if just for a little while.

FOURTEEN

I woke up at Levy's place before dawn, the light barely starting to creep through the windows. Despite his insistence that I take the bed, I'd crashed on the couch. Felt safer somehow—like I needed to keep my guard up, even in my friend's tiny, neat apartment. But sleep hadn't been kind. My dreams were a mess—shadowy figures chasing me through dark, damp tunnels, the smell of rot and decay clinging to me no matter how fast I ran.

I woke up covered in cold sweat, my heart hammering, but I was determined not to let panic take over. Instead, I lay there, breathing slowly, forcing myself to focus on the sunrise filtering through the high-rise windows. The city looked peaceful at this hour—still asleep, with no idea what kind of chaos was about to unfold. The world was always like that, though—quiet right before everything went wrong.

Soon, Levy was up, too. He started the coffee machine in the small kitchen, and as the smell of freshly ground beans filled the room, I felt grounded enough to join him.

"You hungry?" he asked, sliding some bread into the toaster.

I wasn't, but nodded anyway. "Sure."

We sat at his small dining table, coffee and toast between us, as the sun painted the sky with shades of copper and yellow. For a few minutes, neither of us spoke. Just two friends sitting there, sipping coffee, picking at toast, and pretending the world wasn't about to fall apart.

"What are you going to do?" He finally broke the silence after I finished. He pointed at the pot. "More coffee?"

I nodded. "It's obvious. I need to find the rest of the crew from the picture. Four dead people—Sterling, Diaz, LeClerc, and now Van der Meer were on the same trip. I found three pieces of the key—so far. LeClerc's Blade, Van der Meer's Feather. Diaz's Ace was most likely taken when he was murdered. The fourth one is probably in Sterling's home. Unless they took it already. We've moved way past coincidences."

Levy nodded, got up, and disappeared into his bedroom, only to come back with his laptop. "You sure it's him, though?"

"Who?"

"The senator."

"Find a recent photo of him," I said, already grabbing my phone. I swiped to the image I'd taken in LeClerc's storage and zoomed in on the face. Levy typed quickly, and within seconds, a picture of the late senator popped up on his screen. I held my phone next to it, comparing the two side by side.

The difference was jarring. Van der Meer in LeClerc's photo was a young man. Tall, lean, with long, wavy hair and sharp features. The man on Levy's screen was bloated, with a second chin that sagged like it had been carved out of dough. His hair was now cut short, almost buzzed, and it was fully gray. But there were things even time couldn't change. The nose, slightly hooked, was still the same. The deep-seated eyes. His thick eyebrows, wild like they'd never been tamed, were unmistakable.

"Yeah. You're right. This is him."

"I told you."

"Let me see the pieces," he said, pushing his coffee aside. His tone was casual, but I could tell by the look in his eyes he was intrigued.

I got up and brought the small metallic key pieces to the table. Levy leaned in, hovering just above them before he picked one up—the Ace, the one I'd found in the club.

He turned it over, inspecting every angle, the intricate detail, the way the metal seemed impossibly delicate but tough. "Incredible craftsmanship," he muttered.

I nodded and slid the second piece across the table—the one I hadn't had a chance to look at properly myself yet. A shiver ran down my spine as I remembered prying it from the senator's dead hands. It was slightly longer than the other, with a gentle curve.

"This one's different," he said, handing it back.

I took it and turned it in my hand. "This has to be the Feather."

He glanced at me but said nothing as he waited for an explanation.

"The journal—the one I found in LeClerc's stuff. They all had names like this."

I list them one by one, recalling the page from the journal:

The Mind's Eye—held by the Scholar
The Ace—held by the Joker
The Blade—held by the Soldier
The Helm—held by the Captain
The Elixir—held by the Alchemist
The Feather—held by the Hawk
The Shade—held by the Phantom

"We've got three out of four now," I said. "Diaz is the Joker. LeClerc's the Soldier. Van der Meer is the Hawk. We don't know who Sterling was, but if I'm lucky, the piece is still at her place. Once I find it, I'll know who she was."

Levy let out a low whistle, shaking his head. "Too much damn theater for my taste. And what good does it do us, anyway? All we've got are four dead ends." A smile tugged on his lips. "Pun intended."

I wanted to argue, tell him I had another clue, maybe a theory or two. But everything I thought to say seemed to vanish the moment he used that word. *We.* He didn't say *It doesn't help you.* He said *It doesn't help us.* I found myself staring at his lips, my brain short-circuiting for a second. I had to pull it back, fast.

Focus, Alex.

"Are you all right?" Levy's voice cut through the haze, snapping me back.

"Yeah, I'm fine." I blinked hard, trying to reroute my brain to the task at hand.

He eyed me, clearly unconvinced. "What else do we have? Besides four people?"

"Two things. First, I saw something at the club—it's got to be a clue. When I went to check if Van der Meer was still alive, I saw a tattoo on his chest. Wait—hold on." I fumbled with my phone. "I took a picture."

Levy leaned in as I opened the photos. My stomach dropped. The image was a mess—completely blurry, nothing but a smudge of skin and shadows. I let out a frustrated sigh. "Shit. It's useless. It was too dark."

Levy peered at the screen. "What was it, though? Can you remember?"

I closed my eyes, trying to summon the details. "Yes. It was heart-shaped, but not like a simple heart design. It was what you'd see in anatomy textbooks—like the actual organ. Only it was made of moving parts, like clockwork or gears, with the same steampunk design as the keys. And the ink—it wasn't your garden variety. It had this strange metallic sheen, like it was both ink and something else. I've never seen anything like it."

Levy frowned, intrigued. "Like the keys, huh?"

"Exactly," I said, nodding.

Levy leaned back, digesting the new information. "All right. We've got a weird heart tattoo that links to the design of the keys, four dead people, and some kind of cult praying in an underground cavern. What else?"

"We need more information," I said. "For starters, we need to know if the other victims had the same tattoo. If they did, it would confirm the cult theory beyond a shadow of a doubt. And we have to figure out who the other people in the photo are."

Levy raised an eyebrow. "And how exactly do we do any of that?"

"We need the resources of the NYPD."

His eyebrow shot even higher. "You're not seriously thinking—"

"That is precisely what I'm thinking." I held his gaze. "DD could tell me if the others had the tattoo. He's got access to the autopsy reports. He either knows this already, or he can get this information in one simple phone call. And he's got the age progression software. We get him to run the faces from the old photo, and he'll give us a pretty good approximation of what they look like now."

"That is a great idea," Levy said, but the sarcasm was impossible to miss. "Just one teeny little problem—you're the prime suspect in Van der Meer's murder. The moment you pop up, he'll slap cuffs on you faster than you can say 'wrong number.'"

"I'm not actually going to show up at his door and ask him for a favor," I said, shaking my head. "I'll call him."

Levy's expression shifted from skeptical to concerned. He opened his mouth to respond but then paused, thinking. After a few seconds, he disappeared into his bedroom without a word. I heard him rummaging through drawers, the sound of things clattering to the floor. Moments later, he reemerged and placed a small flip phone on the table between us.

I looked down at it, then back up at him, confused. "What is that?"

"A burner," he said casually, as if it were a perfectly normal thing to have lying around. "Bought it with cash when I was in South Carolina last month. A whole bunch of them. Just in case."

I stared at the phone, a laugh bubbling up in my throat despite the mess I was in. "Oh, John. What have I done to you?"

He shrugged, almost sheepish. "Better safe than sorry, right?"

I picked up the burner, testing its weight in my hand. It felt archaic, like holding a relic from another time, but also weirdly comforting. There was no tracking, no internet access, just an anonymous line in the wind. "Are you sure this thing works?"

"I tested it when I got back. Signal's solid. You're good."

I sighed and leaned forward, elbows resting on the table, thumb brushing the buttons on the phone. Hesitating.

"He'll listen," Levy said, his voice soft. "You two have a history. He knows you."

"Maybe." I chewed on my lip. "But he's a play-by-the-book kind of guy. He won't overlook a murder charge, even for an old friend. I've got one shot at this."

I looked at Levy and took a deep breath. "Here goes nothing."

The phone rang once, twice, three times. My heart rate ticked up with each ring, but finally, DD's gruff voice came on the line.

"Detective Deluca. Who is this?"

There was a long pause on the other end, and I could practically see him frowning through the phone.

"You've got some nerve, Alex. Do you have any idea how much heat's on you right now?"

"Yeah, I know," I say. "But this is important. Van der Meer had a tattoo on his chest. I need to know if Victoria Sterling, Milo Diaz, and Drew LeClerc had the same tattoo as well. It would also be on their chest. Heart-shaped. Metallic ink. And I need you to run age progression on some faces. Oh, and, hi."

Another pause. Even longer this time. "You're asking me to stick my neck out for you. Again."

"I wouldn't be calling if it wasn't necessary," I said. "You know me, DD. You know I didn't kill Van der Meer. There was an assassin. He tried to kill me, too."

"That's what you say, but witnesses are pointing right at you. And the video of you snooping around the Pulse and sneaking into the staff-only area isn't exactly helpful for your cause."

"I hear you. But you know how it is. People panic. See things that aren't there. You know I didn't do it." I could feel the heat rise in my chest. "I'm being framed. Come on, man—an anonymous bounty on my head? That's one hell of a coincidence, don't you think?"

He's quiet again. If you can call DD's breathing that sounds like someone was firing up a chainsaw on the other end of the line, quiet. "You're a pain in my ass, you know that?"

"I do," I said. I tried to keep my tone light. It didn't quite work. "But you're the only one on the force I can trust."

That part was true. DD might chew me up for this, but he wasn't going to sell me out. At least, I hoped not. The silence stretched again, and I took that as my cue.

I launched into it—everything I knew so far. The murders, the expedition in Asia. The shipwreck. I laid it all out. The only thing I kept to myself was Pandora's box. DD didn't believe in the supernatural. I still didn't know if I believed in it, either. And mentioning some ancient myth about a cursed box wouldn't score me any points. A valuable piece of art, though? That's something he could understand. People killed for less all the time.

When I finished, he said nothing for a while, but he didn't reject me either. I'd take that.

"Let me get this straight," he finally said. "You're telling me there's more at play here than just a few unconnected deaths."

"Yeah," I said. "A lot more. And they aren't just deaths. They are murders. And they are very much connected. You know they are."

He let out a sigh, the sound like gravel crunching underfoot. "Fine. Tattoos shouldn't be a problem. And send me the photo. I'll see what I can do."

"Thanks, DD. You're a lifesaver. I'll keep you updated on anything I find on my end." I hung up before he could ask me any more questions or second-guess how wise it was to help me in the first place.

"You did well," Levy said.

I gave him a half-smile. "I have my moments."

He smiled back, but it was shallow somehow. "There's something that occurred to me while you were on the phone with DD."

I opened my mouth to ask, but there was something in his face that stopped me in my tracks. I'm not entirely sure I wanted to know what he had to say.

"There's a parallel to Pandora's story," he began.

I said nothing.

"After all, the main idea of the tale is about the introduction of evil and suffering into the world. In Greek mythology, there's a woman who is given the box containing all the world's evils. And out of curiosity, she opens it, letting them out. Sorrow, disease, violence, greed, madness, death. You know the story."

I said nothing still; my hands were suddenly cold.

"But there's another tale," he said, his eyes locked on mine now. "Another woman, tempted. And when she can't resist the temptation, paradise is lost, and she is thrown into the world to suffer. And all her heirs are bound to suffer, too."

The words hung in the air. My pulse picked up. My chest tightened. I didn't want to say it out loud, as if by doing it I'd make it real. *If they know your name, they will always track you* kind of thing. But the thought was there, clawing at the edge of my mind. Screaming to be let out.

I lost that battle.

"Pandora's story is a different version of the temptation of Eve? The box and the apple are describing essentially the same thing?"

He shrugged. "I don't know what's real anymore. But to play devil's advocate, things like that happen a lot."

"Things like what?"

"Different sources describe differently the same event as time goes on. Sometimes, it's subtle differences. Sometimes, the story is disputed altogether. History—real history—is rife with examples. Paul Revere's midnight ride. The story of Caligula's horse in the senate. The Battle of Thermopylae. Mythology—let's call it that, for now—is the same. You get Zeus from the Greeks and Jupiter from the Romans. Odin from the Norse gods and Perun for the Slavs. Why can't biblical Eve have a doppelgänger? And if she does... Perhaps there's something out there. Just because we don't understand it, it doesn't mean it can't be real."

We stared at each other for a moment. I swallowed hard, my mouth suddenly dry.

"You think there's a connection..." I finally said. "To our last case?"

Levy didn't answer right away. Just looked at me, his expression unreadable. When he finally spoke, his voice was low, almost a whisper. "I don't know for sure, Alex. But after everything we've seen, after all the strange...things we've experienced, I think it would be unwise to discount the possibility there's something evil out there. And that it wants to come into this world."

FIFTEEN

I stood across the street, trying to melt into the chaos of the city. The hat and sunglasses weren't exactly high-level spy gear, but considering my current situation, it was better than showing my face.

I watched as John Levy walked into Charlotte Parker's bookstore, the two pieces of the key tucked inside his jacket. The plan was simple: He'd make the drop. I'd stay out of sight.

At this point of the year, the air should've been still thick with humidity that clung to your skin like a second layer, but this evening, there was a chill sneaking in under my jacket. It was sharp, biting, like the city itself was holding its breath, waiting for something to snap. A gust of wind tugged at my hat, rattling the signs of the storefronts. I shivered, more from nerves than from the actual chill, and pulled my jacket tighter. Maybe it was just the weather. Or maybe it was just the pressure getting to me. Either way, I didn't like it.

In theory, it was a good idea to keep a low profile until we got word from DD. The problem? I hated waiting, and I wasn't entirely comfortable using John.

He had picked up a couple more burner phones before we headed out—smart move, considering all the heat on me. The NYPD was breathing down my neck, and thanks to the anonymous donor, every punk in the city was gunning for me as well. DD was working on things, which was a miracle in its own right, but that could take time. In the meantime, we couldn't risk anyone tracking our conversations, so we were back to the basics: cash-bought phones, untraceable.

I stole a glance toward the bookstore. Levy was still in there. I couldn't see anything but shadows through the windows. I leaned against a wall and pulled out one of the burners. While John was still inside, I wanted to try Blackwood again. I dialed his number, listening to the ring. One. Two. Three—voicemail. Again.

I hung up, frowning. He hadn't picked up the last few times I'd called either. I tried again, my patience thinning. Voicemail.

I hung up, jamming the phone back into my pocket, the unease twisting in my gut. This wasn't right. There could be a million reasons he wasn't picking up, but I could feel it was wrong. Like the air before a storm—charged, heavy, dangerous. The rational side of my brain told me to calm the hell down, to wait it out, but the part of me that had seen too much, survived too much, knew better.

Blackwood wasn't just busy. There was trouble.

Across the street, Levy stepped out of the bookstore. He threw a glance my way and gave me a small nod—he'd made the drop. Time to move.

I crossed the street and fell in step with him as we headed down the block toward the car. "How'd it go?"

"She's a strange bird," Levy said, his lips quirking into an uneasy smile. "But I think she believed me. Mostly because I handed over the keys, I guess."

"Did she hear from Blackwood?"

He shook his head. "Nope. Not in a couple of days."

I frowned. "This is just great." The unease in my gut tightened its grip. "I don't like this. I don't like this one damn bit."

He glanced at me. "Are you sure you want to do this?"

"Break into Sterling's apartment?" I chuckled without much humor. "Absolutely not. But what choice do we have?"

He gave a slow nod, his brow furrowing like he was trying to think of some clever way out of this mess. He didn't find one.

Up ahead, I spotted a bank on the corner, the green neon sign glowing like an exit light in a disaster movie. I stopped in my tracks. "Hold up. They'll flag my cards anyway, but I'd rather pull some cash now than scramble later. Go on, I'll join you in a minute."

I reached the bank's front doors, the polished glass reflecting the dull gray of the city around me. I was about to push the door open but paused, my hand stopping just short of the handle. A quick withdrawal from the ATM first might be smarter. If something was wrong, it'd be better to find out without standing in front of a teller. Less explaining, fewer eyes on me.

I stepped away from the door and headed to the ATM at the side of the building. Just a small transaction, I figured—enough to test the waters. If the cards still work, I'd go inside and take out what I needed. If not...well, better to know now.

I punched in my PIN, watching the numbers flicker across the screen. A familiar hum, then a slow beep. The ATM whirred and clicked, but instead of showing the balance menu or offering me options, the screen turned an angry red, followed by an ominous message:

Transaction Declined.

Your transaction has been declined due to illicit activity on your account.

Please contact your financial institution immediately for further assistance.

"Fuck." The word came out like a hiss through clenched teeth. My accounts were frozen. Someone, somewhere, had made their move. It could've been the NYPD. Or, most likely, it was the mysterious donor who funded a large bounty on my head. The police would probably try to track me, not freeze my accounts altogether. It didn't matter. What mattered was I couldn't access a single penny of my hard-earned savings.

I glanced up at the corner of the ATM booth, where a small camera blinked down at me. I raised my hand, gave it the bird, and turned on my heel. If anyone was watching, I hoped they got a good look.

"All good?" Levy said as I got into the car.

"Nope. My accounts are frozen."

His green eyes darkened. "Frozen? As in—"

"Yep," I muttered. "No money. No way to get any. Luckily, I didn't go inside. Just the ATM. But I'm pretty sure I still set off alarm bells loud enough to wake Santa at the North Pole. I'm in deep shit."

Levy frowned, already thinking. "I can lend you some money to keep you going."

"No—" I started, shaking my head, but he cut me off with one of those "don't be an idiot" looks.

"I know you're good for it," he said. "When this all blows over, you'll pay me back."

Before he could say anything else, I leaned in and kissed him softly on the cheek. He went still, like he didn't want to push things one way or the other. Leaving the next move up to me. I pulled back and gave his shoulder a firm squeeze instead, grounding us both. "I owe you, John."

He smirked, eyes glinting as he tried to ease the tension. "Not yet. But you will."

Levy started the car, and a few moments later, we were headed uptown.

The Upper East Side wasn't exactly where most people expected the mayor to live, but Victoria Sterling wasn't most people. While most mayors resided in Gracie Mansion, which had been the official residence of New York City mayors since 1942, Sterling did not. She was the second mayor to eschew the tradition, and instead, she stayed in the apartment her late husband left her when he died of cancer a few years back. Upper East Side, prime real estate—an old-money kind of place where the streets were quiet, the apartments enormous, and the doorman made sure you knew you didn't belong.

Levy pulled the car up about a hundred yards down the block from the building. "What's the play?"

I scanned the area, my brain already kicking into gear. "You up for some breaking and entering?"

Levy chuckled, shaking his head. "Just another day with Alex Watts, isn't it?"

I leaned forward, scanning the entrance. Old-school Upper East Side luxury—a doorman in uniform, thick double doors, and that general air of snootiness that told you they didn't let just anyone inside. But this was where Levy was going to shine. I couldn't fake it if my life depended on it, but he belonged in those circles where air was too rarefied for us mortals. The doorman would pick up on it in a second.

"Here's the plan," I said, nodding at the doorman. "You're going to distract him. Ask him whatever—questions about the building, about Sterling, or whatever else you guys discuss when you meet over black caviar and champagne and conspire on how to fleece us poor folk."

"Ouch," Levy said, but his eyes smiled.

"Hell, pretend you're an old friend of the family. Whatever you need to do, just keep him busy long enough for me to slip past."

Levy shot me a look. "You make it sound so simple."

"It's simple if you're good at it. Are you good at it, John?"

He snorted, shaking his head. "And you? How are you getting in?"

"I'll take the stairs for a couple of flights, so I don't hang out in the lobby for too long, then grab the elevator. Sterling's place is at the top. We'd never pull this off with her mayoral security swarming the building, but now that she's gone, they pulled the extra detail. The place's empty. I doubt it would even have an alarm. Should be smooth sailing—assuming you can keep the doorman busy."

Levy sighed but didn't argue. He threw the car into park, and we both got out. I tugged my hat down a little lower, making sure I didn't look too conspicuous.

"Ready?" Levy asked.

I nodded. "Let's do this."

We started down the sidewalk, Levy peeling off toward the entrance while I hung back, keeping close to the side of the building. As I watched, he approached the doorman with a friendly smile, all casual charm, and asked something I couldn't hear from this distance. The doorman seemed to give him a polite but interested response, turning his attention fully to Levy.

That was my cue.

I slipped past the entrance, hugging the wall, dashed past the elevator, and made my way toward the stairwell door. Once inside, I let out a breath. So far, so good.

The stairwell was deserted and quiet, with the faint echo of traffic from outside. I took the steps, two at a time, moving quickly but not too fast—I didn't want to make noise or give myself away. After a couple of flights, I stopped, listening. No sounds of pursuit, no alarms. Perfect.

I made my way over to the elevator bank and punched the button. A soft ding echoed as the elevator arrived, the doors sliding open with a quiet hiss. A few moments later, I stepped out into the penthouse hallway, taking a quick look around. It was quiet, and I immediately clocked the two penthouse doors at opposite ends: P1 and P2. I remember being thrown off when I first pulled up the architectural blueprints and saw there were two penthouse suites up there. I always thought a penthouse was something that took up the entire floor, but apparently, that's not always the case. Go figure. Sterling's apartment was in P2—I remembered that much.

I scanned the ceiling and the corners, making sure there weren't any cameras. It wasn't surprising there weren't any. Privacy was practically currency in these places, and tenants weren't about to let their movements be monitored. No cameras meant no eyes on me, at least for now.

I moved swiftly, closing the distance to Sterling's door. Kneeling down, I pulled out my lock-pick set and got to work. The metal tools were cold in my hands as I slipped them into the lock, feeling for the familiar tension, the telltale clicks of the pins falling into place.

The seconds stretched, each one longer than the last, but then—*click.*

The door creaked open, and I slipped inside, closing it behind me. The place was quiet, and for a moment, all I could hear was the sound of my own rugged breathing. I was in. Now came the hard part.

For a penthouse, it was...fine. Just fine. Nice, sure, if you compared it to my old house in Bay Ridge, Brooklyn. But not the jaw-dropping opulence you'd expect from someone who could have lived in Gracie Mansion but chose here instead.

The layout was open, with a big, airy space right in front of me. Huge windows lined the far wall, giving a sprawling view of the city below. That part was impressive. I'll give it that. But everything else? Just...eh. To the right was a sizable kitchen, stainless-steel appliances, granite countertops—the works—but nothing I hadn't seen in a dozen other overpriced Manhattan condos. To the left was an entertaining area, arranged in a way that screamed for guests to admire the post-modern art on the walls. Cold. Minimalistic. An interesting glance into Sterling's inner world.

I wasn't here to admire the decor, though. I ignored the living area entirely and headed straight past the kitchen, my steps taking me down a corridor toward Sterling's office. That was most likely where the answers would be.

The office was nothing like the rest of the penthouse. As soon as I stepped inside, it felt like I'd walked into a different world. The walls were lined with towering bookshelves, floor to ceiling, crammed full of volumes. No bare, empty spaces here. Every inch was filled with something—leather-bound books, yellowing papers. A polished rail ran above the shelves, supporting a rolling ladder, giving the room the look of an old European library. It was a place meant for digging, researching, poring over something deeply hidden. Not for show.

And the desk—that was the centerpiece. A massive, imposing thing carved from dark wood, clearly from another time and place, like it had been shipped here straight from some long-forgotten European estate. It stood out starkly against the sleek modernity of the rest of the penthouse. Buried under piles of books, maps, strange contraptions, and other artifacts I couldn't understand the meaning of, it looked like the workplace of a mad archaeologist or a treasure hunter. There were no neat piles, no clean surfaces here—just chaos. Controlled, intentional chaos. The rest of the place was just a front. A mask. But here? This was where Sterling lived, where she was real.

I started with the desk. Obviously. I sifted through everything, looking for something that resembled a piece of the key or a small box that might hold one. Nothing. Just clutter.

I moved on to the drawers. Old letters, notebooks filled with scratchy handwriting that looked like it came from another century— fascinating stuff if you enjoyed that sort of thing. Normally, I might've been interested. Not today. Today, I was on a mission. I rummaged through the drawers but came up with nothing but dust and frustration. I dropped down on the floor and felt around under the desk, checking for secret compartments. Sure enough, I found one. It popped open with a soft click, revealing a golden dagger encrusted with jewels. It looked medieval. Probably worth a fortune.

But not what I needed.

I admired it for another moment and then shoved it back and stood up. I was irritated now. I dragged the chair over and sat down, taking a long look around the room, trying to think like Sterling. Where would she hide something important? She wasn't stupid, but maybe she wasn't all that paranoid, either. People like her—rich, powerful—they think they're untouchable.

My eyes landed on a small box sitting on one of the bookshelves. Innocent. Unassuming.

"No way," I muttered. I stood up and walked over, pulling the box off the shelf. I lifted the lid, and there it was. A tiny gadget with a steampunk-inspired design—intricate parts, gears, and an absurd amount of detail. At first glance, it looked like a cross between a ring and a thimble, but after a second, it hit me. The Helm. Which made Victoria Sterling the Captain.

"Easy money," I said as I slipped the piece into my pocket. Now, I had four out of seven. Almost there.

I reached for the burner phone, ready to call Levy with the good news. Time to get out of here and fast. But before I could hit Dial, something caught my ear—a faint sound, just enough to set me on edge. I spun toward it. Too slow.

A whoosh. Then pain. White-hot and sharp, exploding in the back of my skull. The room spun away from me, replaced by blinding stars and a gray void that swallowed everything. I hit my knees, the world tilting, but I wasn't out yet. Not by a long shot. I pushed and tried to stand.

Another crack to the back of my head. This time, the lights go out for good.

SIXTEEN

I came to in pieces. First, there was the pain—a deep, bone-rattling ache that started in the back of my skull and radiated through my entire body like a shock wave. I tried to blink, but nothing happened. Only darkness and strange pressure on my eyes. My heart hammered. Was I still unconscious and dreaming? No, no, I could feel things. The rough texture of something digging into my ankles and wrists. I could feel the cold metal pressing against my shoulder. The tight space around me wasn't just darkness. It was confined. Way too confined.

Panic hit me like a sucker punch. My breath came in shallow gasps as I tried to move, but something held my arms, my legs. Bound. Blind. My mouth taped. And I was bouncing—my body shifting every few seconds with the erratic movement of whatever the hell I was in.

Then it clicked. It wasn't a dark room. I was in a trunk.

The world jerked again, and my side slammed into something hard. A muffled groan escaped my lips as the car took another corner, gravity throwing me around like a rag doll. I bit down on the pain, trying to calm the storm in my head. Trying to think through the nausea and confusion. I strained against the ropes, my fingers twisting, searching for any slack. Nothing.

Forcing myself to breathe, I tried to calm myself down. I had to get my bearings and figure out how long I'd been out. Where the hell we were going. My pulse thudded in my ears as I tried to focus on the sounds outside the trunk. The hum of the engine, the rush of tires on asphalt. No voices, no radio. Just the steady rhythm of the car eating up the road.

The usual city noise was gone, too. No honking horns, no distant chatter, no rumble of subway trains beneath the streets. Wherever I was, it wasn't in the city anymore.

I winced as another sharp bump sent me crashing into the metal side again. Yeah, this wasn't good. Not at all.

I gave up trying to figure out where I was. I couldn't do it right now. What I could do was narrow down the options. I couldn't have been out for more than an hour—any longer, and I'd probably be dead from the blow. Whoever attacked me would've spent at least ten, maybe fifteen minutes getting me into the trunk. Which meant we'd been on the road for no more than forty minutes, tops.

That didn't leave a lot of options. If we'd gone south, we'd still be in the heart of Brooklyn, where the city never shuts up. Too much noise, too many people. And Long Island? Not a chance. Even this late, the drive to hit quiet parts would take too long.

No, the smart bet was the George Washington Bridge. They'd head north, out of Manhattan, away from prying eyes. The bridge wouldn't be too clogged at this hour. Once they were across, they could make a quick escape into the winding, dark roads of New Jersey. There'd be plenty of places to hide me up there. Whoever these people were, they had a plan. And I was running out of time to screw it up.

Which brought me to another uncomfortable thought—who the hell *were* these people? It had to be about the key. No one else had a reason to bash my skull in and throw me into a trunk like a bad movie cliche. But something else nagged me. If this was about the key, they probably had no clue the other three pieces were safe at Parker's bookstore. I held onto that small victory for a moment.

Then, the realization hit me like a freight train.

The *whole reason* I was in the trunk was because they didn't know Parker had the other pieces. But they'd sure as hell want to know where they were. And they'd be expecting me to cough up that information.

Suddenly, the cramped trunk felt even tighter, my breathing more ragged. My mind flashed through what "questioning" might look like. These weren't amateurs—they were organized. Willing to take the enormous risk of kidnapping a person. People like that didn't politely ask for what they wanted. No, they'd get creative. And in this business, *creative* usually meant *painful*. And there was another side of that ugly coin—once they got what they wanted, I'd be useless. Damned if you do and damned if you don't.

Sweat beaded on my forehead as I fought back the rising panic. My mind raced through the possibilities, none of them good.

I needed to alert someone—DD, John, anyone. But then it hit me like a brick to the face: John. He'd been waiting for me right outside the building. He wouldn't just sit there if he saw me being dragged out and tossed into a trunk.

Which meant he'd tried to stop them. Which meant he could be hurt. Or worse.

My stomach turned, dread snaking through me. John was only in this mess because of me. And now, for all I knew, he could be lying somewhere, bleeding out on the sidewalk.

I gritted my teeth. No. I couldn't let my mind go there. Not yet. I had to stay sharp, figure out where I was and how the hell to get out of this.

The sounds outside shifted. The steady hum of asphalt beneath the tires was replaced by a low, uneven rumble—gravel. We were off the main road. It went on for a few more minutes, and then the car slowed and came to a stop. My brain screamed at me to do something, anything, but I was still blindfolded, still bound, and the trunk was as cramped as a coffin. I braced myself.

I heard the car doors open, then the unmistakable thud of boots hitting gravel. Two pairs, from the sound of it. Two men. Splendid.

The trunk popped open with a metallic groan, and before I could even think of making a move, I felt rough hands clamp down on my shoulders and ankles. They yanked me out like I was a bag of dirty laundry, my body swaying between them as they carried me. I struggled at first—instinct, really—but it was no use. Bound, blindfolded, and disoriented, I wasn't going anywhere.

The air hit my face, cool and clean. But there was something else. An undertone I couldn't miss: manure. Farm country.

They lugged me for a minute, and then I heard the clang of a deadbolt, followed by the groan of an old, heavy door swinging open. My body hit the seat of a sturdy chair, my arms yanked behind it, still bound tight. One of them held me down while the other started on my legs. I kicked out, hoping to catch a lucky shot, but he was ready— he spread my legs apart and tied my ankles to the chair legs like he was doing it for the hundredth time.

Then, the hand on my face. I barely had time to brace before he ripped the tape off my mouth, the sting hitting hard. "Mother—" I bit back the rest, anger boiling. "I'll crush your nuts when I get a chance."

"She's got some mouth on her," one of them said, clearly amused.

Then, the blindfold came off. The room was lit by a single, sorry-looking lamp hanging by a wire near the door. But after the pitch-black I'd been trapped in, it felt like staring straight into the damn sun.

I glanced around. A barn. Small, empty. No windows, no other exits.

I shifted my attention to the two men standing before me, a part of me half-hoping they'd turn out to be nothing more than a couple of hicks. That would have its own set of problems, I supposed, but at least I might have a fighting chance. Instead, the men in front of me were anything but.

These guys looked like they belonged in a different world, one where my chances of escape were slim. They were dressed in comfortable cargo pants and military boots, T-shirts fitted snugly against their fit frames, and light jackets that gave them an air of authority. It was almost like a uniform, a stark contrast to the dusty barn around us.

The older man, maybe in his early forties, was bald, with deep-set brown eyes that assessed me with a cold, calculated gaze. The younger one, perhaps in his early thirties, had tousled blond hair and steely gray eyes. Both of them exuded a professionalism that set my nerves on edge. Former military or law enforcement, maybe.

This was bad—very bad. The way they carried themselves, the confidence in their movements—it was clear they had experience. My mind raced, calculating my odds. I was outmatched on every front, and I knew it.

For a solid minute or two, we were locked in a silent, unspoken standoff, our eyes doing all the talking. No one spoke. No one moved. The barn's creaking in the wind was the only sound. I wanted to thrash and scream, but I wasn't about to give them the satisfaction. They were building a profile of me, sizing me up, trying to figure out what kind of trouble they had on their hands. And I was trying to make sure the profile they came up with was: "Tough bitch. Can't break her. Better let her go before this blows up in our faces."

But if I was being honest, I didn't know if that was working. These guys were pros. They'd done this before, maybe a hundred times over, and I was just another job on their to-do list. It wasn't like they were new to the game—they knew I didn't have a lot of cards to play.

The reality was I didn't even know where I was. I could be on another planet for all the good it did me. And let's not sugarcoat it— the two of them could easily overpower me. Hell, I was tied to a chair, and these guys looked like they could snap my neck with half the effort it took to crack an egg.

Yeah, I was sure they were reading the situation the same way I was: I was stuck. They were in control, and they knew it.

But still, I kept my stare hard, unflinching. I couldn't let them see me sweat. If there was one thing I've learned in this business, it was that you never showed fear. You act like you've got the situation under control. Bluff if you have to. Because sometimes, just sometimes, that's enough to make the other guy second-guess their plan.

The older, bald man stepped forward, squatting right in front of me. His posture, his steady gaze—yeah, if I didn't already know it, now it was clear as day. He was the one running the show. The leader.

"Listen, darling," he said, his voice slipping into a Midwest twang as he drew out the words, rolling his *r*'s in that easygoing way. "I apologize for the way we had to bring you here. But there's no need for all this tension to keep going."

I said nothing.

"Thank you for the piece you already delivered," he continued, as if we were having a friendly little chat. "Now, all I need is for you to tell me where the other three are stashed. After that, we part ways like friends—no hard feelings."

I bit back a laugh. "Friends?" The sarcasm dripped like acid, aimed right at his smarmy grin. If looks could kill, he'd be a smoking crater.

"You betcha," he said, flashing a smile. "We can even compensate you for your troubles. Fair deal, right?"

"Sure."

He rose to his feet, still playing the good cop routine. "I'll tell you what," he said, like he was offering me a gift. "I know all of this is a bit overwhelming. My partner and I will give you some space. We'll come back in a few to see if you're ready to make the deal. How does that sound?"

I kept my mouth shut.

He nodded, satisfied, like he had me exactly where he wanted me. Then he nodded to the blond and strolled out of the barn.

The blond guy paused in the doorway for a moment, pulled an apple from his jacket, and gave it a quick polish on his sleeve. He studied it under the light, then took a slow, deliberate bite. "If I were you, sweetheart," he said, "I'd listen to him." He flashed me a toothy grin and walked out.

As soon as the door clicked shut behind them, my brain kicked into overdrive. My inner state bordered on hysteria, but I shoved it all down, scanning the barn like a madwoman. I knew they left me here to stew, but this was most likely the only time I was going to be alone in the foreseeable future. I needed a plan. Anything—something—there had to be a way out of this.

When I was stuck in the trunk, I didn't know what to expect, but I had a sliver of hope. Now? After my charming little chat with Mr. Midwest, it's crystal clear. There are only two ways this ends: I escape this barn, or they get what they came for, and then they kill me. Simple as that.

Option one—freedom. Option two—death. I'd much rather prefer option one. There's no cavalry coming and no one to call. Just me. And this chair. And these damn ropes.

I caught a glint in the corner of the barn, something metallic buried under the dirty straw. My neck screamed in protest as I twisted to get a better look, but when I finally made out what it was, my heart skipped a beat—a small shovel, the kind you'd use to clean up stalls.

Hope surged through me, a jolt of electricity in my veins.

I tested the chair beneath me. It was sturdy, but I heard a faint creak on the left side. Could be a weakness. Could also be wishful thinking. There was no way to test it, and I didn't have any other options. I was only going to get one shot at this.

I started rocking. Not too much at first, just enough to see if the chair would budge. The legs shifted, but it held. I pushed harder, almost tipping forward, then shifted my weight back and sprang up on my tiptoes. The chair teetered and crashed down with a splintering crack. The whole thing collapsed beneath me, sending me sprawling face-first into the dirt.

With all the excitement, I'd forgotten about the earlier blow to the back of my head. But when the impact jolted my skull—I remembered. Pain erupted, exploding behind my eyes like fireworks. Stars danced in my vision, and the world swam, a boiling lake of agony swallowing me whole.

But it worked—the rope was loose now, and I slipped it off my hands and feet. I couldn't stay down. Not now.

SEVENTEEN

I forced myself to stand, the room spinning like a merry-go-round as nausea hit hard. My legs wobbled, but I stumbled over to the shovel and snatched it up, my grip tight around the rough wooden handle. I whipped around, ready to face whoever was coming through the door.

But no one was there.

The barn was still silent, empty except for me and my pounding headache. I took a few deep breaths, trying to shake off the dizziness as I inched toward the door. I pressed against it gently, hoping for an easy way out.

It didn't budge.

"Damn it," I muttered under my breath.

I scanned the barn again, but there was no other exit. No windows, no back doors—just the large one locked tight with a deadbolt on the other side. The clock was ticking, and when they came back, I needed every bit of leverage I could get.

I glanced at the chair. It was broken, but maybe not useless. I limped over and propped it up, making it look like it was still intact. It wasn't perfect, but it might throw them off. If they think, even for a split second, I've just somehow escaped the barn, that confusion could give me a slight edge. It's not much of a plan, but beggars can't be choosers.

I returned to the door and rested my weapon against it just long enough to unscrew the lonely lightbulb overhead. The barn sank into darkness. I grabbed the shovel again, tightened my grip on the handle, and slipped into the shadows beside the door, ready to strike. Now, I waited.

Seconds stretched into minutes, each one dragging on longer than the last. My body ached, nausea swirled in my gut, and exhaustion weighed on me like a cold, wet blanket. But I stayed ready: standing at attention, weapon in hand, every muscle coiled like a spring. The waiting felt endless.

Then, finally, I heard it. Footsteps. Just one set. Hope flickered—maybe I haven't cashed all my chips just yet.

I heard the deadbolt clank, and the door swung open. A man stood outlined against the moonlit sky.

"Son of a—" he started, but he didn't get to finish.

I slammed the handle into him right below the belt, and he crumpled with a groan, folding in half like a cheap lawn chair. Before he could let out another sound, I brought the shovel down on the back of his head. Hard. He dropped, collapsing as if the ground vanished beneath him.

I waited, heart pounding in my ears, and listened for any signs of backup. Nothing. Still quiet.

I crouched down, checking his pulse. Of course, it's my least favorite blond guy. The pulse was strong, his chest rising and falling in steady breaths. He'd live, but he was going to wake up wishing he hadn't.

I dragged him away from the door and grabbed the ropes from the chair. As quickly as I could, I tied up his wrists and ankles. I checked his pockets, not really hoping to find anything useful—empty.

Figured.

But there was a side holster on his belt, snugly holding a loaded

Glock. There was even an extra magazine in a small pouch. Looked like my shovel had been upgraded. Before I left, I grabbed a fistful of his T-shirt and yanked it down, exposing his chest. And there it was—strange metallic ink gleaming at me in the dim light—a carbon copy of a steampunk heart tattoo I saw on Van der Meer. Gears and cogs, an intricate web of metal etched into his skin. All clockwork and precision.

"How do you like them apples?" I muttered, stepping over him and making my way out of the barn.

I slipped outside, Glock raised, sweeping the area. The bald guy was nowhere to be found. I stayed there for a few moments as my eyes darted around, taking in the scene. To the right, two towering silos gleamed cold in the moonlight. To the left, thick forest loomed, the gnarly branches of oak trees reaching upward like skeletal fingers. No neighbors in sight, no city sounds. Just the quiet of the sticks, where nobody could hear you scream. A perfect place if you're planning on trying some *enhanced interrogating techniques* on the woman you'd just kidnapped. I shuddered at the thought.

Up the hill, there was a rectangular pool reflecting slivers of moonlight, and farther up sat the main house—a large colonial, classic, with two long wings stretching out like arms. Most of it was dark, but the light in the east wing's windows was on. Someone was home.

I threw a wistful glance at the car that brought me here. It sat just a few yards away, an old Crown Vic. I was seriously tempted to jump in and floor it. But no. Not yet. For the time being, I had the upper hand, and I'd be damned if I'd walk away without some answers.

I slipped toward the tree line, keeping myself low. My breathing was steady, but my heart hammered away in my chest. Step by step, I made my way toward the house, Glock leading the way. I was halfway to the pool area when I spotted him—the bald guy, pacing like an agitated animal near the pool's edge.

He was on the phone, but not saying much. Just the occasional grunt or "yes, sir."

I didn't like this. I needed to know who he was talking to. He might be senior here, but in the grand scheme of things, he was just another good little soldier.

I crouched even lower until I was practically crawling, keeping the line of bushes between us. I needed to get closer, ignoring every instinct.

Finally, he hung up, slipped the phone into his jacket, and turned toward the house.

It was now or never.

I rose from the brush, stepping out into the pale moonlight, Glock trained squarely on his chest. "Don't move," I said. My voice was low but firm.

He froze, eyes widening for a heartbeat—no doubt considering his options. But I'd positioned myself perfectly. I was too far for him to lunge at me, yet close enough that if he bolted, I could drop him in two seconds flat. He made his choice, the tension in his shoulders easing as if he'd decided to go along with the game—for now.

"Really?" His voice was casual, like we were chatting about the weather. He glanced down at the Glock, then back up at me, raising an eyebrow. "And what exactly do you think happens now?"

"Take off your belt, drop it next to you, and get on the ground," I snapped. "Do it slow. And don't do anything stupid, unless you want to find out just how loud this gun sounds out here."

He chuckled. Actually chuckled. "You're in over your head, sweetheart."

I stepped closer, the gun steady in my hands. "The last guy who called me 'sweetheart' is still looking for his teeth in the grass."

His smirk faded a little, his eyes narrowing, but he complied.

I circled around him, keeping the barrel of the Glock trained on his back. When I got behind him, I picked up his belt and used it to tie his hands. It was tight—too tight, probably cutting into his skin— but I didn't care. Next, I pulled the laces off his shoes, knotting them around his ankles. He didn't put up a fight.

Once I was satisfied with my handiwork, I flipped him onto his back. His eyes flickered with a flash of anger, but he kept his mouth shut. Too proud to complain.

"Who else is in the house? And who were you calling just now?"

He smiled. There was fury burning behind those dark-brown eyes, but there was no trace of fear. "You know I can't tell you that... sweetheart."

I gave him a tight smile. "Your choice then."

Before he could say anything else, I swung the Glock, the butt of the pistol connecting with the side of his head. There was a dull thud, and his eyes rolled back as he went slack. I crouched down beside him and tugged his shirt down. Just as I suspected, there it was. The same steampunk heart tattoo. For a second, I stood over him, waiting, listening to his shallow breaths. He was out cold, which gave me a little time. I couldn't help but feel some tension ease off my shoulders. But just for a second.

I slipped the Glock back into my grip. "Sweetheart," I muttered under my breath, shaking my head, then turned toward the house. The yard was still empty, the silence unsettling.

When I got to the house, I crouched just below the window and peered through the curtains. The room was simple but clearly well-used. There was a TV on the wall, a small coffee table in the center, cluttered with some leftovers, three glasses, and a remote control. Three chairs were arranged around it—two empty. A man occupied the third. I didn't see his face, only the back of his head and spiky gray hair. I couldn't tell for sure but he seemed older—early sixties, maybe—and there was something about the way he holds himself. The set of his shoulders, the tilt of his head... There's a mental itch in my brain, this nagging feeling I've seen the man before. But I needed to see his face to be sure.

I tiptoed to the nearest door, fingers wrapped around the handle, turning it slowly, quietly. The door gave way without a fight, but the second I stepped over the threshold, the floorboard let out a creak loud enough to wake trolls under the nearest bridge.

"Brian, that you?" a voice called out from the TV room, sharp and annoyed.

Damn it. I inched forward, hugging the wall as the flickering light from the TV danced in the hallway.

"Brian?" The man sounded impatient now. I heard the leather of his chair shift as he moved.

I stepped into the room, my pistol pointing right at the man's face. He was still facing the TV, but now that I saw his profile, I knew exactly who he was.

I wouldn't have recognized him right away just a few weeks ago, but I'd seen his face while digging into Dean Graham's inner circle. There he was, standing off to the side at one of those press conferences, looking like the guy who never wanted to be in the spotlight. Clayton Parish. Not a tall man—handsome in a distinguished way, with an aquiline nose that reminded me of Al Pacino in his prime. His official title was "Senior Advisor," but Parish seemed to be the one running the show for Graham. For the last twenty years, if something needed to get to Graham, it went through Parish first.

As I stepped into the room, I caught him trying to get up from the chair, his face pale as he saw me with a gun pointed right at his face instead of one of his guys.

"Sit the hell down," I barked.

He froze, then lowered himself back into the chair, hands up like we were in some kind of movie. He had that look in his eyes, the one I'd seen before—the "this-can't-be-happening-to-me" kind of look. You see quite a few of those as a cop when you make an arrest. That there were only three chairs in the room gave me some hope. With two of my captors down, maybe this guy was the only one left, and he didn't seem much of a threat.

"Who else is on the property?" I asked, keeping my voice steady but sharp. No need to make it more complicated than that.

Parish glanced at the door, the wheels turning in his head. He was weighing his options, probably thinking about what to say—or worse, whether to say anything at all.

But I didn't give him time to figure it out. I took a step closer, the gun almost touching his face. "I'm not playing around, Parish. Who else is here?"

He swallowed hard, his lips pressed tight. But he was no action hero. He was a guy used to moving pieces around behind the scenes, not dealing with someone who was this close to blowing his whole world apart. Fear flickered across his face.

"Just Brian and Andrew," he stammered, his voice wavering. "They are my...helpers."

"Who else?"

"Nobody, I swear. Just them."

Maybe he was a good liar in meetings, but a loaded gun pointed at your face had a way of stripping away all the confidence. His eyes darted from me to the door, then back again like he was wondering if he could make a run for it. He won't.

I watched him squirm for a few moments and didn't see any signs of deception. I believed him.

"Open your shirt," I said, stepping closer.

His brow furrowed in genuine confusion. "What? Why?"

"Open it," I snapped, sharper this time. "Now."

He hesitated, but only for a second. It was more out of bewilderment than defiance. His fingers shook slightly as he unbuttoned his expensive Oxford shirt. The fabric parted, revealing his chest.

No tattoo. Just bare skin. No steampunk gears, no intricate clockwork design. It was my turn to be confused—I was so convinced he was a part of the club, I didn't really know what to do next.

"Well?" he asked.

"Close it up."

He fumbled with the shirt, buttoning it back up as fast as his shaking fingers would let him. I didn't rush him.

Once he was done, I grabbed one of the empty chairs. The legs scraped loudly against the floor as I dragged it across the room. I flipped it around and straddled it, planting myself right in front of

Parish. My gun hand rested casually on the back of the chair, the muzzle still aimed squarely at his chest.

"I guess we'll start with the basics—where's my stuff?" I said.

He pointed with his chin toward the room behind me. "It's on the table, back there."

"Why?" I asked. It was a simple question, but there was a hurricane of rage building in my chest, ready to tear through.

I wasn't exactly in a great place after the Valentine Killer case. You don't just snap your fingers and shake off the trauma that comes from waking up tied up, helpless, in the lair of a serial killer. But I'd managed. Survived. Hell, I'd even come out on top, tracking the bastard down and putting him in the ground where he belonged. It wasn't perfect, but I was learning to live with it.

And now, these morons—Brian, Andrew, and this smug asshole in front of me—had dug up all the twisted, vile memories I'd spent months locking away, shoving them right back into the forefront of my mind. Like ripping open a wound that was just starting to scar over. And right now, every breath I took made the fury inside me grow, and the only thing I wanted to do was let it all loose on Parish, make him feel just a fraction of the hell I'd been through.

I guessed some of that came across on my face because Parish looked like he was staring down the barrel of his own execution. He had no idea I wasn't going to shoot him—I wasn't like them, not some cold-blooded psychopath. But he didn't know that.

And for a few seconds, I didn't mind letting him think otherwise.

EIGHTEEN

Parish swallowed hard, his Adam's apple bobbing like he was choking on a brick. I'd tied him to a chair now. Perhaps there were only three people on the farm, but if there were more, I didn't want to deal with multiple opponents.

"Start talking."

"You think you know what's going on, but you don't."

"I said, start talking."

He looked at me. He was still afraid of me, but there was something else. A greater terror he couldn't ignore.

"The Heart of Darkness."

"The what?"

His lips twitched, like he wanted to smile but couldn't quite pull it off. "You wouldn't understand. No one on the outside does."

"I'm very much on the inside now," I said. "Your goons made sure of that when they brought me here in the trunk of a car."

He exhaled, long and shaky, his eyes darting all over the place now. "It's a group... I know you're thinking it's just another cult, but it's not some typical group of freaks in robes, okay? The Heart of Darkness...we're preparing the world for what's coming."

"Which is?" I snapped, not in the mood for cryptic nonsense.

"Collapse," he said. "Apocalypse. The world is rotting from the inside. We're on the edge of it. You've seen the news. It's doomed."

I said nothing.

His voice dropped, almost reverent. "It has to end. That's the only way to save it. For something new to be born, the old world has to die. That's what we do—hasten the inevitable."

I stared at him. "You *want* the world to end?"

He nodded, and there was something chilling in how calm he was. "Yes. But it's not just about destruction. We are the chosen ones. We'll be the ones who survive, who lead the new world. And when it comes, we'll rule it."

"Rule it?"

"Yes. As new gods."

I laughed. I didn't mean to. It's not helpful when talking to a lunatic. You want to sympathize and make them feel you're on their side. Or at least could be swayed. But the line was so over the top. So preposterous that I simply couldn't help it.

His face hardened. "You wouldn't laugh if you saw what I've seen. You think this is some fairy tale, but there are forces in this world you can't even begin to comprehend."

"Try me."

His lips curled into a half-smile, more resigned than smug. "You're not ready."

"I'm ready enough to put a bullet between your eyes, Parish."

He shrugged as much as the bonds allowed. "You can kill me. But it won't stop what's coming. It's already in motion."

"I don't have to kill you. You've betrayed your boss and broken the law. You're finished, as far as I'm concerned."

"Dean Graham," his smile was genuine now, "is my boss in more ways than one."

My stomach dropped. I saw it coming, but hearing it out loud still hit like a freight train. I was not just up against some random criminal

—I was going toe-to-toe with one of the most powerful men on the East Coast.

"Where's Graham now?"

"I don't know." He shrugged again. "I'm not one of them. Not yet. I'm just an apprentice. But I've seen enough to know what's coming. And they're everywhere. You can't stop them."

I took a breath, pushing down the chill creeping up my spine. "We'll see about that."

With that, I left Parish to stew and headed for the back room. My stuff was right where he said it'd be. Pistol, phone, wallet—all tossed on a desk like junk mail nobody wanted. The keys to the Crown Vic were there, too. But most importantly, the Helm sat on a napkin, like some half-forgotten trinket. I picked it up carefully, turning it in my hands, wondering how something so small could cause this much chaos. It looked like a sophisticated toy, but I knew better.

I grabbed my gear, traded the Glock for my trusty HK, and headed back outside. As I passed by the pool, I checked on Baldy. The man was still out, sprawled like a sack of potatoes, but his breathing was deep and steady. He was far enough from the edge of the pool, but I pulled him a few feet farther still. He'd be fine until the cops arrived.

Back in the barn, my younger friend was awake—and he got feisty when he saw me. He thrashed against the ropes like a rabid dog, eyes wild with anger. "I'll kill you, bitch!" he spit, his voice raw with rage. "I'll pull you apart, limb by limb!"

I cocked an eyebrow as I watched him struggle. "Easy there, tiger. Save your energy. You'll need it when the cops get here and start asking questions."

He thrashed harder, shouting more threats, but I was already walking away, his voice fading behind me.

I climbed into the Crown Vic, slid the key into the ignition, and punched the address into the GPS. The engine rumbled to life, and I steered the car toward the winding gravel driveway. As I pulled away, the farm faded into the distance, the dark silhouettes of the silos and barn disappearing in my rearview mirror. The road was empty, the interstate only a few miles away, and I couldn't help but feel the weight of what just happened settling in.

The Helm. The cult. The talk of the apocalypse. And now Dean Graham. What the hell had I stepped into?

I knew I should call DD first and fill him in about the farm, the kidnapping, and the acting mayor partaking in an apocalyptic cult. The whole mess. But instead, I dialed John Levy. The phone rang so long I almost hung up, but just as I was about to give up, his voice crackled on the other end.

"Alex?"

There was relief in his tone, and it made me smile like a fool, happy that he couldn't see the ridiculous grin plastered on my face. "John. You okay?"

"Am I okay?" His voice rose a little, like I'd asked the dumbest question in the history of the world. "Are *you* okay? I waited outside but didn't see anything. Then snuck into the penthouse, and it was empty. I was going out of my mind trying to decide whether to call you or the cops. I ended up calling DD."

"I was kidnapped," I said, like it was no big deal. "But I'm fine now. Got away, no scratches. Speaking of DD, I should call him. Left him three nicely wrapped presents on a farm."

His voice dropped, thick with concern. "Kidnapped? Jesus, Alex...what the hell happened?"

I gave him a quick rundown of the last few hours—getting nabbed, the farm, Parish's creepy cult story. I could almost feel the tension building on the other end of the line as I talked. Levy didn't interrupt, but I could tell he was wound up.

"Graham, too?" he said after I finished. "This is...not going to be easy."

"Yeah, no kidding. I'll see you soon." I ended the call and sat there for a moment, the hum of the tires on the interstate calming my buzzing nerves. It was time to call DD.

To say DD wasn't amused when I called him might be the understatement of the year. He didn't blow up—he wasn't the type—but I could hear the strain in his voice, like I'd stretched his patience too thin. Still, after listening to my story and relaying it to someone to follow up, he filled me in on the latest.

First, he'd gone over the autopsy reports for all the victims, and sure enough, all of them had the same strange steampunk heart tattoo as Van der Meer.

He'd also had his friend at the NYPD run the progressive aging software and figure out the identities of the people in LeClerc's photograph. Besides the four I already knew—Sterling, Diaz, LeClerc, and Van der Meer—there were two more: Dean Graham, the acting mayor, and Kai Jensen, a tech billionaire. As DD kept talking, I pulled up the photo on my phone. The guy in the middle—had to be Graham, right? Amazing how much someone could change in twenty-odd years. Even knowing it was him, I struggled to connect the confident, heavyset man I'd seen at the fundraiser with the scrawny kid flashing an awkward grin in the picture. Time did a real number on people.

But then came the bad news. The seventh man in the picture was William Lubinsky, a high-powered criminal attorney. He was a legend in legal circles, known for representing some of the most untouchable people in white-collar crime. The only problem was Lubinsky had been dead for almost ten years. He died...wait for it, from a sudden heart attack. His body was cremated in accordance with his family's wishes, so there was no record one way or the other about the tattoo. At this point, I didn't need it. He must have had it.

But then something else occurred to me. Something that must have been painfully obvious from the beginning. Blackwood. I mean, seriously, how had I missed it? The guy practically spoon-fed me all the clues, and I just swallowed them whole without ever bothering to chew.

First off, he knew about the treasure being found. The wreck was famous, of course, and with Blackwood's interest, it wasn't surprising that he knew about it. But what he never told me was *how* he found out someone found the treasure. And then there were the people from the picture. He was on a first-name basis with at least two of them—Drew LeClerc and Milo Diaz. Now, I was certain had I dug a little deeper, I'd find Simon's ties to the rest of them—Victoria Sterling, Kai Jensen, Van der Meer, and, of course, Graham. The acting mayor himself.

Then there was my kidnapping. I couldn't reach him before that happened. How convenient. He sent me to retrieve the piece while pretending to return to Diaz's apartment when we both knew the piece was most likely gone. And then, when it was time to pick up the spoils, I got ambushed. Right on cue.

And then there was the mysterious donor who put a large bounty on my head. Perhaps Blackwood and that tech mogul guy were in cahoots. My head was spinning. My God, I was such a fool.

As furious as I was at Blackwood, pinning him as the villain in all this would've been too easy. There was a power struggle here—layers of betrayal, all of them trying to get the upper hand. It'd be tempting to think there were two clear factions: one led by Graham, the other by Blackwood. But that's not how these people operated. No alliances. No loyalty. They were all in it for themselves, sharks circling the same bloodied waters. They'd do whatever it took to get the pieces, and if killing was part of the process? So be it. They weren't just fighting for dominance—they were fighting to be the last one standing.

Maybe LeClerc was the only one from the original crew who actually took the oath seriously—the one about keeping the pieces apart, never bringing them together. That would explain why he went to such extremes to hide his piece, setting up clues and riddles. The others? They didn't seem to care as much. Sure, they held on to their keys like trophies, but they weren't really safeguarding them. They were just...waiting.

But then something shifted. Why now? It'd been decades with no movement, so why the sudden frenzy? Why were they willing to kill each other over it now, after all this time?

There had to be a trigger, something that changed the game and made them desperate.

The horn from a passing car startled me, and I snapped back to reality, jerking the wheel to right the Crown Vic in its lane. I glanced at my reflection in the rearview mirror.

I might not have a lot of answers, but one thing was crystal clear. I needed to confront Blackwood. He was the key to all of this. He'd been a step ahead of me, but that was about to change.

Then, something else occurred to me—Charlotte Parker. She was sitting on the pieces Blackwood and I found, which meant she was already on borrowed time. I grit my teeth. Damn it. I knew Blackwood didn't care, but I agreed to drag her into this mess. I was the one who put her on the radar.

And here was the worst part: the quickest way to force Blackwood's hand, to get him exactly where I wanted him, was to tell him I've got the Helm and I was taking it to Parker's bookshop. It'd flush him out, sure, but it'd also put her right in the line of fire.

I chewed on my lip, my hands gripping the wheel harder. I hated this. But I had to use Parker as bait.

NINETEEN

I was back in the city, holed up in a tiny coffee shop that reeked of burned espresso and cinnamon. The place felt like it belonged in a postcard, with its mismatched chairs and scuffed wooden floors, where the bearded barista looked like he moonlighted as a struggling poet. I welcomed the scenery and the aroma—sometimes, the little things could heal your soul in ways no therapist ever could. But I wasn't here for the coffee or the ambiance. I was here to watch the entrance to the bookshop across the street and wait for Blackwood to show his face.

I hadn't slept much. After ditching the Crown Vic near the George Washington Bridge, Levy had picked me up. He read me well—he didn't ask a lot of questions, just gave me that concerned, trying-not-to-panic look as I climbed into his car, filthy and rattled. I spent the night on his couch again, and in the morning, Blackwood was still MIA and not returning my calls. I wasn't surprised, but during my last call, I left him a message. Not a subtle one, either. I told him I'd found the Helm and was heading to Parker's bookshop to drop it off. And if he wanted to see it, he'd better meet me there at ten a.m. sharp.

Levy had argued with me about coming along. "I have to come with you," he said. "You were just kidnapped, for crying out loud. He might have been behind it."

"I don't think it was him. But you aren't coming," I shot back. "I don't want you caught up in this more than you already are."

We went back and forth for a while. In the end, we compromised. He'd come with me, but only as far as the coffee shop. He'd sit there and keep an eye out, ready to call DD if things went south.

Now, here I was, sipping a cup of cold coffee and watching the door of Secret Scrolls. Across the street, people drifted in and out of the bookshop like it was any other day. For them, it was. Just another Tuesday in the city. For me, it was the calm before the storm. I glanced at the door again. Come on, Blackwood. Time to show up.

At 9:59 a.m., I spotted him. Blackwood. Punctual as ever. Even from across the street, I instantly recognized his usual three-piece suit. The man dressed like he was about to attend a royal wedding, no matter the occasion. If it amused me in the past, right now I found it irritating. But there was something else there. Blackwood was the guy who woke up looking flawless, which made it even more obvious when something was off. And right now, something was *definitely* off.

He was tense, his shoulders stiff like he was bracing for a blow. As he moved down the sidewalk, I saw him glance around—quick, nervous flicks of his eyes that screamed paranoia. He checked the street behind him, subtly, but not subtle enough. It was clear he was making sure no one was tailing him.

Interesting. Whatever was going on with him, he was rattled, and that was something new.

"I guess this is my cue," I said.

Levy nodded, but then, just as I was about to stand, he reached across the table and grabbed my hand. A quick squeeze. "Please be careful."

"Always am." I smiled and squeezed his hand back before letting go. "I'll be fine."

For a second, Levy looked like he wanted to say more, but I didn't give him a chance. I pushed away from the table, slipped out of the coffee shop, and headed across the street.

The scent of old books hit me the second I stepped through the door of Parker's shop. It was warm, familiar, like stepping into a different era. The bell over the door gave a cheerful jingle, which felt completely out of place, given the tension coursing through my veins. I glanced around. A few people were browsing the shelves; a girl at the counter rang up an older man with thick glasses. A normal day. For them, anyway.

I scanned the shop and spotted Blackwood near the back, talking to Parker. He saw me too—no smile, no warmth—just a curt nod. He gestured with his hand, motioning for me to follow him deeper into the store.

Fine. We could play it your way, for now, Simon. I followed him past the shelves of hardcovers and paperbacks. The smell of paper and leather was so thick it was almost suffocating.

We passed Parker, and I gave a quick nod. She didn't say anything either, just watched us with a worried frown, her arms crossed tightly. She knew that something was up.

Blackwood stepped into the office, and I followed, my heartbeat already thudding in my ears. Parker entered last, quietly closing the door behind us. No one said a word for a few beats. The tension thickened. I didn't have time for pleasantries.

"All right, Simon," I said. "Let's cut the crap. What's this all about?"

"I beg your pardon?" he said, his tone shaken. "I was terribly concerned for you, Alex. You vanished, for God's sake."

"Oh, spare me the theater." The anger bubbled up, but I watched him closely. His shock at my outburst looked genuine. It made my confidence wobble. He was good—too good at this.

"There's no theater," he said, wounded. "Someone broke into my place. Ransacked it. And I've heard your office was torn apart, and your home...nearly set ablaze?"

"If you were so worried about me, why didn't you answer my calls?"

He threw his arms wide, exasperation bleeding through his polished facade. "How was I to know it was really you? I thought our lines of communication had been compromised. You didn't leave any voicemails. This morning's message was the first I knew it was actually you trying to reach me."

I stared at him, my heart racing. Maybe—just maybe—there was a sliver of truth to his words. But I wasn't ready to buy his story yet.

"Dean Graham," I said. "Do you know him?"

He stiffened. "Of course I know Dean Graham. Everyone and their mother knows Dean Graham. People who don't live in New York know—"

"No." I interrupted him. "Not like that. Do you know him like you knew Diaz and LeClerc?"

His eyes hardened. "Of course not," he snapped. "What a ridiculous accusation."

I said nothing.

Blackwood took a long, measured breath and lowered his voice, his tone almost pleading. "Alex," he said, "I've been as honest with you as I can. I traveled with two of the people in that photograph— Diaz and LeClerc—not on that particular expedition but elsewhere. I haven't met or known any of the others personally. I swear to you."

I crossed my arms, letting his words sink in. He was battering down my defenses bit by bit, but I wasn't ready to fold yet. "Okay," I said, still looking for cracks in his story. "And what about the shipwreck?"

"What about it?" he shot back.

"You told me, when this all started, that you'd heard someone found the treasure," I reminded him. "How did you know that? What proof did they give you?"

For the first time since we entered Parker's cramped office, Blackwood visibly relaxed. His shoulders loosened, and a sly smile curved the corners of his lips. "Ah, darling," he said. "Forgive me for making you think I was being naughty."

I stayed quiet, watching him.

"You need to understand something," he said. "In our line of work, very few sources of information are truly reliable. It's not a world of hard facts and verifiable truths. It just doesn't work like that. You hear rumors, whispers. Sometimes, if you're fortunate, a bit of cash changes hands. But in the end, you're left with a lot of guesswork. Educated guesses, sure, but guesses nonetheless."

I rose an eyebrow, unimpressed. "And you based all of this on a guess?"

"Call it...calculated risk. It's not that different from what the police do. You know the drill—informants, leads, rumors. Some sources you trust, some you don't, but you listen to all of them and make decisions based on the information you have at the time."

"And who was your informant?"

His smile faltered just a fraction. "That, my dear Alex, is where professional discretion comes in. I'm afraid I can't tell you that."

"Can't or won't?"

He shrugged, his grin returning. "Does it matter?"

It did matter, but I knew it was useless to push him.

"He's right." Parker finally chimed in. "I do the same in my business. Lots of unreliable leads. You take what you get and hope it's enough."

I chewed on my lip, anger still simmering just under the surface. I came here looking for a fight, but it seemed Blackwood wasn't going to give me one.

"One more thing," I said. "I want to see your chest."

Blackwood's brow shot up, confusion and irritation flashing across his face. "I beg your pardon?"

"The tattoo," I said. "I want to make sure you don't have one."

The room fell quiet, a palpable tension stretching between us. Blackwood bristled at the request, his body stiffening like I'd crossed some unspoken line. For a moment, I expected him to protest, to tell me I'm being ridiculous. But he didn't, and, with a resigned sigh, he reached for the buttons of his vest.

He pulled the vest open, moved the tie aside, and undid a few buttons of his crisp white shirt, enough to pull it aside and reveal his bare chest. There's nothing but pale skin and patches of gray hair—no sign of the intricate tattoo I'd seen on Van der Meer. But there was a scar. A big one. It ran diagonally across his chest, jagged at the edges, like it was carved out in a fight for survival. It's so large I couldn't even tell where it began and where it ended. The thing was faint now, weathered by time, but I could tell it must've been brutal when it was fresh. This wasn't a scrape or some minor wound—this was deep. Life-threatening. A wound that would have killed most people.

"There. Satisfied?" he asked.

"For now."

Blackwood adjusted his vest and tie, once again the picture of composed elegance, and turned to Parker. "Apologies for my young friend. I was once eager, too. Now, if that's all, I'd appreciate it if we could continue our conversation in a more...productive direction."

Parker cleared her throat to cut through the tension. "How about some linden tea?"

Neither Blackwood nor I wanted any, but after a few beats of awkward silence, we both nodded in unison like a pair of school-children in the principal's office.

When we were situated, I started first and told them about the identities of the people from the picture.

"Graham and Jensen," Blackwood said, as if trying their names on his tongue. "Wow."

I said nothing.

"How do we find the remaining pieces, then?" Blackwood said. "Especially if one of them is, what's his name again, dead?"

"Lubinsky," I said. "He's been dead for a few years now. Heart attack."

"His pieces might be lost then."

"I don't think so." I stopped pretending to sip the tea, put the cup down, and leaned back in the chair. "Think about it. Sterling, Diaz, LeClerc—one after another, dropping dead under suspicious circumstances. DD couldn't confirm if it was a nerve agent or something else, but you know as well as I do those weren't natural deaths. Someone's cleaning the house, and I'll bet my last penny whoever's been taking them out has Lubinsky's piece."

Parker's expression darkened. "So, that leaves us with Graham and Jensen. An acting mayor of the largest city in the country and a tech mogul worth four billion dollars. Neither are exactly your garden-variety villains."

I chewed on my lip, staring at both of them. The thought of going up against those two—men with more power and money than most people could even comprehend—was enough to make any sane person hesitate. But after a trip to the farm, I didn't feel like playing safe anymore.

Most of the time, in detective work, you don't get the luxury of waiting for the stars to align. You work with what you've got. When I was with the NYPD, it was all about budget constraints, personnel shortages, or which political winds were blowing that week. In the private sector, those limitations were even tighter. Resources? Ha. You're lucky if you have enough to cover your gas tank at the end of the day.

But here's the thing. You learn to be creative. When the deck's stacked against you, you find the cracks. You dig deep. You pull whatever threads you can find and weave them into a plan.

"Graham is going to be the toughest one. I know he's got some outside muscle on payroll because they kidnapped me last night."

Both Parker and Blackwood stared at me, their faces frozen. Before either could get a word in, I waved them off. "Spare me the 'Oh my God.' I'm fine."

"Are you—"

"I said I'm fine." I locked my eyes on Blackwood. "Focus, Simon. We were talking about Graham. He's got some thugs on his payroll. He's also got the resources of the city. He can lean on the NYPD, the

DA's office...hell, he can even make the media dance if he wants to. Let's keep him on the back burner for now. We start with the easy target—Kai Jensen."

"I'm sorry," Blackwood said. "Did you just say Jensen? Are we even talking about the same guy? The billionaire boy is the *easy* one?"

I gave him a crooked smile. "You've got one part right, Simon. I'm sure you've seen what kind of lifestyle he's leading. Fast cars, big boats, a new girlfriend every other week. Jensen's got a lot of money and power. But he's still just a boy."

TWENTY

As I approached the towering, twenty-five-story building with Spencer & Spencer spelled out in giant glossy black and gold letters on its side, it hit me—few things had a way of making my life's achievements seem so insignificant as this place. A twist of anxiety coiled in my gut. It was stupid, really. I'd stared down killers and danced with death more times than I cared to count. I could handle back alleys, dodgy informants, and dark tunnels just fine. But this place on Park Avenue, just a short, three-minute walk from the famed St. Patrick's Cathedral, always made me feel as important as a speck of dust on its polished marble floor. My sister, Tina, owned it. She and her husband Chad, to be precise.

It wasn't like Tina herself scared me. She was my sister, for God's sake, and I loved her—even when I couldn't stand her. I could handle her high-end Carroll Gardens townhouse, with its immaculate decor and live-in chef who used truffle oil the way the rest of us used ketchup. I didn't feel intimidated by her constant jet-setting around the world on chartered flights or the unending roster of celebrities vying to be her friend. But this place reminded me of everything I wasn't. I wasn't a power broker. I was just a PI, quite often with more scrapes and bruises than dollars to my name.

I pushed through the revolving door, straightened my jacket, and told myself I could survive this. If I could handle the Valentine Killer, I could handle one measly visit to see my sister in her glitzy Park Avenue kingdom. Right?

Right.

"Good morning," I said to the receptionist as I walked up to the front desk. The lobby at this hour was eerily quiet. Just me, the desk, and a whole lot of space to fill with awkward silence. "I'm here to see Tina Spencer."

The guy behind the desk gave me a quick once-over, a frown tugging on the corner of his mouth. "Do you have an appointment?"

"Of course," I said. "Tell her Olivia Dunham is here to see her."

I could tell the name didn't register at all—why would it? Olivia Dunham wasn't real. Tina and I had made it up when we were kids, a secret identity we'd use whenever one of us was in trouble at school. Tina had used it once. I've used it…well, let's just say some things never change.

"Can I see some ID?" he asked.

"No," I said, giving the man my most charming smile. "It's a very private meeting. You'll understand if you just give her office a call."

He stared at me for a second, probably deciding whether I was worth the hassle, but then picked up the phone. A few moments later, he hung up, and suddenly, his whole demeanor shifted.

"Twenty-fifth floor, Miss Dunham," he said, pointing to the elevator bank. "When you get there—"

"I know my way." I cut him off, already moving toward the elevators. I could feel his eyes lingering on my back. It didn't matter. The second those elevator doors closed, I'd vanish from his radar, just another shadow disappearing into Tina's world. The world mere mortals like him had no access to.

"I haven't heard that name in quite some time," Tina said as I stepped into her office. She sat behind a sleek, polished desk, her bespoke navy-blue pantsuit hugging her in that subtle way none of my dresses ever could.

"Hello, Tina."

"What have you gotten yourself into this time?" she asked. "The police called me a few days ago, asking if I knew where you were. I figured it was only a matter of time until you showed up."

I could see it in her face—the way her perfectly manicured fingers drummed on the arm of that stupidly expensive leather chair like she was holding back a storm. She wanted to be mad. Hell, she *should* have been mad. But there it was, a flicker in her eyes. A ghost of something old and half-forgotten. Olivia Dunham—the name, our secret code from way back, had worked its magic like it always did.

For a moment, it wasn't Tina Spencer, high-powered corporate shark, name partner in a firm who billed more in a day than some people made in a year, sitting in front of me. It was just Tina—my sister, my co-conspirator in a thousand foolish childhood adventures. The girl, who, for some reason, still had my back even though I'd given her plenty of reasons not to.

That name was a time machine. I could see it take her back, just like it took me back. To the days when we were scrappy Brooklyn girls, all big dreams and bigger mouths, without a care in the world. We thought we had it all figured out. We were invincible, or at least we thought we were.

She didn't say anything for a long moment. She just sat there tapping those fingers and studying me like she was trying to figure out who I'd become.

"Tell me now," she finally said, trying to refocus. "What kind of mess are you in this time?"

"It depends on whom you ask." I gave her a smile and took a seat across the desk.

There was a time when Tina would've rolled her eyes at this statement and made some biting remark about how I could never get my life together, but things had shifted between us in recent months. The Valentine Killer case had done that. Our relationship was still far from perfect—the adoration of the real Olivia, Tina's daughter, notwithstanding. But that case earned me something with my older sister. Not quite admiration, but there was now a begrudging respect. An acknowledgment that maybe I wasn't the screwup she always thought I'd be. She eyed me now like she was trying to size up the situation.

"I wanted to call you," she said. "But I wasn't sure if it would mess up your plans somehow. Are you okay?"

"I'm fine," I said, keeping it light. There was no need to make her worried about things she wouldn't have any control over, anyway. "Mostly."

She nodded.

"Do you know Kai Jensen?" I asked, trying to redirect the conversation.

"*The* Kai Jensen?" She raised an eyebrow.

"Yes."

"I do," she said. "I'd love to get some of his business. The last three acquisitions he made were done through our competitors."

"Well," I said, "this will not help you win any of his business, but maybe it'll give you some relief to know he's not exactly the guy you want to do deals with, anyway."

Tina gave me a sharp look. "And why is that?"

"Because he's mixed up in a dangerous cult. They've killed people, Tina. And they will kill again."

"You have proof of this?"

"I do."

Her expression didn't change, but I could see the shift in her eyes —I had her attention now. "I'm listening."

"I need you to play a spy game with me. You've got connections. You know lots of people in the art world. I need you to start a rumor. It can't be obvious. More like—you're not even sure yourself if you know it's happening. It needs to be something juicy, something irresistible. Let's say there's a very rare piece of art up for grabs. Something that would have collectors drooling. Maybe it doesn't even have a clear provenance. I'll give you some options. You do that, and if it's done right, Jensen—being the art aficionado he is—will hear about it. And he'll want in."

"And then what?"

"Once he's hooked, we arrange a showing. Somewhere we can control. Safe, on our terms."

"You're trying to create an illusion that other people are vying for the piece."

"Precisely."

"That," she paused, "requires other people actually doing it. I can't possibly put my reputation on the line for this."

I nod. "I understand, but you won't have to. I have just the right guy."

She tapped a finger on the desk, her mind clearly running through logistics. Probably already sifting through different choices of whom to give the rumor to. "And what happens when he shows up? What are you planning to do?"

"That depends," I said. "I'll try persuasion first. Will have a nice little chat with Mr. Jensen about his extracurricular activities."

"And if it doesn't work?"

"I'll bug him."

"Your goal is to have him admit the crime you say he's guilty of?"

"Nope." I hesitated, debating how much to tell her. "It's complicated. But trust me, he's dangerous. The cult he's in—they are after something a lot more valuable than paintings. And they are willing to kill for it. *Have* killed for it. If not for some quick thinking and a little bit of luck, they'd have killed me, too."

She let out a slow breath, her eyes studying me. I tried to hold her gaze, but it was like staring into a spotlight. My eyes drifted to the windows behind her instead, where the skyline of Manhattan loomed large, sparkling with all the power and ambition Tina thrived on.

"Are you sure this will work?" she asked.

I shrugged. "It's not bulletproof. But it's as good as it'll ever get."

For a moment, she sat there, weighing it all in that cool, calculating way she had. Then she nodded. "Fine. Let me know about the item, and I'll make the calls."

"Thank you." I stood up, ready to leave.

"Alex," she said, startling me. "Be careful. It sounds like you're playing with fire."

I shrugged and gave her a smile. "Not the first time. Certainly not the last."

"If this goes south... You understand this can't be linked to me, right?"

I glanced back as I opened the door, the grin still on my face. "What goes south? I was never here."

I left Tina's office, her words still ringing in my ears. Outside, the city buzzed with its usual chaotic energy that made you feel alive even when you were drowning in it. I took a deep breath, squinting up at the sun blazing high in the sky, a few puffy clouds scattered about against the perfect blue.

My feet carried me in no particular direction, and after a few minutes, the spires of St. Patrick's Cathedral came into view, towering above the street like a sentinel from another world. I stopped at the base of the steps, hesitating.

It wasn't exactly a place I normally gravitated toward. I didn't do churches. But something about it—the way it stood there, solid and immovable amid the chaos—called to me. Maybe it was the Valentine Killer case still clawing at the edges of my mind. Maybe it was Blackwood's case. Either way, I found myself climbing the stairs.

Inside, the air was cool and quiet. There was no service at the moment, and only a few people dotted the vast space, mostly tourists, their eyes wide as they stared up at the stained-glass windows, took pictures, or whispered prayers. I moved down the aisle and slipped into a pew at the back, far from everyone else.

I wasn't one for religion. Never had been. The whole idea of some grand design, of a higher power pulling strings—it never really clicked for me. But sitting here, in the shadow of the cathedral's vaulted ceiling, surrounded by its serene beauty, I couldn't help but wonder.

Maybe there was something more. Something I couldn't see or understand. What if it was a vast, unknowable layer of the world—something humanity had been trying to make sense of for millennia? What if the stories in all those religious texts were just our feeble attempts to explain something too big, too complex for us to ever grasp?

The Valentine Killer case had shaken me more than I liked to admit. It had felt like something out of a myth, where good and evil weren't just ideas but tangible forces at work. And now, with this case —the murders, the artifact, the whispers of ancient secrets—I was starting to feel like I was stumbling into something even deeper. Something darker.

I glanced up at the altar, at the candles flickering in the dim light. Was it possible? Could there really be something beyond what I could touch or see? I wasn't ready to believe. Not yet, anyway. But I couldn't shake the feeling that maybe, just maybe, I was brushing up against the edges of a world I hadn't been aware of until now.

A world where gods and monsters weren't just stories but real— and terrifying.

TWENTY-ONE

The warehouse smelled like dust and old antiseptic. From the outside, the building looked like the place you'd expect to find a body, not a gathering of Manhattan's elite. It used to store medical supplies, though you wouldn't know it now. It wasn't much better on the inside when I first set foot in it—dust hung in the air like it was trying to reclaim the place. But we'd done enough to dress it up, at least for one night. The massive space now echoed with the soft hum of the air conditioning I'd rigged to keep it bearable, and if you didn't know better, you might have thought we were preparing for some high-society gala. I guess, in a way, we were.

Underneath the chipped beams and sagging roof, Levy and I set up a cluster of chairs in neat rows—each one covered in black velvet. A podium stood at the front, polished and gleaming despite its surroundings. The lighting from half a dozen strategically placed lights was dim, just enough to keep everything discreet but not enough to make anyone uneasy. Over by the wall, a table was set with silver trays piled with hors d'oeuvres that would be at home at any Michelin-starred restaurant. Black caviar, because, of course. And lobster puffs and foie gras terrine with fig jam and some tiny thing on toast I couldn't even name despite John Levy telling it to me at least twice. A pair of waiters in sleek masks poured Krug Clos du Mesnil into delicate flutes, serving it like this was just another night out at some five-star hotel.

I leaned back against a cracked pillar, arms crossed, watching the crowd shuffle in. Even with their faces hidden behind Venetian masks, I could sense the wealth, the entitlement, the barely concealed greed. All drawn here by the whisper of a piece of art so rare, so off-the-grid, that it had to be sold in a place like this. Tina had come through, all right. Now, I just had to make sure it worked before anyone figured out I had no art to sell.

"It's not half bad," Blackwood said when I first pitched him the idea of an auction. "But there are a few issues."

We had been sitting in Levy's kitchen, and the air between the two men was thick with distrust, both sizing each other up like two predators deciding if the other was worth taking a bite of. I was the common denominator between them, but that didn't mean they had to like each other.

"Which are?"

"There are three problems." Blackwood raised three fingers to illustrate his point. "One," he folded one finger down, "we need to find a suitable location and make it presentable. That will require some capital."

"I can fund it," Levy said, his voice edged with impatience, like the very fact he was sitting here should've been proof enough of his resources.

I couldn't help being fascinated. This wasn't the John Levy I'd come to know. No, this was the old Levy—a ruthless businessman from his heyday. The man who built an empire before his wife's death took him down a few notches. For a brief second, I saw a glimpse of the powerhouse he used to be when nothing could touch him. The confidence that came with knowing you could make things happen, no matter the cost.

Blackwood nodded, but his eyes were still on me. "Second," he said, folding another finger. "These buyers aren't stupid. You can't just expect them to show up there and be ready to pay millions for an art piece they haven't seen. They'll want proof. Experts."

I said nothing. He was working up to his big point.

"And finally," Blackwood said, raising one finger like it was the trump card. "We have no actual rare artwork to offer. We've got nothing to sell."

"You're not wrong," I said. "But I think I've got solutions for all three issues."

Blackwood watched me, skeptical, his arms crossed.

"First, the location. I know a place—a warehouse in Brooklyn. Smugglers used it back when I was still on the force. After the bust, the lawsuits drove the company out of business. The place has been sitting empty ever since, but since it's part of a pending sale, it's been maintained just enough. Perfect for what we need—off the grid, discreet."

Blackwood nodded.

"Now for your second and third points," I continued. "These people won't be showing up just for the art. They live for exclusivity, the thrill that comes with owning something no one else even knows exists. They love the stakes most people would consider impossible. That's why they're as successful as they are—they thrive on being first, on having access others don't...and on bending and sometimes breaking the rules. We use that against them."

He was listening now, clearly intrigued, but he still wasn't sold. "Okay. But what about the actual art? That's still our biggest problem."

I smiled. "That's where we turn our weakness into our biggest strength. We tell them the piece is so exclusive they can't buy it at the first meeting. Hell, they can't even see it."

Blackwood raised an eyebrow, and I could see the gears turning behind his eyes. "How does that work?"

"We dangle it just enough to hook them. We tell them what the piece is, get them salivating, and let them make blind bids at the auction. But—and this is the kicker—we make it clear we won't be taking their money. Not yet. We meet with each one after the first round and tell three people they are the highest bidders. And because we talk to everyone, no one will know who ended up with the highest bids. We tell them that all the three highest bidders get is an invitation to a second meeting, where they'll finally get to examine the piece in person. They can bring their experts, tools, whatever they need. Then, once they are satisfied, we set up the date for the actual auction, where the highest bid from the first round would be the floor price."

"And when we talk to them one-on-one after the first round—"

"Yes," I said, leaning back with a grin. "We leave Jensen for last. That's how we get him alone. That's the real endgame."

Blackwood's thin lips stretched into a smile. I could see Levy grinning, too.

"It's so preposterous," Blackwood finally said, "that it might actually work. And, as it happens, I think I have an idea of just the right art piece to dangle."

It was my turn to raise an eyebrow. "You do?"

"Well, if you think about it," he continued, leaning back in his chair and steepling his fingers like a professor about to deliver a lecture, "it's almost obvious. Jensen is a billionaire, yes? The others attending our little fake auction will be of similar financial stature. Naturally, the piece must be outrageously valuable—beyond rare. And do you know whose works fetch the highest prices in the world?"

I shrugged. "Jackson Pollock? I've read some of his splatters go for obscene amounts."

"They do," Blackwood said with a nod. "But not quite at the level I'm thinking. No, we need something even more revered, something that speaks to the highest echelon of collectors. There's an Italian name you might have heard—Leonardo da Vinci. His *Salvator Mundi* sold for $450 million—a record for *any* piece of art. And then there's, of course, the *Mona Lisa*. It's quite literally priceless—the French government forbids the sale of it. However, in 1963, when it traveled to the US, it was insured for $100 million. Adjust for inflation, and you're looking at close to a billion today."

"You're not proposing we try to sell the *Mona Lisa*, I hope," I quipped.

"Of course not," Blackwood replied with a grin. "But what I am suggesting is even better. You see, there's a work by da Vinci that's considered lost—a painting of Medusa. If it were ever found, its price would easily rival, if not surpass, *Salvator Mundi*."

"Medusa?" I racked my brain. It wasn't ringing any bells. Judging by Levy's expression, he didn't know it, either. "Never heard of it."

"I'm not surprised. But it's something of a myth in the art world." He leaned forward, eyes gleaming with intrigue. "Believe me when I tell you—*every* self-respecting art collector knows about the piece. The story comes from an Italian Renaissance painter named Giorgio Vasari. You've likely never heard of him, but he's famous for writing *Le vite de' più eccellenti pittori, scultori, e architettori*, mostly known as *The Lives*, a collection of biographies of famous painters, sculptors, and architects including the likes of Michelangelo and Leonardo. In one of those accounts, he tells a fascinating story about young Leonardo, long before he was the master we know him as today. According to Vasari, da Vinci, at his father's request, painted Medusa's head on a wooden shield—a horrifyingly realistic depiction. So much so that it was said to frighten those who saw it. Ser Piero da Vinci, Leonardo's father, was apparently so taken with it he secretly sold the piece off to some art dealer in Florence for one hundred ducats. It vanished shortly after that."

"And we will say—that we 'found' it?"

Blackwood's grin widened. "Precisely. While your sister is sending rumors in her circles, Parker and I will send whispers in ours. As you said, we won't need the actual painting to sell the idea. Just the suggestion that such a monumental piece of lost history has potentially surfaced—and only the most elite can even attempt to get their hands on it? The mystery and allure alone will drive them mad."

"How do we handle the end of the auction, though?" Levy chimed in. "You don't want to leave a bunch of uber-wealthy and powerful people feeling like they were duped. They might lash out in anger."

"I have an idea for that as well. We'd reach out to the winners of the first round and inform them that the seller, overwhelmed by the prices, changed their mind and decided to keep it for the time being. They'd still be disappointed, but the hope of possibly bidding for it again would be enough to keep them from possible retaliation." I looked him in the eye. "One last thing."

He raised his eyebrow.

"You don't show your face at the auction," I said. "They have no idea who you are, and I'd like to keep it that way. You're our ace in the hole."

In the days that followed, we went to work like a well-oiled machine. Tina, with her effortless charm and high-society connections, started planting the seeds. It wasn't a full-on blitz—no, that would be too obvious. She was subtle, dropping hints at the right charity galas, fundraisers, and private luncheons. The idea spread like wildfire through Manhattan's elite circle. A rediscovered da Vinci? The lost work of Medusa, no less? The rumors alone sent a tremor through the upper echelon.

While Tina handled the one-percenters, Blackwood and Parker worked the underworld of art dealers, the ones who operated behind closed doors, dealing in pieces that would never see the inside of a museum. Parker was brilliant in her role. She dropped subtle hints, just enough to pique interest without tipping her hand. Blackwood, with his cultured British accent and impeccable manners, was her perfect match—calculated, precise, and careful to let slip only what we wanted them to know.

The rumor mill did the rest. By the time the whispers hit full steam, the story was gospel: the shield painted by Leonardo da Vinci himself had been rediscovered. A private auction was imminent. A secret location in the heart of New York City was being set up for the auction. No one knew where, and no one dared to ask outright. The exclusivity of it all only heightened the stakes. You weren't just buying art—you were buying into a mystery. A legend.

By the end of the week, we had our players. A dozen participants were handpicked for their wealth, influence, and hunger for the extraordinary. Some were there for the art, others for the prestige, and a few—well, they were just there for the thrill. An opportunity to crush someone else's dreams. All of them were primed and ready, and none of them had the faintest idea they were being played. The stage was set.

I watched them now—twelve masked faces fidgeting in their seats, champagne flutes in hand, nibbling on hors d'oeuvres as they glanced at the disposable phones they'd been handed at the door as they surrendered their own. These phones would be their lifelines tonight, their only connection to the silent bidding war about to unfold. Nine men, three women. They all looked the same in their sleek disguises, but there were tells if you knew where to look. A twitch of a finger, a restless shifting, a too-long glance at someone else's mask.

I watched Jensen. He sat at the edge of the front row, radiating impatience. He waved off the waiter offering him more champagne with a flick of his hand, like a king dismissing a servant. His right foot tapped relentlessly, the heel barely brushing the ground, keeping time with a rhythm only he could hear.

I checked my watch. We needed to let them stew a little longer, let the tension build until it practically hummed through the room. Make them desperate. Bolero was playing softly in the background from hidden speakers, the slow march building ever so slightly, each note winding them up just a little higher.

I could tell some of them were getting close to their breaking points, eyes darting toward the entrance, fingers drumming on the arms of their chairs. Jensen's foot was practically a blur. Then, right on cue, Blackwood appeared from the back of the warehouse. He moved with purpose, his tuxedo immaculate, his steps measured. The mask he wore—a sleek black cat's face with an unsettling, knowing smile as a nod to Leonardo's love for cats—only added to his presence. Every head turned toward him.

"Ladies and gentlemen," Blackwood began as he strode to the podium, his voice smooth and low. "Thank you for attending the first stage of this exclusive auction. I trust everyone has been briefed, but I'd like to go over the rules once more before we proceed."

A few impatient glances but no interruptions. They wouldn't dare.

"No money will exchange hands at tonight's event," Blackwood continued.

That caused a ripple through the crowd. Murmurs, some shifting in seats. Good. They weren't used to this.

"Tonight," he went on, "you are bidding on the opportunity to move on to the second round. Only the three highest bidders will proceed. In the second auction, you'll be allowed to bring your experts, review the provenance, and place your final bids. Tonight's highest bid will serve as the reserve price. After the auction, we'll meet with each of you privately, in random order, to inform you whether you've progressed to the next round. Communication between bidders is strictly prohibited. If anyone reveals whether they've advanced, they'll be disqualified immediately."

He let that hang in the air, his eyes—at least what could be seen of them—sweeping the room like he was daring someone to argue. No one did.

"If we're all clear on the rules, please raise your hand."

Twelve hands went up. Like puppets.

"Excellent," Blackwood said, clasping his hands together. "Then let us begin."

TWENTY-TWO

The bidding wrapped up, but we weren't done with them yet. We let them squirm for a good twenty minutes, giving Blackwood and me just enough time to fake a deep discussion over the bids in the backroom. It was all theater, of course, but they didn't know that. The waiting was part of the game, and we had to play it just right.

One by one, they were funneled into the adjacent room. The interview room, as Blackwood called it—drapes drawn, dim lighting, heavy on the drama. It had the feel of a mob sit-down. They walked in, heads held high, convinced they had this in the bag. And one by one, we shut them down.

Some took it well. A quick nod, a tight-lipped smile behind their mask, and they were out the door before we could blink. Others weren't so graceful. A few tried to up their bids on the spot, but Blackwood was a pro—he brushed them off with a polite, "Unfortunately, the decision's been made," before ushering them out of the warehouse as fast as he could.

We didn't need them anymore. All we needed was Jensen. And there he was in his chair, his mask doing little to hide his impatience, his foot tapping against the floor like it was counting down the seconds. The last one standing. I took a breath. Showtime.

"Mr. Jensen," I said, leaning against the table as Blackwood gestured toward the weathered leather chair in the corner. "Please, go ahead, take a seat. You can lose the mask for now. No need to be uncomfortable."

Jensen strode past us, unhurried, and sat down. Whatever impatience he had shown in the bidding room was now gone—he was in full control of the situation. The mask came off in a smooth motion, revealing a face that defied his fifty-three years. Kai Jensen could've passed for thirty-five, easy. Dark-blond hair, not a speck of gray. His skin was smooth and tight, practically glowing. Whatever it was he was taking, you wouldn't find it at the local pharmacy.

I tried not to let my mind wander, but the rumors flickered in the back of my head. The ones about how he supposedly got transfusions from healthy, young donors to keep himself looking like this—like time had forgotten about him. A tech-made vampire. I almost chuckled at the thought, but staring at him up close, it was not that hard to believe. No fifty-three-year-old I'd ever met looked this...fresh.

He leaned back in the chair, his piercing blue eyes locking on me. "I take it I'm one of the three?"

"About that," I said, keeping my voice calm as I pulled the gun from my holster. I held it out in front of me—not pointed directly at Jensen, but close enough that he got the message. I wasn't trying to send him into a panic yet. I just wanted to make sure he understood where we were headed.

Jensen's head snapped up, and the calm, unflappable billionaire routine evaporated in an instant. His eyes went wide, and he sat bolt upright. "What the hell is this? Do you have any idea who you're dealing with?"

"Well, that depends." I let the words hang there, watching as his face flushed. He was rattled, but not scared out of his mind. Good. "I might be dealing with a man who wants to help me. In that case, you walk out of here unharmed, and we'll never see each other again."

He said nothing, his eyes flicking between me and Blackwood.

"Or," I continued, "I'm dealing with a stubborn fool who doesn't know what's best for him. And that, Jensen...that wouldn't be ideal for either of us."

Jensen's jaw tightened, and the color of his cheeks deepened to Christmas red. "What the hell do you want?"

"I'd like to talk to you about the Heart of Darkness."

His face twitched. It was just a flicker. A shadow so momentary, you'd miss it if you blinked, but I saw it. It struck a nerve.

"You've got the wrong man," he said. He leaned back again, trying to regain control.

"Don't play dumb with me, Jensen," I said. "We both know you're part of the seven. Or do you want me to make you strip and show me your tattoo?"

He swallowed hard, his confidence faltering. "And if I was... hypothetically...part of it, what's in it for you?"

"Hypothetically?" I shrugged. "I care to make sure nobody else dies. And I want your piece of the key."

Jensen's eyes flicked to the gun, calculating, weighing his options. He didn't like where this was going. Not one bit. But he wasn't stupid, either.

"You think you can just...what, threaten me into...?" he trailed off, the realization of what I just said hitting him hard. "What do you mean, *nobody else* dies?"

"Victoria Sterling," I said, watching him squirm as if the words caused him physical pain. "Milo Diaz, Drew LeClerc, Richard Van der Meer, William Lubinsky."

"They all died from natural causes!" Jensen shouted, his voice cracking with desperation. "Well, except for Van der Meer."

I rolled my eyes. "Oh yeah, of course. And when I went to check LeClerc's storage, someone naturally decided to shoot at me in a parking lot. Totally normal stuff, right? And then, when I paid a visit to Sterling's apartment, someone naturally whacked me on the head and kidnapped me in the trunk of a car to a farm in NJ. Just an average Tuesday, huh?"

Jensen's face twisted, his mouth moving but no sound coming out for a second. Finally, he sputtered, "You're lying!"

But I could see it—the crack in his armor, the way his bravado was slipping, his eyes darting around like he was looking for an escape hatch that didn't exist.

I shrugged. "Believe whatever helps you sleep at night, Jensen."

He fidgeted in his chair, glancing toward the door and then back at me. His confidence was crumbling now, visibly falling apart like a house of cards caught in a breeze. He knew I had him cornered.

"You don't know what you're getting into," he finally said, his voice low, like maybe if he said it quietly enough, it would change the stakes.

"The bullet casings in the parking lot and the bump on my head say otherwise." I waved the barrel of the HK at him. "Last chance, Jensen. Either start talking—"

I didn't finish the sentence, letting the silence between us do the heavy lifting. He knew the truth. He just needed the final push. I nodded to Blackwood.

"There were seven people during that expedition," Blackwood said. "Four of them dead, Jensen. Unless you've killed them all, I'd say your life is in jeopardy, too."

Jensen threw a sharp look at Simon, and then his shoulders sagged, his entire demeanor deflating.

"Talk, Jensen," I said. "The sooner you talk, the sooner we can end this."

"It's Graham," he said, his eyes drifting toward the floor. "He's behind it all."

"Behind what, Jensen?" I snapped, my patience thinning by the second.

He flinched, his eyes darting to the floor like he was looking for a trapdoor to fall through. "I didn't know he was taking them out," he said, voice low, shaky. "I guess... I had my suspicions, but when you see 'heart attack' on the news, what the hell am I supposed to think? I brushed it off and moved on with my life."

"Must be nice." I let the words hang in the air, dripping with sarcasm. His excuses didn't exactly tug at my heartstrings.

Jensen leaned in closer, desperation seeping into his voice. "Listen, you have to believe me. I've never been one of the zealots. I swear! I mean, yeah, I did the rituals. Stood there with everyone, humming their stupid chants, got the tattoo. But that's it. I was young, okay? It sounded...cool. Secret society and all that. It seemed harmless. And besides, these people, they were connected. They were in high places. I figured they could help with my career, you know? Greed, that's all it was. I wasn't in it for the crazy stuff."

"Greed," I repeated, biting down on the word. "That's your excuse? Sold your soul for a shot at the big leagues?"

Jensen shook his head, his face twisted with regret. "I didn't know what I was getting into. Nobody talks about the dark side upfront. It's all just whispers, favors, doors opening you didn't even know existed. And, yeah, they helped me. My career took off after I joined. But I didn't know—"

"That people would start dropping like flies once they outlived their usefulness?"

His breath caught in his throat, and he seemed to wilt under my stare. "I didn't know it would go this far, okay? The rituals, the secrecy... I thought it was just part of the game. A weird type of networking. And I had no idea people would die. Guys like LeClerc and Diaz, they were older, stressed-out, not exactly healthy. It didn't seem that far-fetched."

"And Van der Meer?" I pushed. "Did he die from natural causes, too? That must've been a very natural bullet."

Jensen winced, eyes flicking to the ground again. "That one...that one I couldn't ignore. But by then, it was too late. I couldn't just walk away."

"Too late for who, Jensen?" Blackwood said. "Them? Or you?"

His baby face paled, and I could see the gears turning in his head as he realized there was no more running from this. He was in deep, and every lie he'd told himself to justify staying quiet was unraveling, one thread at a time. It must have been weighing on him for a long time, I realized. He wouldn't have crumbled on the spot like this if it hadn't.

"I didn't kill them," he muttered, almost to himself. "I didn't pull any triggers or slip any poison. I just... I just stood by."

I let him stew on it...the confession of a coward who'd been in over his head from day one. But it didn't make him any less guilty. He'd known—*suspected*, at least—and done nothing. That was enough.

"Graham," I said, pulling us back on track. "He's the one behind it all?"

Jensen nodded, his eyes wide, frantic now. "Yes. Graham's always been the real power behind the curtain. He's the one pulling all the strings. I don't know how deep it goes, but he controls everything."

"Why?" I demanded. "And don't give me this apocalyptic bullshit. What's the endgame here? What's he after?"

"I don't know," he stammered. "I swear, I don't. I was never in the inner circle. I was just another cog in the machine. But whatever it is, it's big. Bigger than any of us understood in the beginning."

I said nothing, letting the silence stretch. He was scared, all right, but scared of what, exactly? Graham? Or is the truth finally catching up to him?

"Look, I'll help you," he said, voice rising in panic. "I can give you names. People, places. Anything. Just get me out of this. You have no idea what he's capable of."

"Oh, I think I have a pretty good idea," I said. "And you're going to give me everything you know, Jensen. *Everything*. Because if you don't, you're not just dealing with Graham anymore. You're dealing with me. I have a million-dollar bounty on my head, I'm on the wanted list, my home was burned, and my office was ransacked. I'm all out of fucks to give. Do you understand?"

He swallowed hard, realizing, finally, he had no more cards to play. "Okay," he whispered. "Okay, I'll tell you everything I know."

And just like that, the tables turned.

TWENTY-THREE

"The key, Jensen," I said. "Where is it?"

His eyes flickered with fear, but he didn't hesitate. "It's in a storage unit in Brooklyn. LeClerc rented it a few years back."

The irony wasn't lost on me. I'd already been there—sifting through LeClerc's random junk to find his journal and the photograph. "I was there already and didn't find a key."

"You probably missed it the first time, but it's there in one of the boxes. It's a small safe that looks like a *Pride and Prejudice* hardcover. The code for the combination lock is three sevens."

"What is up with you and the sevens?" I said, "LeClerc used it. It was in the nightclub."

"It's considered a divine number," Jensen said. "A superstition, really. Just like 666 is considered to be the devil's number. The Heart of Darkness members believe they will rise as gods after the apocalypse."

"Yeah." I shuddered. "So I've heard."

"What's the address?" Blackwood chimed in.

Jensen rattled it off, his voice cracking as he spoke. I could almost feel the fear radiating off him. He wasn't just afraid of us. He was terrified of something else. Something bigger.

"And Graham?" I asked, not letting him off the hook just yet. "What's his plan?"

"There's a meeting. Soon. I don't know the details, but I think Graham is preparing for something else. I thought..." He trailed off, his eyes glazing over.

"What?" I snapped. "Speak, Jensen, speak."

"He's planning to do something big," he said. "Where lots of people might get hurt. And don't ask what or where or when because I honestly don't know. You'll know something is about to go down if he skips the city. He has a place upstate to hole up."

A chill ran down my spine as I wrote the address. "Like a terrorist act? Jesus, man."

I glanced at Blackwood and stood up, pushing my chair. "All right. Sit here for another thirty minutes, and you can go. But just so we're clear. If you're lying... I'll find you no matter where you go, do you understand?"

He swallowed, nodding quickly. "I'm not lying. I swear."

We stepped out into the night, the weight of Jensen's confession hanging between us. Blackwood turned to me, his expression unreadable.

"What now?" he asked.

I pulled out my phone and scrolled to DD's number. "Now, we split up. You get the key from the storage. I'm going after Graham."

He gave me a sharp look. "Okay. But I'll need to call Parker first and tell her to expect me. And you're sure Graham's still here? In the city?"

I let out a long breath, scanning the street like I expected trouble to materialize out of the shadows any second. "No, I'm not sure. But if Jensen's telling the truth and whatever they are planning is close, he's probably still here. From everything I've seen about him, he seems to be a control freak. He'll probably stay here until the last moment. When he bails, we know it's go time. Please call Levy as you go, fill him in on the latest, and I'll call DD."

Blackwood didn't say anything for a moment. He just stared at me like he was deciding whether to argue. Then, with a curt nod, he turned and started heading toward his car, disappearing into the gloom.

I watched him go, feeling the pressure ramp up another notch. Time wasn't on our side, and splitting up now made us vulnerable. But there was no other way. We needed the key, and we needed to stay on Graham's tail.

I dialed DD's number—voicemail. Great. I hesitated for a moment, deciding whether to leave a message and hung up before the beep. I imagined DD listening to it, his raspy breathing almost drowning out my voice: *Hey, partner. I don't know how to tell you, but I kidnapped a billionaire boy, Kai Jensen. He looks great, by the way, and he told me, under duress, that the acting mayor of New York City is planning a terrorist attack. So, why don't you just head out there and arrest him before he hurts anyone because your pal Alex Watts told you so? Thanks!*

I got into my car and headed toward the city. The plan was simple: track Graham, get in front of him, and force him to confess. It worked with Jensen, so maybe it was my lucky night.

If only things ever went according to plan.

I'd barely made it out of the tunnel when my phone buzzed in my pocket. I pulled it out, half-expecting it to be DD, but it was Levy.

"John," I said. "What's going on?"

"You watching the news?" he asked, his voice raspy, like he was out of breath. I could hear some shouting in the background and the quick staccato of footsteps.

"No, why? Why are you out of breath?"

"Graham's gone. Just popped up on the news. He left the city, Alex. Headed for some retreat in the Catskills."

Great. Just great. "Are you okay?"

"I'm fine." There was a hesitation in his voice. "Probably. I gotta go."

He hung up before I could say anything else. My mind was racing. If Graham was gone, that meant Blackwood was walking into a trap. Jensen was a coward. If he told us about the location of the piece, he must've told somebody else. And Graham somehow must have connected the dots. If he could get Jensen's piece and get the location of the other four from Blackwood, he'd have the full set. I blew a red light cutting across the West Side Highway and looped around, heading straight back into the tunnel I had just come from.

The moment I came out on the other side, I called Blackwood, but it didn't connect. I floored the gas pedal, weaving through traffic like a madwoman with a death wish. My phone sat on the passenger seat, glowing up at me every few seconds with the same maddening response: Call Failed.

I dialed again, gripping the wheel tighter with every ring. "Pick up, Blackwood. Damn it, pick up."

Nothing. No voicemail, no curt British greetings. Just empty silence. The cold feeling in my gut twisted a little harder. Something wasn't right. I could feel it in my bones. The silence on the other end told me everything I needed to know. Blackwood was in trouble.

The storage facility loomed ahead, a gray concrete slab at the end of a parking lot. The second I pulled in, my instincts were screaming. I didn't even bother parking properly—just jumped out of the car and ran. My boots hit the concrete hard, echoing down the lot. And then I saw them. Jensen was on the ground, his body convulsing, his skin pale as death. He was trying to speak, but only broken, garbled sounds escaped his lips. Standing over him, clutching a small object in his hand—the key—was Blackwood.

I stopped dead in my tracks, heart pounding. There he was, standing over a dying man, holding the last piece of the key that could unlock who knows what levels of hell.

"Blackwood," I shouted, my voice ricocheting off the walls. "What the fuck?"

He didn't flinch, didn't even look up at me. Just stood there, his face shadowed and unreadable, like a man who'd just crossed a line he couldn't uncross.

Jensen made a strangled sound, his hand twitching toward Blackwood, his eyes wide with fear, and then his entire body just *froze*. He looked like a science experiment I once saw on the internet—when a student dipped a live frog into liquid oxygen.

Rage hit me like a freight train. I didn't even think—just moved. In two strides, I was on him, shoving him hard enough he stumbled back.

"What the hell did you do?" I snarled, my voice shaking with fury.

Blackwood caught his balance, eyes narrowing. "Alex, wait—"

"Are you kidding me?" I snapped, cutting him off. "Jensen's dying at your feet, and you're holding the key. The one thing we've been chasing this whole time."

He raised his hands, palms out, but there was something else in his eyes—cold, calculating. "You're jumping to conclusions."

I took another step toward him, fists clenched. "I'm not stupid, Simon."

His face hardened. "Neither am I. And it's a little suspicious, isn't it? You show up here when you were supposed to be tailing Graham?"

"I'm not the one standing over a body."

"I didn't kill him," Blackwood said, his voice low. "I spooked someone when I arrived, and they ran off before taking the key. I didn't do anything wrong. But if you want to keep pushing me, Alex, I'm not going to stand here and take it."

I threw a jab before I even realized it was happening. One second, we were shouting, and the next, Blackwood's hand shot out, deflecting my punch like it was nothing.

I went for him again, throwing every ounce of my frustration, my anger, my betrayal into the strike.

He blocked, countered, and moved back. He might have been

older than me, but he'd danced like this before. I aimed for his ribs, but he caught my arm and twisted, forcing me to break free with a spin. My foot caught his ankle, and I used the momentum to sweep his legs out from under him. He hit the ground with a grunt, but before I could pin him down, he rolled and lashed out, knocking me back.

"Stop this nonsense," Blackwood growled, pulling himself up.

Just as I was about to go for him again, the distant wail of sirens cut through the chaos. My head snapped toward the road. Cops.

"Damn it," I muttered under my breath. This wasn't how it was supposed to go. I needed answers, not handcuffs.

Blackwood's eyes flicked toward the road, then back to me. "You've got two choices," he said, his voice calm despite the tension. "Fight me, or run."

He was right. As much as I hated it, he was right. The sirens were getting closer by the second, and I couldn't afford to stick around. Not with this mess.

I shot him a glare, fury still boiling beneath the surface, but I knew I had no choice. "This isn't over, Blackwood."

"I hope not," he said.

I turned and bolted toward the car, the wheels spitting smoke as I gunned down the street, away from the sirens and lights.

The wind howled through the open windows as I sped down the highway, carrying with it the scent of asphalt and something vaguely metallic. In my rearview, the city lights blurred into streaks of gold and red. The road stretched ahead, dark and empty, just like the answers I was chasing.

Jensen was dead. I couldn't get the image out of my head—him lying there, his body jerking, the last sparks of life sputtering out while Blackwood loomed over him with the key. It didn't look good. Hell, it looked damning. So why did it feel so wrong?

The distant wail of sirens finally faded, but their echo still rumbled in my chest, a reminder of how close I'd been to getting caught. Too damn close.

But I couldn't dwell on it now. Graham was heading to his retreat far from the city, which meant whatever plan he had in motion was nearing its conclusion. That should've been my next stop, but instead, I was speeding back to the city. I had to.

Secret Scrolls. The other pieces of the key were there and either Blackwood or Graham's people would come for them, and if I didn't get there first, Parker was as good as dead. I couldn't leave her defenseless.

I glanced at the speedometer. It was creeping toward the high end, the engine roaring beneath me, but I didn't let up.

My phone vibrated in the seat beside me, but I didn't even glance at it. There wasn't time. Not for explanations, not for backup. This was on me. Just like it always had been.

I let the call, whatever it might be, go to voicemail. I needed to save Parker; everything else was going to have to wait.

TWENTY-FOUR

I parked my car a block away, cutting the engine and letting the silence settle in. The night around me was still, too still for a city that never slept. My eyes locked onto Secret Scrolls, its sign barely visible in the low light, but I didn't need to see it.

Blackwood's Corvette was parked right next to the entrance, gleaming under the streetlamp as if it was a part of some sort of exhibition. So much for beating him here. I'd driven like hell to get ahead of him, but apparently, he'd been one step ahead of me all along. Typical.

The lights inside the shop were on, glowing faintly through the drawn blinds. I could see two figures moving inside—shadows more than people. They were close enough to each other that I couldn't tell if they were just talking or fighting.

I stayed low, moving toward the shop's entrance, my breath steady but my pulse racing. Every instinct screamed at me to keep my distance, scope it out first, but there wasn't time for caution.

I reached for my gun, the cold steel in my hand reassuring and familiar. The games were over. No more second chances, no more deals. If Blackwood was in on this, I'd find out right now.

I edged toward the door, gun drawn. The creak of the hinges cut through the silence as I stepped inside, eyes scanning the room.

I stepped into Secret Scrolls, gun raised, heart pounding, ready for whatever nightmare awaited me inside—Blackwood assaulting Parker, Graham's goons tearing the place apart. Hell, I even imagined a few other scenarios that would require a lot more ammo than I had on me. What I didn't expect—what I couldn't have imagined in a thousand lifetimes—was this.

Blackwood and Parker. Kissing.

I froze, brain screeching to a halt as I tried to process what I was seeing. The gun in my hand, steady just a second ago, was now lowered. I blinked. Nope, still happening. Blackwood's hands were gripping her shoulders, gently pulling her closer as if they were on some romantic getaway.

"What the hell," I muttered, loud enough they broke apart like two guilty teenagers. Blackwood's hands still rested on Parker's shoulders, but the moment was shattered.

"I'm sorry, Alex," Blackwood said, finally letting go of the woman. "I haven't been entirely honest with you."

"It's on me, too," Parker said, stepping forward. That's when I noticed the faint bruise blooming on her cheek. It was still fresh, its intensity increasing by the second. "I didn't want you to think there was a conflict of interest."

"Conflict of interest?" I snapped.

"There's a bigger problem," Blackwood said, cutting me off before I could let loose. "Graham's people were just here."

My stomach dropped. I spun around, gun in hand, expecting to see someone barge through the doors of the bookshop. "When? What did they do?"

"It's too late," Parker said, shaking her head. She stepped back from Blackwood. "They took the pieces."

I cursed under my breath, eyes scanning the room for any sign of the struggle I hadn't noticed at first. Now that I had a moment to focus, it was obvious. A stack of books was overturned, and one desk had been shoved aside. The bruise on Parker's face and the scratch on her forehead were the final pieces that made it click.

She fought. And lost.

"Let me get this straight," I said, holstering the gun. "Graham's people were here, they beat the crap out of you, and now they've got all the pieces of the key."

Parker nodded and gingerly touched the cut on her forehead with the back of her hand. "That's the gist of it. We don't know for certain if Graham has Lubinsky's piece, but it's a reasonable assumption that he does."

Silence hung between us. Thick. Suffocating. I clenched my fists, every nerve in my body screaming at me to run, to do something. Anything. I needed to talk to John. He'd have some advice. He'd always had good advice.

I pulled out the phone, only now remembering the missed call and the voicemail. I pressed Play without thinking, putting it on speakerphone.

Hello, Alex. It was a man's voice I didn't recognize. *I hope this finds you well. My name is not important, but I trust you know the person I represent.*

I saw Blackwood and Parker lean forward as they listened to the message.

You might not know this, but as it happens, the voice continued, *the next few days are going to be very important. Something we've been preparing for a very long time. While we appreciate your assistance in locating the few missing pieces, at this point, we really need you to stop interfering. My employer is well aware that you would be unlikely to listen unless you were given an incentive. He asked me to ensure that you did. Your friend, John, is going to stay with us for a while, and I would like you to join him. We are out of town at the moment. I trust you have the address. And just to make sure you don't get any brilliant ideas, let me be as explicit as I can. If you try to save your friend—he dies. If you go to the police—your friend dies. If you take longer than four hours to get here—well, you guessed it—he dies. We will see you soon.*

The voicemail cut off with a click. For a second, no one spoke. My hands trembled around the phone, fingers tight like it was the only thing holding me upright. Levy. They had John Levy.

I took a few shaky steps, pulled out a chair from the nearby desk, and lowered myself down.

I shouldn't have dragged him into this. I had no right. Not after what we'd been through last time. I should've known better. But I brought him in. And now they had him. Because of me.

"It's my fault," I muttered, the weight of guilt squeezing my chest like a vise. I struggled to pull any air into my lungs.

"Alex..."

Blackwood's voice was soft, without the usual hint of sarcasm, and that just made it worse. I didn't need sympathy. I didn't *want* sympathy. I wanted to rewind the last few hours and make it all stop.

"This isn't on you," Parker said, stepping forward. "You couldn't have known. None of us could."

I looked between them, their faces etched with worry. They were trying to help, but they didn't get it. Levy had been in over his head from the start. And now, Graham's people had him. I forced myself to take a breath, blinking back the stinging behind my eyes.

"They want me there," I said, my voice rough.

"Why?" Blackwood frowned. "I don't get it. Graham's got all the pieces."

I clenched my jaw, staring in the distance. "Because I'm the only one who can stop him. He knows that. And as long as I'm alive, I'll be a problem for him. It's a one-way ticket."

Parker crossed her arms. "What is his plan, then? He gets you there, kills you both, and finishes whatever the hell he's up to?"

"Exactly." My fists clenched tight. "That's why I have to call DD."

Blackwood's eyes widened. "You heard the message, Alex. They said no police."

"Of course they said no police," I snapped. "I don't care. DD's the only chance we have of getting Levy out of this alive. I won't just walk into a trap and let Graham take us both. Once I'm there, what's possibly stopping him from killing us? He'll just sit there as his goons bury John and me somewhere in the grounds of his stupid castle."

Parker threw a glance at Blackwood before taking a step toward me. "Wait," she said, her voice suddenly hesitant. "Did you just say *a castle?* There aren't many castles upstate. What's the actual address?"

I rattled it off without thinking, and her eyes went wide.

"I know the place," she said. "I've been there dozens of times. Oliver, the guy who owned it...you probably don't remember, but I even told you when we first met, that you reminded me of him. Sold him some rare books and a few other trinkets and then...had a little... fling with him."

Both Blackwood and I blinked at that, but she pressed on before either of us could say anything.

"The place is beautiful, but it's like a real medieval castle," she continued, her hands gesturing in the air. "Huge. And I'm not just talking about the mansion itself. There are secret passages beneath the place. He showed them to me. Probably not *only me*, to be honest. He wasn't a particularly monogamous guy, so I suspect he used the tunnels to sneak his love du jour in and out."

Blackwood raised an eyebrow. "You're saying you can get us in?"

She nodded. "Maybe? If the tunnels haven't been sealed, I can help you both get inside without being seen. We can at least have the advantage."

I stared at her, processing the information. Secret passages. A way into the castle Graham's people weren't guarding. It was almost too good to be true. Almost.

"And you're sure this will work?" I asked, not bothering to hide the skepticism in my voice.

Parker shrugged. "I'm not sure, obviously. I haven't been there in a while. They might have closed the tunnels. Or they might have changed the passwords. But I think there's a possibility we can still use it. It's our best shot."

"All right," I said, the decision firming up in my mind. "We'll go in. But I'm still calling DD."

"We can't," Parker said.

I opened my mouth to argue, but she cut me off.

"No, listen to me. We can't bring anyone else. There's lots of open space. I'm sure the entire area is crawling with Graham's guys. I don't know how serious he is about killing your friend, but if he is, the moment they see flashing lights and helicopters—it's over. The only chance we have to get there undetected is to keep a low profile."

"We?" I gave her an incredulous look. "There's no we. You tell me how to get into the tunnels and I go there myself."

"Yes, *we*," Parker said. "It's not easy. You won't be able to get there without me. You won't find it. And Simon, despite his fragile looks, can be quite useful."

"I'm not staying behind," Blackwood said, his thin lips pressed into a line.

"See?" Parker shrugged. "We are all going."

I exhaled slowly, the tightness in my chest refusing to let up. Everything about this screamed *bad idea*, but Parker had a point. Graham's men would be on high alert. If we showed up with a loud team, Levy was as good as dead.

"Fine," I said, the word tasting bitter. "But if either of you gets in my way, we're going to have a problem."

Parker gave me a tight smile. "Understood. I'll grab a bag. We'll leave in five."

Blackwood nodded and glanced at me. "I'll help her pack."

I waved them off and made my way to the back of the bookshop. The bathroom door creaked as I shoved it open, and I stepped inside, staring at my reflection in the mirror. My face was pale, streaked with dirt and sweat, my eyes bloodshot from lack of sleep. I leaned against the sink, splashing cold water onto my face, letting it shock some sense into me.

What the hell was I doing? Charging into Graham's stronghold with Blackwood, who I couldn't truly trust, and Parker, who I didn't really know—on a rescue mission for someone who shouldn't even be in this mess. I felt like I was walking into a hurricane, naked and blind. But what choice did I have?

I scrubbed my face, letting the water drip down my neck, the chill waking me up. When I looked back at my reflection, it didn't look any better, but at least I didn't feel like a walking corpse. I dried off and headed back out into the shop.

Parker and Blackwood were already waiting by the door, both carrying bags. Blackwood's face was as unreadable as ever, and Parker looked focused. Sharp. She gave me a once-over, her eyes lingering for a second.

"All set?" I asked, avoiding the awkwardness that was clearly building between the three of us.

"Ready when you are," Parker said.

The second I stepped out of the bookshop, I made a beeline for my car. My mind was already racing, plotting out how fast I could get to the Catskills and what I'd do when I got there. I yanked my keys out of my pocket, but Parker's voice cut through the night before I even made it to the sidewalk.

"No offense, but your car won't cut it where we're going."

I turned around, one eyebrow raised, watching as she walked toward a garage door near the back of the shop. She pulled out a key, unlocked it, and swung it open. Inside, under the dull garage lights, sat a black Mercedes G-Wagon that looked like it had been waiting for this moment its whole life.

I blinked. "You've got to be kidding me."

Parker grinned, walking over to the car and patting the hood. "We're going up into the mountains, and those roads get tough. This baby's built for off-road terrain."

Blackwood opened the back door and threw in his bag. "She's right, Alex."

I couldn't argue. I took another look at my car and grimaced. "All right, fine. But I'm driving."

"I don't think so." Before I could say another word, she slid into the driver's seat, firing up the engine. The G-Wagon's low growl echoed off the garage walls.

I stood there for a second, shaking my head. Then, I gave up and climbed into the passenger seat. Parker might have won this round, but I had bigger things to worry about.

The streets were still quiet as we pulled out of the city. Parker drove with a calm precision that irritated me. I wanted her to punch the pedal to the metal. We needed to save Levy. My stomach knotted up, and I forced myself to think about the facts, about what I could control. The mansion. Graham. Our next move.

The G-Wagon sped along the highway, the city lights disappearing behind us. In the distance, the dark shapes of the Catskills soon rose, ominous against the night sky. I stared out the window, my mind ticking through possibilities.

We didn't have much time. Four hours. That was the deadline. That was all we had to get to Graham and rescue John. And, somehow, pull off a miracle.

No one spoke. Blackwood sat silently in the back, his face a thin-lipped mask popping up and down in the rearview mirror. Parker stayed focused on the road, her fingers gently tapping the steering wheel from time to time.

I hated waiting. Not knowing what was coming next. But if Parker was right, if she really knew a way into this mansion that didn't require kicking down the front door, maybe we had a shot.

Maybe.

The highway stretched out before us, a ribbon of asphalt winding through the dark, shadowy landscape. The headlights cut through the gloom, illuminating nothing but the road ahead.

"Get ready," I muttered, mostly to myself.

Because when we hit the mansion—it was all or nothing. Graham had no idea just how far I was willing to go to get John back. But he was about to learn.

The hard way.

TWENTY-FIVE

The G-Wagon creaked as we parked on a rocky ledge, wheels inches from the cliff's dizzying drop. The sunrise was just cresting over the hills, casting a surreal glow over everything—the sprawling forest, the silver ribbons of lakes cutting through the green. Under different circumstances, I'd have paused and let the view sink in. But right now, every minute was one more that Levy didn't have.

"Up there," Parker said, pointing to the manor's spires that clawed at the sky like a medieval fortress. "The main road's on the other side of the hill. With some luck, they won't notice us until it's too late."

The place was massive, and it looked deserted—at least from this side.

Blackwood shaded his eyes, squinting toward the hulking estate. "And the entrance?"

Parker pointed to a twisted rock formation tucked right under the cliff face, half-hidden in brush and shadow. "There. Leads to a tunnel that comes out into the lower basement. No one else is supposed to know about it."

I glanced over at her, then at the house. A hidden tunnel cut right into the rock, with nothing but a thin line of bushes to disguise it. It sounded like something out of an old spy movie, but if Parker was right, it was our best shot.

"And you're sure Graham's people haven't found it?"

"Oliver was...very possessive of this secret," Parker replied.

Blackwood gave her a sideways glance. "He's dead, then?"

"Yes. Skiing accident." She shrugged and started walking. "Let's move."

The path to the rock formation was rough, steep, and overgrown with vines and slick moss that threatened to knock us down the cliff side. I was grateful the sun was getting higher—at night, the climb would've been damn near suicidal.

Up close, the hidden entrance was barely noticeable—a narrow crevice in the cliff wall concealed by a tangle of vines, with just enough shadow to keep it in the dark. Parker paused, punched the code into a small panel, and then ducked into the cool, musty air of the tunnel beyond. A string of small lights along one wall flickered and came to life, and I pulled the door closed behind us.

"This will take us right under the manor?" Blackwood's voice was barely a whisper.

Parker nodded. "There's an old cellar. It'll lead us straight in. They built this during the Prohibition era to bring in supplies for the parties. Oliver's father wanted to seal it off sometime in the sixties because it was not even close to being up to code, and he was paranoid that someone was going to die in the tunnel. But Oliver persuaded him to keep it and later modernized and reinforced the structure."

"Let's keep on moving," I said, feeling every heartbeat echo through the tight walls around us. I pulled the HK out of the holster, its weight reassuring.

I kept my gun drawn, creeping forward in the dim tunnel with Parker leading the way. Before long, we were in front of another door, a metal keypad blinking in the dim light. Parker punched in the code, each beep ringing out in the silence like a dare.

The lock clicked. We stood there, holding our breath, waiting.

Nothing. Just silence thick enough to choke on. I positioned myself next to the door and gave Parker a nod as she pulled on the massive handle.

The smell hit me as soon as we crossed the threshold. It was damp, musty, and tinged with that unmistakable whiff of old alcohol. I swept my flashlight around, taking in row after row of wooden shelves stacked with dusty wine bottles. Labels clung to the glass, faded and peeling, like the names of old lovers you're trying to forget. Behind them, towering industrial wine coolers lined the walls, humming softly like giant cats purring in their sleep.

"Looks like somebody's compensating for a dry personality," I quipped, letting my light trail over the endless rows of bottles illuminated by a faint emergency light.

Parker shot me a sideways glance, more annoyance than amusement. "I'd save the jokes."

We moved deeper into the cellar, our footsteps swallowed by the thick silence around us.

Somewhere above, the house was waking up, and not in a lazy, stretching-to-the-sun kind of way. This was the sound of a disturbed hornet's nest. A low thrumming buzz was seeping through the ceiling —footsteps pounding in all directions, furniture screeching across the floor, and a muted murmur of voices blending into one frantic hum.

I shot a look at Parker, raising an eyebrow. "Busy night up there. You think they're expecting company besides me?"

"Doesn't look like the fun kind," Blackwood said, his eyes scanning the dark as if he could see through the walls. "That's a lot of activity for this hour."

We pressed on, slipping between rows of shelves stacked with dusty bottles. Every creak, every muffled word made the hairs on the back of my neck stand up. Somewhere in this mansion, John Levy was being held captive by Graham's people. If they knew we were here, they hadn't come looking yet. But that hum of activity wasn't a good sign. It was only a matter of time before someone poked their head down here, and I had a feeling they wouldn't be offering us a glass of vintage merlot.

"There." Parker pointed to a set of stairs that disappeared up into a steel door at the top. "That'll take us to the main basement."

I squinted, taking in the layout, my mind running through possibilities. "Is this where they would keep Levy?"

She hesitated, her lips pressed tight. "I don't know for sure," she finally said. "But if I had to guess, he's probably in the old kennel. It's on the other side of the house."

"Outside?" Blackwood muttered, a slight edge of exasperation in his voice.

"Yes."

"Which means—" I started, only to freeze as the door handle up top gave a metallic creak, and a sliver of light sliced into the cellar.

"Hide," I hissed, already moving. I darted to the side of the stairs, pressing myself against the cool stone wall, barely breathing. Parker and Blackwood slipped back into the shadows, vanishing into the dark recesses between shelves.

From my vantage point, I saw the door swing open wider, the light spilling into the cellar, casting long shadows across the rows of dusty bottles. A pair of black, scuffed military boots appeared, followed by a set of faded jeans, and I heard a man's voice, casual, annoyed.

"Just two bottles?"

His feet angled toward the open door, and I heard someone respond—something muffled and unintelligible from above. The man sighed and started down the stairs, one slow, lazy step at a time. "No problem," he said, the words punctuated by the thud of each step.

I held my breath, my hand tight on my gun, every muscle coiled like a spring. He was close enough that I could hear the faint rustle of his jacket and smell his cheap cologne. I calculated my options—drop him quietly or wait him out and pray he didn't linger. Either way, one wrong move, and we'd have the entire house on us.

The guy took another step, his boots hitting the floor just

inches from where I stood in the shadows, his back turned. He went to the end of the first row and leaned over a crate, one hand reaching for a bottle. I looked over at Parker and Blackwood, catching the glint of Blackwood's eyes from the dark, and pressed my finger to my lips.

I returned my attention to the man. The angle, the rhythm of his movements—it didn't look good. The second he turned, he'd be looking straight at me, and no amount of shadows was going to save us. I tightened the grip on the pistol, crossed the distance between us, and lifted it, aiming to drop him fast and clean with a blow to the back of the head.

But before I could bring the gun down, something heavy crashed into *my* skull from behind. White-hot pain burst through my vision, and I staggered, barely holding onto consciousness. I whirled, the world tilting dangerously, my pulse roaring in my ears.

Parker.

Her face twisted with something that looked almost like regret— but it didn't stop her from raising a metal pipe, ready for a second swing. She brought it down hard, a blinding, brutal crack against the side of my head. My knees buckled, and I hit the ground, my vision blurring and fading to black at the edges.

Through the haze, I caught one last glimpse of Parker lowering the pipe, nodding to the man in military boots, and picking up my gun. Then she turned to Blackwood, who was still crouched in the shadows, frozen in shock.

The last thing I saw before darkness took over was Parker's finger sliding onto the trigger, her cold, calculating gaze locked onto Black- wood. And then—nothing.

I came to with a start, my mind swimming in pain and confusion. I wasn't out for long—seconds, really, but it was long enough. My wrists were bound behind me, ankles zip-tied, my face pressed so hard to the dusty cellar floor as if it belonged there. A moment later, Black Boots, I'm assuming, was dragging me up the stairs, bump by agonizing bump. My head felt like it had been split open, filled with molten lead, each movement sending fresh waves of agony pulsing through my skull.

But that was nothing compared to the sight I glanced from the top of the stairs as Black Boots maneuvered me sideways to get me through the door.

Blackwood. Facedown. His usually sharp, elegant figure reduced to a lifeless heap, splayed out on the ground. A dark puddle, viscous and slowly spreading with brutal inevitability, pooled beneath him. It crept in a line toward my captor's boots like a silent accusatory finger in ink-black crimson.

"Nice of you to rejoin us." Parker's voice drifted over, light and unbothered, as though she were discussing a catering menu. She stood in the doorway, framed by the harsh light from the hallway beyond, my pistol still in her hand.

"Parker," I rasped, the word scraping my throat like a thorn.

She gave me a thin smile and a little shrug.

Black Boots tightened his grip, yanking me up and over his shoulder. The movement knocked the air out of my lungs. Bright pain flashed behind my eyes as blood pooled in my head, and I bit down on my lip to stifle a moan. I didn't want to give Parker the satisfaction.

Through the haze, my eyes flicked to Blackwood again, trying to make sense of the mess. This whole time, as I remained suspicious about Simon, she'd played me like a fool.

Parker smirked as she watched my gaze linger on Blackwood. "Don't worry, darling. He was just collateral. You're the one I need." She gestured to Black Boots. "Get her inside and make sure she's secure."

I dangled, slung over Black Boot's shoulder—a study in humiliation and pain, each step jostling my bruised body. Each bounce was a fresh reminder that I was no longer in control. But hell if I was going to let that stop me from keeping my eyes peeled.

The place was like something out of a vampire movie—sprawling rooms and endless corridors, everything covered in that gaudy, polished sheen of obscene wealth.

We passed through a ballroom that looked like it was hosting the setup for some grand, twisted masquerade. Caterers in black, servers hauling piles of linen and gleaming silver trays and setting up flowers and candelabras. And right in the center, like the master of ceremonies at a devil's gala, stood Graham himself.

Our eyes met for a second across the room, and he grinned—with an honest-to-God wave like we were long-lost pals finally catching up at a high school reunion. The smug smile made my skin crawl, a silent "Welcome to my party, Alex" that I could practically hear over the bustle.

Finally, Black Boots lumbered through a side door and out into the open air, hauling me around the mansion to an isolated outbuilding—a kennel. He pushed the door open and dumped me onto the hard floor with all the grace of unloading a sack of potatoes. The impact rattled me, knocking the air out of me in a sharp gasp, a cry slipping out despite my best efforts to hold it back.

I looked up through the haze of pain, squinting in the dim light filtering through a small window, and there he was. John Levy, tied to a post across from me, his head slumped forward, unconscious. His shirt was torn, his face pale, with a fresh bruise blooming across his right cheekbone.

Black Boots yanked me up, strapping my wrists to the post beside Levy's with a level of efficiency that told me he'd done this before. Real professional, this one. He checked the knots once, twice, then gave a satisfied grunt and turned on his heel, slamming the kennel door shut as he left. I heard the lock click. We were in this hellhole alone.

"John," I called out. Nothing. I turned as much as the rope holding me to the post let me and nudged Levy's leg with my foot. Still nothing. He didn't so much as twitch. "Come on, John," I muttered under my breath. "Now would be a great time for you to wake up."

I twisted my wrists, testing the bonds. Zip ties—tight and unforgiving—dug into my skin with every movement. No wiggle room, no give. Brilliant. I scanned the floor around me. I wasn't betting on it, but maybe, just maybe, there'd be something to work with—an overlooked nail in the wood, a gap in the floorboards beneath me, anything.

Nope. Nothing. Zilch. Nada.

"Shit," I muttered, frustration pooling into anger and desperation.

What the hell did Parker mean by "You're the one I need?" I forced myself to focus, to rein in my breathing. I had to figure out a way out of this, and fast. Because if Graham was planning a vampire ball, I sure as shit wasn't on the guest list—I was the main course.

TWENTY-SIX

I'd tried every trick in the book: twisted my wrists until they burned, scraped my zip-tied hands against every bump on the post I could reach. It was useless—Black Boots knew exactly what he was doing. There was no escaping this right now for now, so I stopped fighting the binds and settled in, breathing, listening, trying to ignore the ache in my shoulders and the pain in the back of my head. Preserving energy was more important than thrashing about. I counted minutes, each one stretching longer than the last, until finally, I saw John's eyelids flutter.

His eyes opened, sticky and bloodshot, and squinted at me through the low light.

"John," I whispered, relief flooding through me despite the hopelessness of it all. "My God, I'm so sorry I dragged you into this."

He gave me a weak, lopsided smile. "I guess it makes us even then. Last time, it was me who got us into a shitty case."

A chuckle slipped out of me before I could stop it, bitter and rueful. "We really shouldn't be seeing each other, should we?"

He grinned, or at least tried to. "Got any brilliant ideas?"

I shook my head, the edge of panic biting at my composure. "Nothing yet. But we'll find it. How'd you end up here?"

"They must've tracked me somehow." He shrugged. "I was walking home when I called you and noticed these two guys hanging on my heels. I thought I'd shake them, but...well, here I am. You?"

"Parker," I spat, the taste of betrayal still bitter. I laid it all out for him, down to the shot that took Blackwood out. "She used my gun, John. Shot him point-blank right after we broke into the cellar."

His eyes widened, a flicker of horror just behind the fatigue. "She what? Blackwood's...dead?"

"Dead," I confirmed, voice flat. "I spent days convinced he might be a part of the conspiracy. Turns out he was clean. And I... God, I feel like an idiot."

Levy let out a low whistle, his gaze distant. "But Parker? How the hell does she fit into this?"

"That's the five-billion-dollar question, John. The theory I had— the one where everyone from that expedition was after each other's throats—almost made sense. We figured two camps, right? One more subtle. Used a chemical agent to fake heart attacks and tried not to draw any attention to itself. The other used straight-up force— kidnapping and assassinations. And I pegged Graham as the brute. Straightforward, iron-fist, it's-a-nice-business-you-have-here mobster."

"Still could be," Levy muttered. "Maybe they were at odds initially but then joined forces. Figured teaming up gave them a better shot at pulling it off. What if Jensen wasn't as clueless as he wanted us to think? Maybe he was in on it, too. It actually tracks when you break it down—Graham had the institutional power and the muscle, Parker had the treasure-hunting connections. And Jensen bankrolled the whole operation."

"Maybe." I mulled it over, the pieces not quite fitting, some jagged edge in the logic catching like a splinter in my mind. "There's still a problem. Parker wasn't even in the damn photograph, John."

He stayed silent for a while, the dim light catching the furrow of his brow as he pondered it.

"And here's the real kicker," I said, the words heavy in my throat. "After Parker...shot Blackwood, she said something that didn't make any sense. She looked me dead in the eye and said, 'You're the one I need.'" I paused, letting it hang in the stale air between us. "I have no clue what that means, John."

"You're sure that's what she said?"

I chewed on my lip as I replayed the scene in my head. "It was crystal clear. She's supposed to want the keys, the box, the power—or whatever the hell this twisted treasure hunt's all about. But that? 'You're the one I need'? It just doesn't track."

As the sun climbed, the kennel turned into a tin can of sweltering heat. Sweat pooled under my collar, trickling down the back of my neck, and every breath felt like inhaling warm soup. The noise outside ramped up, spilling over from the house into the yard. Footsteps, low voices, the clatter of equipment—it was like the prep for a carnival, only darker.

Closer to noon, the hammering started, sharp and steady, echoing off the walls of our makeshift prison. They were building something out back, something big if the racket was any clue. We waited, watching the door. And then waited more.

An hour later, Black Boots strode in, his shadow slicing across the kennel floor. He checked our bonds, yanking on the zip ties with a grunt of satisfaction. Not a word, not a drop of water, not so much as a passing glance of acknowledgment. He was all business.

"A ray of sunshine, that one," Levy said when Black Boots was gone. His voice was raspy. Tired. "Whatever they're setting up, it doesn't sound like they're planning on us sticking around to enjoy it."

"Yeah," I muttered, barely hearing my voice over the pounding in my head.

"Do you think they've actually got it?" He looked up at me, blinking sweat out of his eyes.

"What?"

"The box."

"I don't know for sure." I shrugged. "But just judging by all the ruckus, I'd say they've got all the ingredients for whatever it is they are cooking."

The hours rolled like tumbleweeds in dry heat—slow, hazy, and directionless. By the time the sun went down, I was teetering between exhaustion and feverish delusion. Every breath felt like dragging in hot gravel. My head was pounding, my vision blurring. At some point, I must've slipped into a foggy Neverland because one moment, Levy and I were alone in the kennel, squinting against the sunset's last defiant glow, and the next, it was pitch-black outside. The day's heat faded fast, replaced by the creeping cold of the mountain night.

And then Parker was there.

I didn't hear her come in, didn't see the door open. She just materialized in front of me, torch held high, its flame licking the air and casting long, spindly shadows across the kennel walls. The flame crackled, spitting fiery sparks as if a captive spirit was wrestling to break free. In that wild glow, Parker looked like some ancient priestess come to life.

She'd ditched her regular clothes. In their place was a long, black robe, hood pulled back, her face flushed from the heat of the torch. She moved with a slow, ceremonial grace, her bare feet soundless against the concrete floor. The robe hung loose and heavy, and from the way it clung to her as she moved, it didn't look like she was wearing anything underneath. The effect was unnerving—a figure straight out of a fever dream.

"Evening, Alex," she said. Her voice was surprisingly normal. Like she was welcoming me to her bookshop instead of talking to me in a decrepit kennel.

"Parker," I croaked, trying to sit up straighter against the post. "If you're going for the whole villain vibe, it's not working. You just look cheap."

She ignored the dig, her gaze sweeping over us with a clinical detachment. She studied Levy, but only for a second, and then her gaze slid back to me, all steel and ice.

"You've been quite the nuisance, you know that?" she said. "All your poking and prodding. It's time you saw things from our perspective. Understood why this is all necessary."

"Necessary?" I spat. "You mean all the murders? The kidnapping?"

A flicker of a smile. "Sacrifices, Alex. For a cause much bigger than you or me. The box... It requires things. Obedience. Respect. And those who fail it? They simply don't last."

Levy shot me a look, his face pale in the torch's fiery glow. "You're out of your damn mind."

Parker laughed softly, the sound floating in the air, cold and indifferent. "I guess you could call me that. Or you could just accept that some things are beyond your understanding." She took a step back, her face shrouded in shadow again, leaving only the fiery torch between us, the twisted halo of a zealot preparing her altar.

And suddenly, I knew—we weren't there so we wouldn't cause trouble. We were part of whatever unholy trial she and Graham had in store.

I watched her, barely able to keep my head up. The pain from Parker's earlier smack was still fresh, throbbing with a pulse that echoed through every inch of my skull. But it wasn't the ache that was getting to me—it was Parker, standing there like she was about to drop some grand truth on me.

"Why are you doing this?" I asked. I didn't give a damn about her motivation. What I cared about was stalling long enough to figure out an escape route or at least to learn something that would allow me to delay whatever wicked plan she had for me. "And why do you need me, Parker? You've got a whole bunch of idiots ready to do your bidding. Why me?"

She studied me, her head tilted, a faint smirk tugging at the corner of her mouth. "You really want to know, Alex? Fine. You see, most people only know the beginning of the Pandora story. Zeus is pissed off about the fire debacle. He wants to punish humans, yada, yada, yada. Pandora is made. Pandora gets the box. Pandora opens it. The end. People like neat endings, don't they? I've seen some versions where Pandora lives happily ever after and even has a daughter, Pyrrha."

"Neat endings work," I muttered. "You open a box, all hell breaks loose, box stays shut from then on out. Makes sense."

"Oh, it's much messier than that." Her eyes glinted with gleeful malice, like she was savoring a secret too juicy to keep to herself. "Pandora doesn't go on to live happily ever after. No, in the actual story—the version the gods tried to erase—Pandora suffers. And not just some emotional, 'woe is me' crap. I mean physically."

I raised an eyebrow. "Physically?"

She nodded, her expression now somber. "Her body breaks down. Boils, lesions, pain that makes death look like a luxury. She's cursed and crippled, Alex. Poetic if you ask me, since Hephaestus, the very god who made her on Zeus's orders, was a cripple himself. She's damned to a life of agony, and her punishment lasts a lifetime."

"And this is relevant because...?" I asked, rolling my eyes despite the headache. "I mean, you're not Pandora. This isn't ancient Greece. And in case you missed it, Parker, the whole thing is a goddamn myth!"

"Oh, sure. Sure," she said, her tone laced with condescension. She waved her torch with a dismissive flourish, sending another spit of sparks dancing into the air. "But see, myths have a funny way of sticking around for a reason. People always want to dismiss them as fairy tales, but there's truth buried in them, Alex. Truth that's been passed down...distorted, but real. And the truth is only a woman can open the box. It's part of the curse. The divine stipulation."

I stared at her. "So that's it? You're planning to use me as some kind of Pandora proxy?"

"Exactly," she said, her lips curling into a smile that made my skin crawl. "You're going to do it for me. You'll open the box, and I—well, I'll be waiting to reap the benefits."

I laughed at her madness. "You get the power, and I get the boils."

Parker's smile grew wider. "Something like that."

Her hand slid under the robe, parting the fabric to reveal her chest. Nestled between her breasts was the tattoo, the mechanical heart like some twisted piece of clockwork anatomy. But this one had an extra detail—a crown perched atop the heart. She tapped the tattoo with her index finger. "I'm the high priestess of the Heart of Darkness, Alex. I'm the *only one* who can receive the power."

I gave her a dead-eyed stare. "Cool story. There's just one tiny wrinkle."

"Really?" She arched her brow. "And what's your magnificent plan, then?"

"The story is just a myth, but I won't play your games, anyway. I won't open your stupid box."

"Oh, darling." I could almost swear there was some pity in her voice. "We aren't your enemy. We could've used somebody else, but we chose you. You should be proud—you'll be the martyr who opens the door to the new world. The old gods were jealous and tricked us. They released all the evils upon this world just to slight us for getting fire. But they made a mistake. Something else was left in the box. Some call it *Hope*, but we don't think it was. You see, that's why myths aren't just myths. They try to tell you the truth. Anything truly powerful needs to have a weakness. The way to undo it. Achilles could be shot in the heel. The monstrous Cyclops only had one eye. The Hydra, who regrew its heads, would lose the ability if confronted with fire."

"And what's the weakness of the box?"

"It stored the power to undo the gods themselves. When we reopen it, the gods will die, and we will take their place. And I don't need you to actually *do* anything. Once I assemble the key and attach it to the box, your blood will open it. And his blood will seal the old gods' power in it."

"Blood?" Levy spat, his face a mask of fury. "You even think about touching her—"

Parker didn't bother with a response. She'd already turned and headed toward the door, signaling the conversation was over.

"Charlotte, wait," I said.

She paused in the doorway, glancing over her shoulder. "Yes?"

"When did you learn about the box?" I asked, eyes locked on her. "You played surprised when we told you, acting like it was all brand new. But clearly, you knew all along. You must've been part of this for years."

She didn't even blink. "Of course, darling. I didn't just know about it. *I* led the expedition. *I* found the box. And yes, there were only seven people in the photograph. But *I* was the one who took that picture."

TWENTY-SEVEN

After Parker left, I looked over at Levy, and his expression mirrored the dread pooling in my stomach. The odds were stacked so high against us they might as well be insurmountable. For a minute, we just stared at each other, defeated, each lost in our own private purgatory. Levy tried to force a reassuring smile, but it was nothing more than a ghost of what it should be. Neither of us said it, but we were both bracing for the worst.

Minutes slid by. Then, an hour. Nothing happened. No more Parker, no more Black Boots storming in. Just...nothing.

As the night marched on, the temperature dropped fast, a chill seeping into my bones as I leaned my back against the rough wooden post. The air grew thin, sharp, and cold, and every breath I took caused shivers that racked my body. The night felt endless and weighty, with the unsettling stillness pressing down around us. Even the distant buzz of activity we'd been hearing all day had faded. It was like the entire place just stopped, frozen in time.

I glanced at Levy again, and he looked back, his face tight. A question flickered in his eyes, one I couldn't answer. It was the quiet that set alarms blaring in the back of your mind. There's a finality to it—a sense that whatever happens next will change everything. The silence was so absolute it practically roared in my ears.

And then, just as I thought I was losing my mind, a sound floated through the chilly night air.

It was soft, delicate—a series of plucked notes drifting toward us like a whisper. It sounded like a small guitar or maybe a harp. There was a lifting, haunting quality to it that was almost beautiful. Almost. The melody slid into something mournful and melancholy. The tune wound its way under my skin and took root.

Levy fidgeted at his post, and I could see him tense up, his breath hitching as the eerie notes reached us.

The melody grew louder, and for a second, I swore I saw a faint flicker of movement through the cracked wood slats of the kennel. Shadows slid across the ground outside, dancing with the music, like dark tendrils beckoning us closer to something I wasn't sure I wanted to see.

The melody continued to swell and then—a drum. A sound like thunder rolling in slow motion, coming from somewhere beyond the flickering shadows.

Boom. Boom. Boom.

The beat was steady, unnervingly slow at first, each pulse heavy enough to feel in my chest. It was like a heartbeat, primal and raw, syncing with my own pulse until I couldn't tell where one ended and the other began. The melody twined around the beat, growing more insistent, and then another drum joined.

Boom-boom. Boom-boom. Boom-boom.

The tempo picked up, a layered rhythm building on itself, louder, more frantic. It was no longer just music. It was a call, a summons. It sent a chill up my spine, making the hair on the back of my neck stand.

And then, just as suddenly as it started, the drums cut out, leaving only the faint echo of the haunting melody hanging in the air.

As if on cue, the kennel doors crashed open. Black Boots stormed in, flanked by three more men, each one radiating the cold efficiency of someone who does this sort of thing for a living.

Two of them made a beeline for Levy, and the other two came for me. The moment they cut the ropes, I launched myself forward, aiming to slam my forehead into the jaw of the guy gripping my shoulder. He was expecting it. He ducked smoothly, sidestepped, and before I could try anything else, his fist slammed into my gut. Pain hit me like a sledgehammer, sharp and sudden. My stomach twisted, a cruel knot of fire, and the air—*my God, the air*—wasn't there. I gasped, desperate, but all that came out was a ragged wheeze.

In the fog of pain, I barely felt the men grab me under my arms, lifting me as my zip-tied legs scraped across the ground.

Behind me, I heard the sounds of a scuffle—Levy's muffled grunt and the unmistakable thuds of a few punches. I twisted my neck, fighting the dead weight of my body as I turned to look. Black Boots had Levy locked down, another brute steadying him as he struggled, defiant even in the face of a losing fight. They didn't give him much chance. Another quick blow landed and Levy went limp, his body slumping as they hauled him toward the doorway.

The second we're yanked outside, the haunting melody cut off, replaced by a relentless rhythm from the drums. There wasn't a hint of softness to it now, no eerie notes drifting in the breeze. Just a hard, driving beat—ra-ta-ta-ta, ra-ta-ta-ta. It gained speed, drilling into my skull like the countdown of a bomb.

I shivered. I wanted to say it was from the cold, but no—it was fear, unfiltered. Primal.

I forced myself to look around, to take it all in, to memorize every detail I could. They've transformed the backyard into some kind of demented outdoor theater. A raised stage loomed at the far end, crude but massive.

Leading up to it, a path lined with torches carved a bright streak through the darkness, casting everything in flickering gold and shadows. Sets of benches lined either side, filled with hooded figures. The sheer number hit me—easily a hundred, maybe more—all cloaked, faces hidden. The hum of anticipation was almost tangible.

But it was the stage that pulled my focus. In one corner, two burly men were pounding away on enormous drums, their skin bare and slick with sweat despite the chill of the night. Every muscle flexed with the beat, their faces locked in expressions that were equal parts trance and fury. Across from them, a woman—also nude—cradled a lyre in her lap, fingers poised to pluck its strings, though it was silent now, as if holding back for some grand crescendo. Her eyes were half-closed, her expression serene, like she was already somewhere else.

At the center of it all stood Parker, framed by the twisted choreography of firelight and shadow. Her robe rippled in the breeze, a black wave against the night, and flames cast jagged shadows across her face, giving her an eerie, otherworldly look. She was positioned behind a low, foot-tall podium. Flanking it, there were two six-foot-long platforms, each tilted toward it, ending in narrow chutes that met just above the podium's center—together forming the shape of a stylized arrowhead. It pointed to the object on top of the podium.

My stomach dropped as I zeroed in on it, half-hoping it wasn't what I thought. But there it was. Not a box—a stout little vase, unremarkable but for its one glaring feature. The smooth surface was plain, undistinguished—except for the cork sealing its mouth. It was shaped like a rose, its metallic petals catching the torchlight, the gears and cogs gleaming with the same steampunk design I'd seen etched into Parker's skin. The light animated them, turning the cork into something alive, as if it breathed on its own. Waiting.

I couldn't look away. This was it. The Heart of Darkness. Pandora's box.

Levy was silent beside me, but his gaze was glued to the stage, too. I could feel his tension, his fear, mirroring my own. There was no wriggling free, no last-minute plan. The crowd began to chant with the drums. It was low at first, barely more than a whisper carried by the wind, but it built, growing stronger with each stroke of the drums.

And as Parker lifted her arms, I realized—this whole demented circus had been building to this moment.

The drumming hit a crescendo as they pulled us down the torch-lit path toward the stage. After we reached the foot of the steps, I finally saw Graham. He was the only one not cloaked in black robes. Instead, he was dressed in a tailcoat so perfectly cut, so impossibly black, it almost seemed to absorb the torchlight around him. His white shirt and bow tie hovered against the void of his jacket, making him appear both spectral and solid, like a figure stepping out of a nightmare. Graham caught my eyes and winked, the smirk as chilling as the night air.

The thugs jerked me forward, pulling me up each step; my bound feet thumped against the wood, sending jolts through my body.

At the top, they dragged me to the platform on the right while the other two hauled Levy over to the left. This close, I spotted details I missed before—leather straps bolted to each platform, waiting to secure a body in place.

My body.

Panic clawed at me, and I started thrashing, fighting for every inch, but their hands were like iron vises. With rough efficiency, they lifted me onto the platform, head down.

I barely processed it as they sliced through the zip ties at my wrists and ankles, only to replace them with thick leather straps. One by one, they cinched them tight, locking me down. A final strap looped around my neck, holding my head immobile. The platform was set at a slight angle—fifteen degrees at most, but it was enough to let the blood rush straight from my legs to my head, amplifying the throbbing behind my eyes.

The drums pounded relentlessly in frantic bursts, each beat colliding into the next until it was a single, fevered pulse. And then, at once, it stopped. The silence was so sudden and complete—for a split second, I was convinced my own heart had stopped beating.

It was quiet for some time, and then I heard the steps. I wanted to see what was going on, but my head was fixed, and from my vantage point, all I saw was Parker, looming over me like a statue of the sphinx.

But then Graham stepped into my peripheral vision. His posture was regal, ceremonial, as he cradled something in his arms.

"My brothers and sisters," he said, his voice swelling like thunder. "For thousands of years, we have toiled and suffered. We fought and bled and died for the cause. To avenge our betrayal. To take back the power that is our birthright!"

The crowd rose as one and started the chant again, hooded figures moving in perfect synchronicity, swaying back and forth. I yanked against the strap around my neck, teeth gritted, and felt it loosen—just enough to angle my head and glimpse Graham's hands. He was holding something, but I still couldn't make it out.

"But our time has come," he declared. "Blood shall be spilled, and the box shall open."

The chanting built, voices merging into a chaotic, primal roar that reverberated off the walls and rattled through me. I glanced to my left and saw Parker drop her robe, her skin glistening bronze in the torchlight. She was every inch a living, breathing idol. A large bandage covered her left arm, and despite everything, I almost laughed out loud as the realization hit me—Parker was the assassin. She was the one who'd shot Van der Meer, the one who'd nearly taken me out in the tunnel under the nightclub.

If only my aim had been better.

Graham turned away from the crowd and stepped closer, holding up the object he'd been cradling. Now I could finally see it: a golden dagger, its hilt encrusted with rubies and sapphires. *The golden dagger*. The one I found in Sterling's apartment.

He handed the dagger to Parker and then knelt beside the vase on the podium. I couldn't see anything, but the crowd hushed, and the only sound left was the soft whir and clicks of the gear as he assembled the key. A final click rang out, and the crowd gasped.

I guessed it worked.

I should be thrashing, screaming, fighting. Doing anything but lying here like a lamb brought to slaughter. Instead, a strange calm settled over me, the knowledge of what was coming washing over me with a numbing inevitability. I was frozen in place, my eyes glued to the razor-sharp edge of the blade.

"We are the Heart of Darkness," Parker said and raised the dagger high.

TWENTY-EIGHT

Time stretched thin. Parker raised the dagger, poised to strike, her muscles taut like a coiled spring about to snap. The blade gleamed in the torchlight, golden and hungry, shimmering as if alive, thirsting for my blood. I shut my eyes, bracing, unwilling to know the exact moment it would tear into my flesh.

A gunshot cracked the silence. It was sharp and unexpected. I flinched, and my eyes flew open as warmth splattered across my face, shocking me with its metallic tang. Blood. But it wasn't mine.

Parker stumbled, a small dark circle blooming over her tattooed heart. Blood pumped out, steady and rhythmic, spilling down her chest in sync with her faltering heartbeat. Her eyes widened, then glazed, and her body swayed.

Another shot rang out, this time catching her shoulder. The impact spun her, and she crashed down on me. Pain exploded in my thigh as the dagger buried itself deep, the searing edge slicing through the muscle. I cried out in pain, my fingers grazing the hilt, but with my restraints, I couldn't quite reach far enough. The blade slipped from my grip just as her weight settled over me, pinning me under her body.

Over Parker's blood-smeared shoulder, I saw the crowd scatter, dark robes flying as more shots rang out, chaos erupting like a dam breaking. I heard another thud of a body falling and saw black boots pointing to the sky. Graham's voice shouted orders, but the robed figures were already fleeing in every direction, their cultist zeal crumbling in the face of real danger.

Shots faded into silence; the shrieking and scrambling dwindled into the low growl of cars fleeing the mansion. For a few tense seconds, it was just the quiet drip of blood pooling under my leg and the faint hum of crickets edging back into the night.

"Are you okay?" Levy's voice broke through the stillness.

"I think so," I said. "She nicked me, but it doesn't feel too deep. You?"

"I'm fine," he said. I could hear the strain in his voice. "Shit. I don't think I can undo these cuffs."

The sound of footsteps, deliberate and unhurried, sent a fresh jolt of dread through me. I tried to shift, to see past Parker's lifeless body draped over me, but it was no use.

"I leave you two alone for a few hours, and this is where you end up?"

The voice was calm, dry, and all too familiar. A moment later, Parker's weight lifted off me, and I found myself staring up into Blackwood's pale face, his expression caught somewhere between exasperation and relief.

"Simon?" My voice broke. "How?"

He raised an eyebrow, kneeling beside me with a knife in hand. "Relax, Watts. You look like you've seen a ghost."

"Nearly did," I muttered as he sliced through my restraints, each cut sending relief through my cramped limbs.

When he was done, I sat up on the platform and gingerly pulled up my pant leg. The cut was deep, but it looked like Parker had missed any major arteries. The bleeding had mostly stopped. Blackwood moved over to help Levy, working quickly to free him. I couldn't help but stare at the dark stain on Blackwood's shirt.

"How are you not dead, Simon?" I said. "I saw her shoot you point-blank."

He gave a sly, almost embarrassed smile. "I'm a Terminator of sorts," he quipped, tapping his chest. "Part human and part machine. When I was a kid, I went swimming in a muddy river, wasn't watching where I was going, and rammed right into a tree branch hidden under the water. Nearly did me in. They had to put a steel plate in my chest. Luckily for me, that's where the bullet hit. They put me on the stack of pallets in the back of the cellar, just out of sight. Presumably, to get rid of me after the ritual. And that's where I regained consciousness."

"I'm guessing Parker didn't know about the plate."

"Let's just say it's not a tale I share often," Blackwood replied. "But it looks like I wasn't the only one not sharing stories."

I shook my head, still not quite believing we were all here—sore and thoroughly battered but still alive.

Levy nodded toward the empty podium. "The box."

"Graham took it," Blackwood said, his face tight. "I didn't want to shoot anyone I didn't have to." He looked down at Parker's body, a mix of regret and something darker crossing his face. "I really didn't want to shoot anyone at all. But I had no choice. She was going to kill you, Alex. And then I had to shoot the thug with the gun. He left me no other options."

I rested a hand on his shoulder. I'd seen it before—the aftermath of the first kill. There was no way to make it easier, no magic words that could untangle what it did to someone's psyche. Even when the deceased deserved their fate.

Blackwood and Parker had been close, which was only going to make it tougher. Shock would give way to something worse soon enough. And there wasn't much I could do to save him from it. Therapy helped. But time, as bitter and relentless as it was, was the best cure of them all.

"Let's get out of here before anyone comes back or the police show up," Levy said.

"Agreed," I said, trying to ignore the throbbing pain in my leg.

Levy helped me down the platform as Blackwood hovered nearby, his usual aloofness gone, replaced by distracted urgency. He kept glancing around, scanning the torch-lit grounds as if expecting someone to burst through the shadows at any moment.

"Give me the gun," I said.

He looked at me in surprise, as if he had no idea what I was asking, and then stared at his hand, still clutching the pistol.

"Simon," I said. "It's okay."

He flashed a quick smile and then gave me the gun, handle first.

We made our way down the makeshift aisle between the torches, the eerie quiet pressing in on all sides. Blackwood helped steady me as we walked.

I caught a last glimpse of Parker's body sprawled on the platform, her lifeless hand dangling over the edge, but I pushed the image from my mind. There would be time to process all of that later—right now, survival was the priority.

"We'll take the back road," Blackwood said, guiding us toward the edge of the property and heading down. "Just watch your step so nobody goes over the cliff."

"Fine," I muttered, clenching my teeth against the pain radiating up my leg. "Just keep an eye out. If anyone shows up, I'm in no mood to chat."

As we neared the tree line, the light from the torches receding into the distance, I glanced back at the house—its dark silhouette against the starry sky, shadows stretching like claws over the lawn. Whatever secrets it still held, they could stay buried for now. We had our hands full with the ones we were already carrying.

We reached the G-Wagon, and Blackwood fished the keys from his pocket, the engine roaring to life in the quiet night. I slid into the back seat, my leg throbbing as I tried to find a comfortable position.

Levy climbed in beside me, casting one last look over his shoulder. "You think they'll come after us?"

I shrugged, glancing at the rearview mirror, but there was nothing but the dark forest. "Probably. But we'll be gone by then. We need to find Graham. He won't stop until he finishes what he's started."

Blackwood floored it, gravel crunching beneath the wheels as we sped away from the mountain and the house of horrors, leaving the Heart of Darkness behind us—at least for now.

The headlights sliced through the night, sharp and cold, cutting a path down the road that seemed to stretch on forever.

Levy broke the silence first. "What now? Graham might've lost his high priestess, but he's got the box *and* all the keys. And we've got no clue where he's going or what he's planning next."

"It's worse than you think," I said. "Jensen told me Graham was planning something big. I don't know what exactly, but it sounded like a terrorist attack. I'm guessing it was supposed to coincide with the ritual back there—either during or right after."

I could see Blackwood frown as he reached for the radio. "Let's see if anything's happened."

He flipped through the channels, and the air filled with the crackle of static and the familiar hum of late-night broadcasts: weathermen droning on about cold fronts, a sports recap for the latest game, pop music, and a religious channel. Finally, he turned it off. "Nothing so far. Maybe Graham was going to send a signal and start whatever he was planning once the box was open. We might still be running on borrowed time. Which brings us back to John's question—what's our next move?"

I let out a long sigh. There wasn't going to be an easy way to say this. "We need to call in the cavalry. The NYPD has to know there's a potential terrorist threat on the horizon. DD needs to know."

Levy shot me a glance. "You think he'll believe you when you tell him you were almost used as a human sacrifice in a cult ceremony perpetrated by the acting mayor?"

"Believe me?" I shrugged. "Probably. Be able to do something about it? That I don't know, because that would depend on DD being able to convince other people. But that's out of our hands. He knows better than to ignore a warning—even if it sounds like it's coming from a lunatic. He'll get the message out."

"Okay."

I looked at Blackwood. "Find us a gas station. We'll stop there, and I'll make the call."

Fifteen minutes later, we pulled into a gas station wedged between stretches of pine trees and flat, empty fields. The place had the aura of a lost relic, the single, flickering neon sign and peeling paint giving it the unmistakable, seen-better-days look. A convenience store squatted next to the pumps, its windows plastered with faded ads for off-brand soda and beer. I doubted it had seen real business in years.

The only sounds were the soft hum of an ancient pump and the buzzing of a bulb hanging from a wire overhead, casting a half-light that made shadows jump.

Inside, the air hit me like a wall—stale, thick with the scent of cigarette smoke and the sharp, synthetic tang of microwaved burritos. Behind the counter, the lone clerk—a gangly, scruffy guy with a beard that looked like he'd been growing it since high school—stared at us, instantly on edge. His eyes darted from me to Levy and then lingered a beat too long on Blackwood's shirt.

"Evening," I said, sliding up to the counter and giving him what I hoped passed for a non-threatening smile. "Any chance we could use your phone?"

He blinked, flicking a glance over his shoulder as if he expected to see a manager he could pass us off to. No one. Just shelves stacked with old magazines, candy bars, and mystery meat jerky. His Adam's apple bobbed once, and he gave us a curt nod, reaching under the counter to hand over a dusty cordless.

"You folks look like you've had quite the night," he said, clearly not entirely sure if he wanted to know the details.

"You could say that." I took the phone, turning my back on him to give us a thin layer of privacy, and punched in DD's number.

He picked up on the second ring, his voice low and groggy. "Detective Deluca. Who's this?"

"It's Alex," I said.

"Watts, what in God's name do you want at this hour?"

I took a long breath. "I've got some intel on a threat in the city. Potential terrorist attack."

There was a rustling noise on the other side of the line as if DD sat up straight. "Go on."

"It's Graham, the acting mayor," I said. "He's part of a doomsday cult. Call themselves the Heart of Darkness. And they're planning something big—like a full-blown terrorist attack."

The silence stretched, and I could almost see DD scrunching his face as if he was trying to decide if he was being pranked. "The mayor? In a cult? And you know this how?"

"Because less than an hour ago, I was tied to a table while a bunch of hooded freaks chanted as they waited for someone to slice my throat. To sacrifice me, DD, do you understand? And Graham was in charge of it all."

I heard loud breathing on the other side of the line for a few seconds as DD tried to digest. "I gotta say, Alex," he finally said. "Somehow, you always end up getting mixed up in some of the weirdest shit."

"I know," I sheepishly agreed. "And Graham isn't the only prominent person in the cult. There were others."

"Like who?"

"Van der Meer."

"The senator stiffed a hooker, and she shot him dead in anger," DD snapped. "Hardly a cult."

"Oh yeah? I thought I shot him?"

"The witnesses changed their story. You're still a person of interest since you were there, but no longer the prime suspect."

"No," I insisted. "That's not what happened. This is a cover-up. I saw the murder with my own eyes. And there's also Jensen."

"Wait." There was a beat of silence. "Do you mean—Kai Jensen? The tech billionaire?"

"Yes, that Jensen. He's up to his neck in this. Well, *was* up to his neck in this."

"What do you mean *was?*"

"Because he's dead, DD," I said, losing patience. "Keep up with me here. Somebody killed him the same way they killed Sterling. I actually think Graham killed him because he was trying to consolidate power."

"Oh, shit." The breathing became thunderous as DD's gears seemed to start clicking into place. "Christ. Watts, Jensen's actually been on federal radar for a while. A former spy made some accusations about one of the companies Jensen owns."

"What accusations?"

"There was no solid evidence," DD said, his voice strained. "But there was a rumor of a stash of old Soviet chemical weapons in Eastern Germany that allegedly went missing when the wall came down. Nasty stuff. But like I said, no credible evidence. Accusations like that are enough to put you on a watch list, but unless something tangible comes up, that's all it is."

"What do we do?" My voice came out tighter than I'd meant it to.

"We need more than rumors. Locations, names, dates. Do you have anything concrete?"

"Not yet," I said. "But Jensen was convinced it was something big. And I think it's coming down soon. In the next twenty-four hours. Maybe even less. And it'll be in New York."

"All right. I'll talk to my captain and see what we can do given our...limited mandate. But, Alex, if you get a whiff of anything action-able, you call me first."

"Understood."

"And, Alex?"

"Yeah?"

He paused for a second, his laborious breathing thundering in my ear. "Please watch your back."

TWENTY-NINE

We staggered into Levy's apartment just as dawn bled through the skyline, painting everything with an anemic glow. Blackwood slumped on the couch, his hand clutched against his chest—the plate might have saved his life, but it didn't spare him from the pain. Levy cleaned my leg, his fingers steady as he pressed a damp cloth to the wound. It stung, but I could hardly complain. After he dressed my wound, Levy offered his help to Blackwood, but the stubborn Brit only shot him a sidelong glance and shook his head as he unwrapped a bandage roll, pulling it around his chest, his jaw clenched tight enough to crack teeth.

I texted DD from yet another burner, but he didn't respond. I guessed there wasn't any exciting news to share yet.

"Well, we have about one option left," I said. "We need to pay Graham a visit."

"Visit him?" Levy shot me a look like I'd suggested robbing the Federal Reserve. "You realize where he lives, right? Gracie Mansion? It's got twenty-four-seven surveillance, checkpoints, an eight-foot-tall fence, and a cop detail who don't take kindly to trespassers."

"We won't go to the mansion," I replied. "Think about it—Graham knows we could've gone to the police by now. Whether we have enough to get them to do anything is irrelevant. The point is, it's too dangerous. Especially considering he's about to do something from which there's no turning back. He'll go somewhere safe. Somewhere familiar. He must have a safe house somewhere."

"That's probably true," Blackwood said. "But how do you propose we find this elusive safe house? It's not like it's going to be listed under his name."

"Yeah," I said. "If only we knew a PI who could do something like that."

Levy chuckled but didn't say anything out loud.

"I'd started looking into Graham already. It's ironic, really, as Graham himself authorized my access to the NYPD database. When Sterling died, he wasn't even close to being a suspect, but I thought it might be a good idea to look into the man who benefited the most from the mayor's demise. I don't have the address, but I won't be starting from zero, either. Can I use your computer, John?"

"By all means," he said and headed toward the kitchen. "I'll fix us something to eat while you're at it."

By the time Levy had a pot of coffee and some sandwiches started, I narrowed it down to two locations. Both were leased under shell companies, but I was able to link them to Parish, Graham's advisor. It wasn't bulletproof, but it was good enough, and *good enough* was going to have to cut it. By the time I looked up from the screen, Levy had outdone himself—sandwiches piled on a plate, the comforting smell of coffee filling the room. My stomach growled, reminding me it had been a long while since anything more than adrenaline was holding me up.

"Oh my God," I muttered as I gobbled the last bite of ham and cheese, "I didn't realize how hungry I was."

"What's the word?" Levy asked, pouring three cups of coffee.

I took a last look at my notes, gathering my thoughts. "There're a few possibilities, but two stand out the most. Graham's advisor set both up through shell companies. One's here in the city. Hell's Kitchen, to be exact. The other's a bit more out of the way—on Staten Island, near Bloomingdale Park."

"Hell's Kitchen is close to the Lincoln Tunnel," Blackwood said. "He'd have a quick escape route if things got hot."

"Staten Island is arguably even better positioned then," Levy said, shrugging. "It's near the Outerbridge Crossing, which would make it even easier to get out if he's in a hurry."

"Maybe." I chewed on my lip, mulling it over. "But I'm leaning toward the place in the city. Let's be real—Staten Island's a hike. Graham might not want to be far from the city. He was a deputy mayor. It's not exactly practical to bolt out of Manhattan to visit a place nearly an hour away."

"There's something else to consider," Levy said. "We've been assuming Graham's planning a terrorist attack. If that's the case, he's almost definitely doing it in the city."

Blackwood nodded slowly. "Sounds like we're going to Hell's Kitchen."

"Yeah. But let's make this decision together—let's vote. Hell's Kitchen?"

Two hands shot up.

"Hell's Kitchen it is."

By the time we got to Forty-Eighth Street, the morning was in full swing, bustling like it had somewhere better to be. The building—a faded-brick, four-story relic from an era when the city had more grit and fewer skyscrapers—sat on the corner across from an empty lot slated for yet another condo project. On one side of the building, a hardware store clung to life, a smattering of early risers in work boots coming and going. On the other side, a small cafe buzzed with regulars and the scent of freshly baked bread drifting out.

We crossed the street, our steps falling into sync as we reached the main entrance and headed up. The stairway was sunlit, warm, and open, which only added to my unease. Each step felt louder than the last, competing with the echo of someone's radio playing a morning station from one of the lower floors.

A messenger jogged past us going down the stairs, barely sparing us a glance, and then a woman with a toddler in tow sidestepped us, muttering apologies as her kid trailed behind.

We reached the third-floor landing, and I held up a hand, tensing as I listened. It was quiet here. I couldn't hear anything beyond the background noise of the building, waking up for a new day.

"Keep an eye out," I whispered, just about to kneel and inspect the lock when I noticed it—the door was closed, but not quite. The latch hadn't caught. Whoever had been here last had either been in a hell of a hurry or didn't care. Perhaps both.

I pulled my gun, holding my breath as I turned the handle and nudged the door open. It swung with a faint creak, revealing a room barely big enough to be called an apartment—a studio with grimy walls and a mess that made it look more like a crime scene than a living space. There was no furniture except a cheap metal desk and a folding chair. Both were swamped in a sea of takeout containers. Coffee cups and papers littered the floor.

I checked the bathroom, the door hanging off one hinge, but it was empty, too. I nodded at Levy to close the door behind us as he stepped in, his eyes scanning the chaos.

"Not exactly what I pictured," he said, frowning.

"And we're obviously too late," Blackwood added, his tone edged with frustration.

"Looks that way," I said and moved to the desk.

A large, topographical map of the city covered most of the surface, the edges curling up. On top of it, diagrams lay scattered like puzzle pieces. They were circular and jagged, with spokes jutting outward, each a unique combination of colors. Their length varied, too, creating a strange geometry that made them resemble flowers.

I tilted my head, staring at the map. "That almost looks like..." I hesitated. "A wind rose?"

"A wind rose?" Blackwood echoed, moving closer.

A shiver ran down my spine. "Yeah. Look at it."

Levy and Blackwood leaned over the table, their eyes shifting between the strange, petal-like spokes radiating from each compass point.

"A wind rose is a tool to show prevailing wind patterns," I explained to Levy, tapping one of the colorful wheels. "Each spoke tells you the direction and frequency of winds. The longer the spoke, the more frequent the wind. Now, think—what does that tell us?"

Levy's eyes darted across the map; his brow creased. "That prevailing winds blow mostly west this time of year?"

"Or northwest," Blackwood added, squinting as he traced the lines on the map. "If you want to be exact."

I nodded. "Precisely. Now, consider the angle of the New York metro area, stretching from Staten Island all the way to the western-most part of Long Island. What direction does it mostly run?"

"Northwest," Levy and Blackwood said, almost in unison.

"Right," I said, lowering my voice. "Now imagine you're a deranged terrorist with a large stash of an airborne chemical agent."

"Damn it." Levy's face paled. "You release it on Staten Island, and the winds would do the work for you. The entire metro area would be covered in hours. We're in the wrong place."

"That's it," I said, my eyes locked onto the colorful spokes on the map. "That's Graham's plan."

"But here's the snag," Levy said. "The Staten Island place is just a small house. Not exactly a suitable place to store large amounts of chemicals. What's he going to do? Spill them off his porch?"

"You're right," I said. Frustration twisted in my gut like a knot of barbed wire—we were running on fumes, half-formed theories, and scraps of evidence. We'd been playing catch-up since the moment Blackwood walked into my office. And time was slipping away. Fast. "Our leads are flimsy at best, and this one's a stretch. But maybe—just maybe—we'll get lucky and find something there."

Levy gave a nod and pushed himself up. "Then Stranded Island it is."

Blackwood raised an eyebrow. "*Stranded* Island?"

Levy chuckled. "It's a local thing. Some people call it a forgotten borough. Or *Stranded Island.*"

Blackwood gave a small, distracted nod, and the three of us left the apartment and headed outside. We had a mayor to catch, and time was running short.

THIRTY

The midday sun hung high and blazing, casting everything in glaring, crystal-clear light as we tore down the Verrazzano Bridge toward Staten Island. The sky was cloudless and bright, like some cosmic irony, as if the universe was out to remind us no one else knew what we did.

"What if the whole thing's just nonsense and the vase is filled with...I don't know, a thousand-year-old orange juice?" Levy muttered. "Do you think Graham actually believes it's real?"

"The box? I don't know." I watched his tight jaw, sunglasses masking whatever storm was brewing behind his eyes. "The chemicals are real. We have to stop him before he releases them."

"I guess." He gave a small, almost imperceptible shrug. "I was just shocked to see so many people taking part. Intellectually, I knew cults existed. But it's so jarring to see one out in the open. Especially populated by some of the most sophisticated people you can find. Graham. Jensen. Sterling. These aren't some small-town folks who'd never been farther than a fifteen-mile radius outside their home."

"You give too much credence to so-called *sophistication*," Blackwood said from the back seat. "It's the story as old as the world itself. Strong but twisted minds taking advantage of the weak."

I watched the buildings of Lower Manhattan in the distance, glistening in the bright sun. People were in those buildings going about their lives: working, chatting with friends, watching the news.

"It doesn't matter if the box's real," I said. "Look at what they've already done. People died for this—all on belief alone. The Valentine Killer believed in something, too. People cling to these stories, especially when they think it'll make them something bigger than themselves."

We rolled up to Graham's safe house a few minutes later. It was a squat, detached place that looked about as innocuous as a dollhouse. It was in a charming cul-de-sac, set back from the road, wrapped in an overgrown hedge that might've been trendy at one point in the late '90s. Levy parked us half a block down, and we all climbed out, surveying the place.

"Not exactly the villain's lair I was expecting," Blackwood said, squinting at the peeling white paint and the slouching porch.

"Yeah, well, evil doesn't always come with a neon sign," I muttered and headed for the door. "Let's go take a peek."

The front door lock was laughably easy to pick—so much so that I spent a few minutes checking the doorframe before stepping in, looking for booby traps. There were none, and I pushed the door open and slipped in, letting my eyes adjust to the dim light.

It didn't look like a safe house. A few old-fashioned furniture pieces stood on a carpet that'd seen more than a handful of presidents. A layer of dust was so thick it was clear no one had stayed here long.

Levy let out a low whistle. "Looks like a dead end. I don't know if Graham's even been to this place."

I scanned the small space. "You're probably right. But we need to search it, anyway. Anything even remotely out of place, I want to see it."

We split up. Levy started with the kitchen, Blackwood with the tiny excuse for a bedroom, and I started with the living room. It was almost bare, with stacks of old magazines and papers on the table, some outdated china behind a dusty glass of a buffet, and a gray sofa with dented pillows.

When nothing turned up, I headed upstairs, sending Levy to the basement and Blackwood to the garage.

A few minutes later, Levy drifted in, empty-handed. "It's all clean. Well, not clean, but you know what I mean."

Blackwood emerged from the garage a moment later, shaking his head. "He either didn't stay here long or didn't stay here at all."

"Seems that way," I agreed. "Perhaps he got this place just in case but never actually used it."

My stomach churned. This was our final clue, but it yielded nothing. And now we were back to square one, with Graham free to move the game further.

"Damn it," Levy said, kicking a cardboard box with his boot. "It's like we're chasing a ghost."

"We must be missing something," I said, more to myself than to anyone else. But the bare-bones house stared back at me, as silent and empty as ever.

"Let's go back to my place," Levy said. "We'll regroup and think of something."

"Okay. Wait for me outside. I'll give it one more look and meet you there."

Levy shot me a look as if he was going to argue but then just nodded, and they stepped through the door into the bright afternoon. I walked through the house again, slowly scanning each room, hoping for something, anything, to stand out. But there was nothing.

Just as I was ready to cut my losses and leave, I heard the sounds of tires crunching gravel. Lots of tires. My heart leaped into my throat as I registered the unmistakable blue and red lights flashing outside, spilling through the dusty windows. Cops. It seemed they'd found the safe house just like we had. I looked around—there was nowhere to go. There was no back entrance, and hiding in an empty house that was about to be turned upside down by a forensics team seemed like a silly idea. I took out the gun, put it on the couch, and then moved to the middle of the room, my hands high in the air.

A moment later, the front door rattled open, and a pair of officers stepped in, guns drawn, looking more than ready to use them.

"Hands up!" one of them barked. "Stay calm."

"Oh, I'm calm," I replied. "And my hands are already up. I'm unarmed, and my only weapon is over there on a couch."

They slapped cuffs on me, ran through the Miranda spiel, and shoved me out the door, down the front steps, and into the police van idling at the curb. As they pushed me inside, I snuck one last look around. No sign of Blackwood or Levy. They'd slipped out, at least— a small mercy, but I'd take it.

I took a seat on the hot metal bench inside, steeling myself for what was probably going to be one long, uncomfortable ride back to the city. But before I could settle in, the back door swung open again, and a familiar figure climbed inside, giving me a half-smirk as he took the bench across from me.

"Detective Deluca," I said, half-sighing, half-growling. "Here to save the day?"

DD raised an eyebrow and made a few rumbling noises as he breathed in and out. "I sort of hoped I wasn't going to find you here. You want to tell me why you're trespassing on a city official's property?"

"Sure," I said, leaning back. "How much time you got?"

He gave me that piercing stare of his. "I thought we had a deal, Alex. You tell me things if you find something new."

"I did."

"Not about this place." He rubbed his face. "Okay, now that you're here, why don't we start with the big picture and work our way down to this breaking-and-entering?"

I wanted to roll my eyes, but I had to put myself in his shoes. Unlike me, DD was under orders. He didn't have the luxury of galli-vanting all over the city, so I bit down on my pride and went over the basics—the box, the cult, the wind rose we found in the Hell's Kitchen apartment. He listened, and though he kept his expression blank, I knew DD. That's how he processed new information. With all his faults, he probably had the best bullshit detector in the NYPD. If DD wasn't listening to someone or something, it was probably not worth listening to.

"You think he's going to disperse it from here," he finally said when I finished.

"Yes." I nodded. "Well, not from *here* here, but from somewhere on Staten Island. Are the feds involved?"

"Nope." He shook his head. "I'm not supposed to tell you this, but so far, we are simply looking into Graham's disappearance. Technically, he's not even a suspect for now.

"Look," he reached out, and his thick, rough fingertips gently touched my knee, "I'm sorry we had to take you in. You know I've got no choice, right?"

I blinked and nodded, not quite trusting my own voice.

"I got your back, Watts," he said and stood up. "No matter what."

Inside the van, the minutes ticked by, indifferent to my plight. Through the narrow window, I caught glimpses of the cops going in and out of the house, moving through the yard. One ducked under a window; another kicked through a patch of weeds. Frustration twisted in my gut, tight and hot. They were out there searching, rifling through empty drawers, tugging at dusty furniture—wasting time. The cuffs cut into my wrists, the walls of the van crowding in. We were so close, and yet I stayed locked in this stupid van, the pieces slipping further away with each passing second.

I pressed my forehead against the wall, trying to tune out the idle chatter of two officers standing nearby. But the noise outside was growing—a few shouts, the crunch of feet on gravel, the occasional static crackle of police radios—building into a commotion that had my senses prickling. I craned my neck, trying to see what was going on, catching a view of two officers rushing into the house, their pistols drawn.

The van's door rattled and flung open. I squinted against the bright light, and there was Blackwood, smirking like the Cheshire Cat. "Well," he said, extending a hand. "I'd say this is our cue to leave."

"Don't mind if I do." I let him grab my elbow, swinging myself out of the van, casting one quick look at the house.

We ducked low, cutting through a line of parked cars until we reached the G-Wagon with Levy behind the wheel, grinning like he'd just pulled off the biggest heist of the century.

As we peeled out, I let out a shaky breath, heart pounding. "How did you manage that?"

Blackwood leaned in and unlocked the cuffs with a flick of his wrist. "Magic, love."

"Impressive," I said, rubbing my sore wrists, feeling the heat of the adrenaline that hadn't quite worn off. "Because I think I've just figured it out—where Graham's keeping his stash."

"Well," Levy said, leaving the blue flashing lights behind, "let's make sure this time he doesn't see us coming."

THIRTY-ONE

The dim glow of the streetlights outside filtered through the car windows as the evening crept in. As we drove in zigs and zags across the borough to make sure we weren't followed, the clear sky gave way to a mean-looking cloud. By the time we finally found a quiet street and pulled over, the first few raindrops gently spattered across the windshield, little beads of water creeping down in messy lines as the drizzle picked up. Outside, the world turned into a soft blur of streetlights and shadows. It suited my mood perfectly.

We sat there, the three of us, each lost in our own thoughts for a moment, and then I spoke, putting the pieces together out loud.

"Here's what occurred to me," I said. "I got so caught up with Graham and the cult and everything else that I forgot where it all started."

"The box?" Blackwood said from the back seat.

"No. The first domino to fall was Victoria Sterling. She wasn't the first to die, but she was the first to make an impact. And as I remembered that, I started thinking back. She was on her way to a groundbreaking ceremony when she collapsed and died from a *heart attack.*" I paused for effect, watching my friends' faces. "A ground-breaking ceremony on Staten Island."

Levy looked over at me, clearly catching my drift. "You think he's stashed the chemicals there?"

"What's a better place to hide something than an active construction site? Plus, I've looked it up—the construction has been postponed after Sterling's death."

"Where is it?" Blackwood asked.

"Todt Hill," I said as I pulled it up on the phone. "And listen to this. *Todt Hill is a 401-foot-tall hill formed of serpentine rock on Staten Island, New York.*"

"Four hundred feet high?" Levy said, surprised. "That's...pretty high."

"That's better than high," I continued. "*It is the highest natural elevation on the entire Atlantic coastal plain from Florida to Cape Cod.*"

Levy gave a low whistle. "Holy shit. It fits."

"Yep. But there's something else."

"Other than the highest elevation on the East Coast?"

"High elevation is obviously beneficial," I said. "But it got me thinking—it doesn't mitigate the dispersal problem. It's a hill, not a spire. If he spills it off the hill, most likely, it'll just blanket the surrounding area. He needs to get off the ground somehow. And then it hit me—do you know what they use on construction sites?"

"Cranes," Levy said. "He's going to release it off the crane."

"Exactly. That's going to give him another hundred feet of elevation. At least."

"So how do we do this? Call the cavalry?"

"No." I shook my head. "What if he has some kind of remote trigger, and the cops spook him? No, we need him to think he's finally by himself. We'll sneak into the site, find a place to hide, and watch the cranes."

"He'll probably have the box with him, too," Blackwood said.

"Just another reason not to alert him."

Blackwood nodded. "There are usually building crew trailers near the site. We could set up camp there—monitor the area without being visible."

"It's a good plan," Levy said. "Straightforward. Not a lot of moving parts. I'm in."

He started the car again, and we headed through the streets. The drizzle turned into a steady rain that drummed against the roof of the car. The headlights cut a narrow path through the thickening mist as we approached the area, searching for the entrance to the construction site.

Soon, the place loomed up ahead—a hulking shape outlined by faint construction lights against the rapidly darkening sky. The entire area looked deserted, with no signs of late-night shift crews or security personnel. As we parked down the road, I could make out the shadows of two tower cranes looming over the site, like some prehistoric beasts, their booms stretching against the sky.

We stepped out into the rain and set along the perimeter, searching for a way in. It didn't take long. One section of the fence had sagged, the chain-link flapping loose where it hadn't been properly secured. With a quick glance around, I slipped through, Blackwood and Levy close behind.

Inside, the site sprawled in every direction—stacks of concrete blocks, metal rebar, coils of industrial cables. And, of course, two massive cranes. Their towering frames disappeared into the low-hanging clouds, each looking like it was ready to reach down and scoop up the city. Thunder rumbled in the distance, and Levy tilted his head up, squinting through the rain. "Might not be the best time to operate one of those."

We crept through the maze of equipment and debris, keeping low as the rain plastered our clothes to our skin. Finally, we spotted a row of crew trailers lined up along the far side of the site, out of sight from the main road. Blackwood stepped up to the door, glancing around before he pulled out a lock-pick set. It took less than a minute before we heard the soft click, and the door creaked open. We slipped inside, out of the rain, and shut the door behind us.

The trailer was dim and dusty. It was filled with the faint, stale scent of coffee and cheap air freshener. In the corner, there was a small foldable table and two mismatched chairs. I crouched by the window and wiped away a layer of grime to get a better view of the site.

Blackwood leaned over my shoulder. "Think he'll come in through the main gate?"

"Get away from the window," I said. "Your silhouette can be visible."

Levy settled into the chair and stretched his legs. "Now we wait."

"Yep," I said. I could feel my heart pumping. "Now we wait."

The rain was coming down in sheets now, lightning flashing in staccato bursts that threw the construction site into sharp relief. I stood by the edge of the window, watching the area, when I saw the sleek black sedan pull up along the far edge of the fence. Graham stepped out, a dark figure against the glowing headlights, an umbrella in one hand, the unmistakable shape of Pandora's box cradled in his other arm.

Blackwood drew a sharp breath beside me.

"Here we go," Levy muttered, his voice barely louder than the rain hammering on the trailer's roof.

Graham moved through the downpour, slipping past pools of light cast by the scattered security lamps as he made his way toward the crane on the other side of the field. I watched him discard the umbrella as he approached the ladder inside the tower. He clutched the box tight under his arm like a football and started the climb.

"That's a long climb," Blackwood said as we watched the dark silhouette slowly ascend through the night. "Somehow, I always assumed they took an elevator to get up there. I guess not."

It took him a solid ten minutes to reach the top. Finally, the cab lights flicked on, cutting sharp beams through the rain, and the hum of the crane's electric motors pulsed through the night as the boom moved.

I waited, watching, expecting him to lower the boom to grab whatever was hidden somewhere in the field.

Instead, he began swinging the boom slowly, the long metal arm slicing through the misty air like a scythe. The boom stretched across the site, and just as a bolt of lightning cracked the sky, we saw it: Graham swung the crane's arm around to hook the counterweight of a second crane. There was a jolt as the cranes collided, a metallic groan vibrating through the storm.

"What the hell's he doing?" Levy hissed, pressing closer to the window.

The second crane shuddered under the strain, swaying back and forth like a drunk losing his balance. And suddenly, I knew what he was doing.

"Oh no," I whispered. "The chemicals. They were stored under the counterweight, not in the field."

The metal shrieked as the cranes buckled under the forced weight. Graham gave one last yank and a final swing, and the hook came away with a rectangular box. There was silence for a moment, but then we heard a deafening crack as bolts and steel gave way, sending the second crane careening down like a wounded beast. The entire structure swiveled, stopped for a second as if suspended in the air, and then crashed to the ground, barely missing our trailer.

The impact threw us backward, sending tremors up through the floor and shattering the window. The storm barged into the room, throwing handfuls of rain into my face and whipping the dust and papers around the trailer.

Blackwood cursed, stumbling back and steadying himself against the desk. "Damned fool near took us out."

I saw Graham angling the boom upward, the crate with chemicals dangling above the dark void below. Then, he switched off the controls and climbed out of the cab. But instead of heading down, he climbed over the railing and onto the boom itself.

I didn't think—I just acted. I shot out of the trailer, boots pounding the wet ground as I sprinted around the twisted hulk of the fallen crane. Its tangled metal groaned as it settled, and I slid in the mud, narrowly avoiding a set of mangled steel beams jutting out like spears. I recovered, Blackwood and Levy's voices barely cutting through the roar of the storm behind me, and bolted forward. Just then, someone lunged out, slamming into me and driving me to the ground. I snarled, twisting to kick my attacker square in the chest—only to halt as DD's face filled my view.

"Where do you think you're going?" he snapped, voice barely audible over the thunder.

"To the top," I shot back, scrambling to my feet. I could see Graham's figure starting to climb the boom, perched precariously over the abyss with a box clutched under one arm.

"Like hell you are. Let me handle it."

"Get out of my way, Dom," I shouted, pushing him. "I'm faster, goddamn it!" I stuck my hand back at Blackwood and Levy. "Stay down here with them. I need you ready if anyone else is coming."

A muscle ticced in DD's bulldog-like jaw, but he pulled up his pants leg, took out a small pistol from his ankle holster, and shoved it in my hands. "Go."

I didn't waste time on a response. I launched toward the crane, rain soaking through every layer and chilling me to the bone. Graham's men arrived just as I grabbed the first rung, their shouts cutting through the storm.

As I ran up the ladder, the night below me burst into muzzle flashes and screams as bullets tore through the air. I forced myself to ignore the chaos and climbed, my fingers gripping the slippery steel rungs, each step taking me closer to Graham and the crate hanging like a death sentence above us all.

Thunder crashed around us, the storm's fury matching my own, but there was no turning back now.

Rained hammered down, driving into my skin as I scrambled up the slick ladder, each rung threatening to toss me all the way down.

The storm had only escalated, lightning clawing at the sky as if the heavens themselves had joined the fight. A bullet chipped the frame a few inches away from me, and then another whistled by; close enough, I felt the heat graze past my neck. I ducked and kept going, teeth gritted as I forced my way up, every muscle burning.

When I reached the top, the wind roared even louder. I went through the cab, its metal door rattling with each gust, looking for Graham. As I stepped inside, he appeared in the doorway, his heavy frame filling the narrow entrance. He lunged, catching me off-guard, and we crashed backward, limbs grappling, slipping on the rain-slicked metal as we fought.

He pinned me against the frame, his weight crushing the air from my lungs, making it almost impossible to breathe. With one brutal twist, he wrenched my arm to the side, slamming it against the unforgiving steel again and again until my grip broke, my gun clattering down and disappearing into the black void below.

Summoning my strength, I planted my heel, swung my leg up, and drove it hard into his knee. Graham lost balance, his grip slipping, and I pushed forward, twisting free and throwing an elbow into his ribs. He reeled, barely regaining his balance before I landed another punch square to his jaw. He staggered back, his head smacking against the cab wall with a profound thud before he slumped to the floor.

Gasping for air, I looked around the rain-slicked cab. There it was —Pandora's box, right where it needed to be, safe by the cabin seat. Relief washed over me as I tied Graham to the cab frame. He wasn't going anywhere. I let myself sink to the edge of the platform, my feet dangling over nothing but rain and open sky. My body ached with the deep, bruised kind of pain that comes after you've gone a few rounds.

Down below, the gunfire had stopped. Through the fading haze of rain, I spotted Blackwood, Levy, and DD, drenched and worn but upright. They were all watching, faces turned up at me, alive and breathing. I raised a hand, gave a small wave, and leaned back, letting the rain pelt my face. The box, Graham, the keys to his twisted plan—all of it ended here, on this steel perch in the middle of a stormy sky. And for the first time in what felt like forever, with the rain washing over me and the wind howling through the metal beams, I felt a strange, blissful calm.

THIRTY-TWO

It was still drizzling when I finally stepped out of the precinct. The fog hung thick and low, curling like tendrils around the streetlamps and drifting lazily down the road, where the early morning sunlight turned it into a soft, golden haze. I paused on the granite steps, taking it all in. The city looked surreal, a morning where you couldn't tell where the fog ended and the clouds began—like a watercolor painting left out in the rain, everything bleeding together.

A car pulled up to the curb, and the window rolled down. Levy leaned over, one eyebrow raised, grinning. "You coming down, or should I call and book you one of those lovely interrogation rooms?"

I snorted, shaking my head as I started down the steps toward him. "Believe me, I've had my fill of the hospitality here."

Sliding into the passenger seat, I sank back against the worn leather and felt a flood of exhaustion settle over me. It was the tiredness that digs deep into your bones, the aftermath of too many close calls and too little sleep.

Levy started the car and merged into traffic, glancing over at me. "I'm guessing you're in the clear?"

"More or less," I said, glancing down at my mud-splattered

clothes. "Can't leave town while they are wrapping things up, but I'm no longer a suspect in Van der Meer's murder case. Or anything else, for that matter."

"That's great. What's next?"

"I'm meeting Blackwood in the evening. He still needs to pay me. But I need a nice, hot shower. And a set of clothes that doesn't look like I've been sleeping on the sidewalk for the past two weeks."

"You can crash at my place if you want," he offered. "Faster than going all the way back to Brooklyn."

I looked at him, tracing the angles of his face as he kept his eyes on the road. I wanted to go to his place. Take a shower, have some tea... I shook my head. "Thanks, but I need to get home. My place is a mess, and I've got a cat to pick up from my neighbor's."

"Fair enough."

We drove in comfortable silence for a while, the hum of the engine and the soft patter of rain the only sounds. The city streets drifted by, shrouded in fog, giving everything an eerie stillness.

"While I was waiting for you," Levy said, "I heard on the radio Graham's being charged."

"Yep," I said. "DD told me. Terrorism, conspiracy, half a dozen other charges. DD said we got really lucky. The pallet had a remote-controlled dispenser. Originally, one of Graham's goons was supposed to hit the switch during the ritual, but they bailed after hearing about the mess that went down upstate. And when Graham tried to take care of it himself, he couldn't get it to work because the storm was messing with the receiver. He's singing, by the way. Hoping for some kind of leniency, I guess, though I don't see how. He's most likely looking at a life sentence."

"And Parker?"

"DD filled in some gaps for me," I said. "But not all. Parker was an exceptionally good diver, and it was she who discovered the wreck. She made a few dives, and the vase was one of the items she pulled from the sunken ship. It came in a box that had an inscription on it with a prophecy that would eventually inspire them to start the cult. Part of it was the date in the future when the box could be opened and turn those who did into new gods. That's why they sat on it for so long and didn't try to open it right there and then."

"What happened to the rest of the treasure?"

"They tried to hire a vessel and return to the site with proper tools to get the rest of it out. But Sumatra is apparently located at the boundary of two tectonic plates in what they call the Ring of Fire. Earthquakes are very common there and by the time they hired the crew and came back, the tremors reburied the ship. It's still there somewhere, but they couldn't find it. They made a pact to keep things under wraps and went back to their lives, waiting for the time to unseal the vase. The only guy who didn't want to open it was LeClerc. Milo was on the fence."

"Sounds like a lovely group of people," Levy said.

"It's a one-sided story, told by Graham," I said. "I don't know how much of it I'm actually buying. He says everyone was terrified of her. That part, I believe, as Jensen easily gave us Graham but still wouldn't name Parker. The now-former mayor claims Parker initially wanted to kill them all, but after a short civil war, Graham convinced her he'd be a loyal servant, and she agreed to work with him in the end. Partially because he was in a position of power and had access to the resources she didn't. Well, he also thought she'd die during the ritual and he would be there to collect the power."

"Jesus. A love affair of a scorpion and a rattlesnake."

"Yep." I sighed. "I feel bad for Simon, though. I don't know how long his affair with Parker lasted, but clearly, she was using him. That must've hurt. Well, at least the snake is dead, and the scorpion is about to serve a very long sentence in jail. I don't think he'll ever see the light of day again."

Levy chuckled. "Kind of poetic, don't you think?"

"What is?"

"Graham was trying to unseat the gods, if you take his and the cultists' nonsense literally. Storm the heavens—and what stops them? A little bad weather. Guess Zeus had the last word after all."

I raised an eyebrow. "What does that make us? The lightning rods?"

He flashed me a grin. "Hell if I know. All I know is that anyone would rather be on the ground than up in that tower last night. But you didn't even hesitate."

I shrugged. "Do you believe in any of this?"

"Believe what exactly? The gods? Zeus?" Levy scratched his chin. "No. But I do believe there might be something we don't quite understand."

I said nothing.

"Which reminds me," he continued. "How on earth did Blackwood pull that Houdini act with the vase? I'm sure DD's still livid about it."

I had to laugh at that. "Yes. Yes, he is."

My mind drifted back to those chaotic moments. By the time I'd climbed down from the tower, the so-called Pandora's box—the vase that had been the center of all this madness—was finally in my hands. For something supposedly imbued with the power to end the world, it felt surprisingly, almost anticlimactically light. Like a fake prop. But the weight of the thing wasn't in its heft, of course. It was in the blood spilled and lives ruined in its name.

And, of course, as soon as I hit the ground, DD's eyes locked onto the vase like a hawk eyeing its next meal. He wasn't interested in conversation. He wanted it fingerprinted, tagged, and cataloged— locked down in evidence where it belonged. But before I could even consider handing it over, Blackwood materialized out of thin air, sliding up beside me. Without missing a beat, he snatched the vase right out of my hands, holding it behind his back like it was some parlor trick.

I didn't even have time to blink before DD's attention was entirely on Blackwood. He demanded the vase, spitting warnings and threatening to lock up the Brit on the spot. But Blackwood just shrugged, opened his now empty arms wide, and replied, "What vase, Detective?" Like he'd never laid his eyes on the thing in his life.

DD was ready to throw him in cuffs right then and there. He searched every inch of Blackwood's pockets, patted him down, and ordered the officers who had by then arrived on the scene to search the area. But Blackwood just stood there, calm and defiant, his face a mask of polite disinterest.

Minutes ticked by, and DD finally ran out of places to look—and, judging by his muttered curses, patience, too. He stomped off, his pride clearly bruised, leaving Blackwood standing there with that damnable grin still plastered on his face.

"Did you find out where he hid it?" I asked Levy as we drove.

He shook his head, a wry smile tugging at the corner of his mouth. "Not a clue. After they cut us loose, we headed back to the car to wait it out. But the second the cops cleared out, Blackwood wandered back to the scene, as casual as you please, and, just like that, he reappeared with the vase in hand. No big reveal, no explanation, nothing."

I groaned. "Classic Blackwood."

Levy chuckled. "When I asked him how he did it, he just looked at me and said, 'Magicians never reveal their tricks.' Like he was Houdini's long-lost heir."

"Of course he did." I shook my head. Blackwood could probably walk into the Vatican and come out with the pope's hat, and no one would be any wiser.

By the time we got to Brooklyn, the sun had climbed higher, burning off the last of the fog and leaving the street clear and sharp in the morning light. Levy eased the car to a stop in front of my place, and I took a good, hard look at the front of my house. The door was charred around the edges from the Molotov, blackened and rough, but somehow, it didn't look as bad as I'd imagined. Small mercies.

Levy tapped the steering wheel lightly, watching me survey the damage. "If you need any help," he said, "you know where to find me."

"Thanks," I said, holding his gaze. "I really don't know what I'd do without you, John."

He said nothing. Just gave me this look—steady, warm, and knowing. It said everything he couldn't and what I probably wasn't ready to hear out loud, anyway.

I leaned in, closing the space between us, and pressed a gentle kiss to his cheek, just at the corner of his mouth. I felt him hold his breath, the faintest catch. Then I pulled back, gave him a small smile, and slipped out of the car.

"Take care, Watts," he called after me, his voice a little rougher than usual.

I didn't look back. Just gave him a wave and headed up the steps.

I lifted the small rug in front of the door, fingers brushing the familiar rough texture, and pulled out the spare key. With a quiet sigh, I fit it into the lock and pushed open the door. It groaned in protest, a few charred bits of wood flaking off the frame and dropping on the floor like dead leaves.

Stepping inside, I was met by a thin, chalky film of fire extinguisher residue coating everything in the foyer. The smell hit me next —sharp and acrid, like burnt metal. Perfect. Welcome home, Alex.

So much for just crashing and forgetting the world for a few hours. If I was going to stay in this place, I'd have to make it livable again. I sighed, kicking off my shoes and heading to my room to change into a worn T-shirt and shorts. And then I got to work.

I started in the foyer, wiping down surfaces and scrubbing the floor, my mind drifting as I worked. Each swipe of the sponge, every sweep of the broom, felt strangely grounding. The events of the past few days—the cult, the box, the human sacrifice—continued to play in my head. But as I scrubbed away the grime, I felt a sense of control I hadn't had since Blackwood first showed up in my office.

By the time I was finished, the place didn't look perfect, but it was mine again. The metallic scent had faded, replaced by the clean smell of pine soap. And in the quiet of the now-clean house, I finally let myself feel the weight of it all, exhaustion creeping in.

I took a breath, long and deep, and let it out slowly. It was finally over.

THIRTY-THREE

The street outside Secret Scrolls was dead quiet. I kept to the shadows, just beyond the reach of the single streetlamp casting a weak, flickering glow over the sidewalk. The windows were dark, the blinds pulled tight, the place as lifeless as Parker herself. But I wasn't taking any chances.

Parker might've been gone, but her network wasn't. Some cultists were still out there. The police were working overtime, dragging them in one by one, but I'd been in this game long enough to know it didn't mean much. There were always those who slipped through the cracks.

I scanned the street again, just to be sure. Not a soul in sight, only the sound of some stray cars passing a few blocks away. I took a breath, keeping my nerves in check, and headed to the shop's door, ducking under the yellow police tape.

The lock didn't put much of a fight—a simple twist, a soft click, and I was in. I slipped inside, shutting the door behind me and stood there for a few moments, letting my eyes adjust.

The place smelled like it always did—the comforting mix of leather bindings and old wood, but today it didn't have the same charming effect on me. The shop bore unmistakable scars of a recent police search. Shelves were half-emptied, books and artifacts scattered haphazardly, and papers lay crumpled on the floor like discarded confetti. The usual order of Secret Scrolls was gone, replaced by a sense of violated chaos, as if every hidden corner had been forced into the open.

I skipped right past the main area and went straight for Parker's office—the heart of her little operation, where she'd worn the mask of the quirky, harmless shop owner with a taste for rare books. I wasn't holding my breath for anything obvious; if there'd been something easy to find, the cops would've snagged it. But maybe she'd hidden a few crumbs they'd missed.

I circled around the heavy oak desk, pulled out the tall leather chair, and settled into it. The joints let out a long, tired creak that echoed in the silence, like the office itself was protesting my presence.

I started pulling open the drawers one by one, rifling through them with a growing sense of frustration. Loose papers, old receipts, dried-up pens, and a few dog-eared notebooks with Parker's neat handwriting cataloging the front store—nothing that screamed "ancient secrets." I dug deeper, even tipping the drawers to make sure there weren't any false bottoms, but came up empty-handed.

After a few minutes, I leaned back in the chair, my gaze drifting to the dead double monitors on the desk, their black screens staring back at me like two empty, unblinking eyes. The office had given up nothing. I sighed and pushed myself up.

I made my way upstairs, each step creaking underfoot as I climbed to Parker's living quarters. The place wasn't much—just a bare-bones studio with the essentials and not a hint of personality. To describe it as Spartan would've been generous. No photos, no books, not even a stray coffee mug on the counter. The police had already scoured the room; I could tell by the half-open drawers of the dresser and the closet left wide open, its emptiness somehow making the space feel even colder. But for all their rummaging, there was hardly anything to search through.

I took a seat on the edge of the hard mattress, letting out a long breath. I'd come here hoping for a lead, for something—anything—that might answer a few of the remaining questions rattling around in my brain. But as far as I could tell, Parker had left nothing behind. Just an empty place, picked clean by the cops. I was about to stand, ready to leave, when something caught my eye.

A small wooden number screwed into the wall over the doorframe—a "7," no bigger than a fingernail, worn down with age. I cocked my head, examining the piece, a little spark going off in the back of my mind. An itch that told me to look closer.

I found a small step stool and dragged it over, climbing up to get a better look. The number seemed like nothing at first glance, just a cheap piece of wood fastened with a single screw. But as I reached up with my tools and twisted it free, the piece came off the wall easily, revealing a tiny hollow behind it. I pulled out my flashlight, shining it into the space, and my pulse quickened.

There, tucked away inside, was a hard-wired switch.

"Oh, great," I muttered under my breath, feeling a cold trickle of sweat down my back. I had no way of knowing if this switch would reveal a hidden safe or blow me up to pieces. But I hadn't come this far to walk away now.

"Well, here goes nothing," I whispered, bracing myself as I pressed the tip of my finger against the switch. It clicked, and then there was a faint mechanical whirring somewhere behind me.

I turned, watching in disbelief as a section of the wall beside the bed slid back, revealing a hidden entrance. Heart pounding, I stepped down from the stool and moved cautiously toward the opening.

Inside was a small, brightly lit room that looked like a vault crossed with an armory. "Holy shit," I breathed, taking in the scene before me.

One wall was lined with firearms—everything from pistols to a sniper rifle—all meticulously arranged. The walls on both sides of it displayed artifacts, old and exotic, their origins no doubt spanning centuries and continents. And running along all three walls was a counter lined with glass cases, each containing treasures of its own: jewels, ancient coins, gilded relics that looked like they'd been pulled straight from a museum.

But my eyes were drawn to the center of the counter, where one object sat alone. It was a helmet. The skullcap was etched with scenes of battles, men with swords locked in eternal struggle, every detail masterfully carved. Across the brow, a lion-headed griffin with outstretched wings, its fierce gaze seeming to watch me as I approached. The years hadn't been kind to it—the lining was gone, eaten away by time and seawater, and empty slots where pins once held a regal plume now sat barren.

I brushed my fingers over the helmet, feeling the cold, ancient metal, smooth and solid under my touch. This wasn't just any artifact —it was *the* helmet, the one that had once rested on the head of Alexander the Great himself, the man who'd conquered half the world.

I lifted it carefully, turning it to get a look inside, hoping to spot whatever Blackwood thought might've played a role in Alexander's sudden, mysterious death. But then I stopped short, my breath catching as I took a step back. Right there, beneath where the helmet had sat, hidden from view, was a small glass vial filled with light-amber liquid, gleaming in the light like it had been waiting for me all along.

I stared at the vial like a rabbit hypnotized by a python, muscles locked, the air barely going in and out of my lungs. But as the seconds ticked by, my brain kicked in, logic catching up to instinct. If there'd been poison in the air, I'd have been dead before my fingers ever touched the helmet.

I made my way back out to the main store, found a shopping bag, and returned to the hidden room. Using one of Parker's dresses as a buffer, I lifted the helmet and carefully placed it inside the bag. Then, as an extra layer of caution, I set the dress back down on the counter next to the vial. The helmet probably didn't have any lingering poison on it, but I wasn't interested in testing that theory on myself. It would get a proper soak once I was back home. After a few centuries at the bottom of the ocean, a dunk in New York City tap water wasn't going to hurt it.

I cast a last glance at the hidden room, shaking my head with a wry smile. Parker was a great poker player, after all. To the world, she was a harmless antiques dealer and a book collector with a penchant for dusty relics. Meanwhile, she'd been a lethal, globe-trotting murderous version of Lara Croft.

I retraced my steps and slipped out of the shop. Then I crossed the street and slid into my car. I pulled out my phone, scrolled to DD's number, and let out a long sigh. Poor guy was going to blow a gasket when I told him what I'd just gotten myself into.

THIRTY-FOUR

The Seraph, the ship Blackwood said he would be boarding, was a sight to behold. A sleek, three-hundred-foot-long yacht bobbed as it sat docked at the Manhattan Cruise Terminal. Its hull was painted a striking, polished blue that glistened under the setting sun. The gentle lapping of the dark waters against its sides filled the air with a rhythmic hum, like a heartbeat.

As I stepped onto the pier, my footsteps soft on the weathered planks, I spotted Blackwood leaning against the railing, looking out over the Hudson River. He didn't look like a man gearing up for a long journey. His Air Force-blue suit was sharp enough to look like he'd just stepped out of a magazine spread, every detail immaculate. Not a hair out of place, no sign of the weariness you'd expect after the past few days—just the polished, unshakable confidence of a man who had all the time in the world.

I walked up to him, the cool river breeze tugging at my hair, the final notes of daylight stretching across the sky. He turned as I got close, a warm, genuine smile breaking the usual guarded mask.

"Hey, Simon."

"Alex." He squinted against the sun's last rays, his smile deepening, that slight glint of mischief still dancing in his eyes. "She's a beaut, isn't she?"

I glanced at the yacht, its sheer size, the smoothness of its lines, the glint of metal on its deck fittings. It was a thing of perfection, built to be admired, to sail somewhere far beyond what most mere mortals could even imagine.

"Yeah," I replied, turning back to him and putting my bag down. "It's something else. No luggage?"

"Oh, it's already on board."

"I see." I hesitated. "How long are you going to be gone?"

He didn't answer right away, just held my gaze, like he was trying to read something in my face. Finally, he turned back to the river, his eyes fixed on the water as if he could already see the miles ahead of him.

"Hard to say," he said. "We're not in a rush. We'll take our time. Take her down along the East Coast, then through the Caribbean. We'll stop in Brazil for a few weeks. After that, we'll head down to the southern tip of Argentina." He paused, his gaze drifting farther as if tracing the route in his mind. "From there, it depends on the weather. The Drake Passage is unpredictable, but it's at its calmest November through March, so we might get lucky. All in, probably eight to twelve weeks. And then, whatever time we spend in Antarctica and the voyage back, of course."

"That's...long," I said.

He gave me a small smile. "A long journey, indeed. But Antarctica's been on my list for years. And, as it turns out, the timing couldn't be better."

I said nothing, just leaned against the railing and watched the Hudson with him. The boats drifted along, some close, some farther out, leaving small ripples in their wake, like ghosts passing each other. I wanted to bring up Parker, to ask if he was holding up all right. I had no idea how close they'd been before her betrayal, and I doubted he'd share much if I asked. For all his warmth, Blackwood kept his own world tightly sealed.

"Oh," he said. He stood straight, reached into his pocket and produced a small envelope. "Before I forget, here are your wages. Your services were very much appreciated."

"My pleasure." I took the envelope and stashed it in my jacket. "Have you decided what to do with it?"

He turned, his eyes locking onto mine. "Yes. I wanted to keep it. I *really* wanted to keep it. But I think it would be best if it was hidden away—where no one, not even me, can ever get to it."

"Hidden? And by that, you mean...?"

"The Drake Passage," he said, glancing out at the horizon, his face shadowed by the dying light. "There are areas that go down fifteen thousand feet, maybe more. Once we get out there, I'm going to throw it overboard." He said it calmly, like he was informing me he was going to dispose of an old sofa rather than a millennia-old artifact that had turned our lives inside out.

"And you're sure that's where it belongs? At the bottom of the ocean?"

"Alex," he said quietly, "some things are meant to stay buried. I don't know whether it's real or not. Some people believe it is, and that's more than enough. That box is dangerous. It has a way of finding those who seek it. The ocean is the only place I can be sure it'll stay lost."

"All right." I straightened up, pushing off the railing. "It was... interesting meeting you, Simon. I hope you enjoy the trip. I never asked—just a pleasure cruise, or is there something specific you're after out there?"

He gave a small, knowing smile. "Both."

Before I could say anything more, he opened his arms, and somehow, before I knew it, I was hugging him. He smelled like sandalwood and a hint of smoke, warm and rich. "Take care, Simon."

"You too, Alex." He leaned back, winked, and then produced a single red rose with an impossibly long stem, offering it to me with a flourish. "Maybe I'll see you again sometime."

I took the rose, half-amazed and half-annoyed. Only Blackwood could pull something like this off. "How, Simon? Just how?"

"Magic, love."

"Well," I said, picking the bag up off the ground and handing it to him, "I have something for you, too."

"Oh?" He cocked his brow, taking the bag. "What's that?"

"Magic, love," I said, deadpan. "Goodbye, Simon."

He turned, gave me a wave, and headed for the gangway, disappearing into the belly of the yacht as if he'd never really been here at all.

I walked back to my car as the last slivers of sunlight vanished, the sky melting into twilight. The streetlamps blinked on one by one as if catching the last rays and keeping them alive through the night, just to give them up again and send them back to the sky in the morning.

I put the rose into the back of the car and then slid into the driver's seat. I tossed my phone into the cup holder and started the engine. The cell buzzed and rattled, and the screen lit up with a blocked number. I frowned.

I picked it up, thumb hovering over the screen before I answered. "Hello?" I said, waiting.

At first, there was nothing—just dead air, thick and empty and... somehow...vast. But then, faintly, something shifted. I leaned in, concentrating, catching a faint crackle mixed with something else. It was a deep rumbling, distant and raw, almost like thunder rolling in the great distance.

"Who is this?" I demanded, my voice firmer now, a hint of irritation creeping in. But still, no reply. "I'm hanging up."

"Alex," the voice whispered, low and distorted, scraping along the edge of my hearing like nails on a chalkboard. I froze, an icy jolt running down my spine. It sounded less like a person and more like a storm that had learned to talk—thunder layered over itself, twisted and warped, barely holding together the illusion of human speech. "We meet at last."

I straightened up, gripping the phone so hard my knuckles went white.

"Who are you?" I demanded, the fury overpowering my fear.

The voice paused, like it was savoring the moment, letting the silence stretch and crawl under my skin.

"I have many names, my child. But you may call me Prince."

JOIN THE STORY

Thank you for reading DARKNESS. I hope you enjoyed it.

If you liked this book, please take a moment to leave an honest review. Reviews are important for authors because they help us sell more books and, thus, spend more time writing new stories.

And, of course, don't forget to join the newsletter to learn about upcoming releases, exclusive free content, and more. You can do it right here:

wesleycross.com

Thanks again for reading, and I hope to see you soon!

ALSO BY WESLEY CROSS

ALEX WATTS

MADNESS

DARKNESS

THE UPGRADE SERIES

BOOK 1. THE BLUEPRINT

BOOK 2. VERTIGO

BOOK 3. THE LOOP

BOOK 4. SPARE PARTS

BOOK 5. FATA MORGANA

BOOK 6. DEUS EX

Also in The Upgrade Series:

ROGUE (A short story) Exclusively available

at www.wesleycross.com

Copyright © 2024 by Wesley Cross

All rights reserved.

No part of this book may be reproduced in any form or by any electronic or mechanical means, including information storage and retrieval systems, without written permission from the author, except for the use of brief quotations in a book review.

www.ingramcontent.com/pod-product-compliance
Lightning Source LLC
Chambersburg PA
CBHW061801190726

48289CB00007B/2027